THE
NIGHT
VILLAGE

Zoe Deleuil was born in Perth and studied Communications at Murdoch University. She moved to London in her twenties, working as a magazine subeditor for the BBC. Like many a sub before her, she realised while polishing other people's copy that she would prefer to be writing her own, so completed a master's in Creative Writing at Bath Spa University. She now works as a freelance writer, and her stories and features have appeared in *Westerly*, the Margaret River Press short story anthology *Pigface and Other Stories*, *The Guardian*, *The Big Issue*, *The Australian* and *Green* magazine, among others. Her manuscript *The Back Shed* was shortlisted for the 2012 Hungerford Award and longlisted for the *Australian*/Vogel's Literary Award. *The Night Village* is her first novel.

ZOE DELEUIL

THE NIGHT VILLAGE

 FREMANTLE PRESS

For Felix

'I have my dead, and I have let them go,
and was amazed to see them so contented,
so soon at home in being dead, so cheerful,
so unlike their reputation. Only you
return; brush past me, loiter, try to knock
against something, so that the sound reveals
your presence, Oh don't take from me what I
am slowly learning ...'

From *Requiem for a Friend*
Rainer Maria Rilke

1

Every so often I'd escape that clean, metal-bright hospital room by looking out the window. I'd stare out at the council estate across the road, at the sprinkling of powdery snow on its tiled roof. Was the snow getting heavier, or was it stalling, like me? Sometime before dawn the midwife excused herself, then returned with her arms clamped around a careless pile of white sheets. A sleepy-looking porter trailed her with a fold-out bed and set it up next to mine, and then the midwife made Paul a rough nest with the sheets and raised her eyebrows at him like he was an overtired child.

'You need to sleep now,' she said. But when she left the room for her break he squeezed my hand and I knew he wouldn't rest until it was over. As we stared at each other I couldn't believe we were about to become parents, when a year ago we were just getting to know each other.

'Whatever you need, tell me,' he said, close to my ear.

We'd arrived hours earlier, the lift opening onto a brightly lit hallway. In front of us was a double door with a security guard stationed in front of it. *Postnatal Ward*. Spelled out above another set of doors, a little way down the corridor, were the words *Labour and Delivery*. The letters were bold and red and impossible to miss, even as another contraction fastened around my belly like a steel claw. As I doubled over with my hand against the wall, wondering how I would ever reach those big red letters, a man

7

emerged from the postnatal ward. He looked like someone I might have walked past at Broadway Market on a Saturday morning, a *Guardian* tucked under his arm. He seemed composed, if a little tired. But when our eyes met, his face crumpled in sympathy or horror or exhaustion, and he shook his head and turned away from me. It wasn't encouraging. He veered off in the direction of the lift and I staggered towards the labour ward entrance, where Paul was already speaking to someone through the intercom. The double doors swung open and we were in a hectic waiting room with a strangely disinhibited atmosphere. In front of the rows of chairs, like a performance-art piece, a woman lay on what looked like a yoga mat, face down, knees apart. The room filled with the sound of a low, persistent alarm, and after a few confused minutes I realised it was coming from her.

As the night went on, we did laps of the ward, along deserted corridors with a hallowed Sunday-night feeling, our voices dropping to whispers each time we passed a Hasidic Jewish man who rocked on his knees, eyes closed and deep in prayer, next to a closed door. At first my contractions were easy to breathe through, but as the hours passed they loomed over me like grey waves on a winter beach, each one harder to scale until I was exhausted and panicking. I felt like a small child again, knocked over and held down, except that it was pain and not sea water crushing me. Paul was falling apart; he wasn't going to save me. Framed by a blue headscarf, the midwife's serene face was my lifeboat, all that stood between me and certain death, and I kept my eyes on her until each contraction faded.

'It's only going to get more intense until it's over,' said Paul, and I tried not to swear, knowing that if I started I probably wouldn't stop. 'If they're happy to give you an epidural, you should take it.'

'Fine. Whatever works. I don't care.'

'Is there anything else I can do?'

'*Stop talking*,' I muttered between clenched teeth, as another wave hit.

Sometime later a man with tightly curled hair and green eyes appeared, waiting patiently for me to stop thrashing around on the bed so he could slip a needle into my spine, delivering a numbing anaesthetic that halted both the pain and the momentum of labour.

On it went, the night getting old and the snow falling outside and my blood pressure soaring higher as the epidural wore off and more people appeared, soft-focus strangers coming into the room, checking a machine that rolled out a message of mountainous lines.

I had never realised that in childbirth the baby is working with you, striving as hard to begin its life as you are to deliver it, and that you are doing this intense labour together. No-one told me that. Nor did I realise that through all the external chaos of childbirth there would be a silent centre, enclosing the two of us. We communicated – that's not the word, exactly, because the word doesn't exist – but I felt the baby's intention and animal focus as it made its slow way into life.

An empty hospital crib plugged into the wall was the finishing line, waiting to be turned on at some indefinite end point. Outside was that grotty dawn that always appears after a sleepless night, and then it was Monday morning and there were more people in the room: an obstetrician and his students, another doctor standing at my side, two more for the baby, a student midwife. Finally the baby was yanked from me in two distinct pulls, a sudden blue form in the antiseptic air, landing on my belly for a second, long enough for my hand to cup the warm, wet head and slide down the slippery back, and for Paul to tell me it was a boy, before someone snatched him away and took him to a far corner of the room.

Raising my head, I looked past the faces of the obstetrician and the medical students to the two silent figures, their heads down, their backs blocking whatever they were doing in that corner. Silence. On and on and on as I stared in the direction of the baby, willing him to breathe. And then, finally, a weak yet distinct scream. I dropped my head back to the pillow and closed my eyes. The night's grip released me and slipped from the room.

When I opened my eyes the doctor standing at my side, an Asian woman with the kind, tired face of a mother herself, smiled and said, very quietly, 'Well done.'

'Thank you.'

Another doctor walked towards us, holding the baby, now wrapped in a white towel. Paul held out his arms and took the bundle, and he was no longer a potential emergency, a problem to be solved. He was ours.

'Do you want to hold him, Simone?'

Through half-closed eyes I shook my head. He was here and he was alive, and that was enough. Right now I needed to monitor everything that was still being done to me, and let my breathing return to normal. Paul gazed down at the bundle in his arms. Was he stunned, like me, that there was suddenly a baby in the room? He looked so solemn. What was it? Apprehension? A kind of despair? Was he regretting it? He'd seemed so keen. After a moment, he turned to me.

'I should go and call my parents,' he said, looking like he was about to pass out.

'You can call them in here,' I said.

'No. I'll step out. You did so well, Simone. I want to tell them how well you did, and that he's okay.'

He handed me the baby and was gone.

For years I'd dreamed of a baby, its solid fatness and cool gleaming skin, the two of us splashing in clear green water on some sunny beach. But that dream-baby was nothing like the real one that I now held. I could never have imagined such dark eyes or the tiny creaky sounds he made as he experienced his first moments of life out of water.

Everything was blurred and bleached of colour apart from him, as I watched him take in his surroundings without fear or surprise. It was as if I was an alien, recently arrived on Earth and seeing a human baby for the first time. He was the one who had just landed in the world, yet he was self-possessed and curious from the start. And I understood, looking at him, why throughout the pregnancy I had been filled with such a sense of wellbeing. He had an assurance about him, an innate calm, which I had rarely experienced before falling pregnant, but which, with him living inside me, I had been able to relax into and draw upon. Even after he was born, it was as if he had left a faint cellular trace of himself in me, so that I felt subtly altered by his stay. I knew it to be a fact, and much later on, when I began devouring articles about pregnancy and birth and child development, I read about a scientific discovery called microchimerism, which is when a remnant of DNA is left by a baby in his mother's brain and stays there for decades after he has left her body.

Later on, I wished I could go back to that moment, or even earlier, when he was living in my belly and no-one could separate us. When it all seemed so simple. I didn't know it then, but outside that suddenly peaceful room, someone else was waiting, too.

The labour suite was quiet now. The doctors and students and midwives had rushed away to some other woman's bedside, taking their instruments and controlled panic with them. Swaddled under a warming lamp in the hospital crib, the baby slept, his face grave and still. The midwife, so focused and energetic and decisive during the birth, now sat by the door, deep in her notes.

Paul came back in and put his arm around me, then leaned closer, whispering into my ear. 'I have so much respect for you, after seeing you go through that.' He kissed me. 'It was horrendous. So long. I didn't think it was going to end.'

'Me neither.'

How weird that he sat there and saw it all happen. I felt a bit jealous. I'd never been present at a birth and would have found it exciting. But he didn't look like he'd seen something exciting.

He looked wrecked. His face had that same traumatised pallor as the man I'd seen last night, staggering out of the postnatal ward.

'I might have a shower,' I said, suddenly keen to restore some normality.

As I got up, wrapping myself in a sheet, the midwife looked away discreetly. After everything she'd seen, it was sweet of her to afford me that dignity.

'Try to keep your arm out of the water,' she told me. Looking down, I saw my hand was still pierced with a pronged needle attached to a plastic box with tubes coming out of it.

I stood under the warm water, rinsing away the night, all the people who had touched me with their blue-gloved hands, and my legs shook and my arm kept drifting down into the spray. Paul appeared at the door with my bag of clothes.

'Lift your arm, lift your arm,' he said, again and again, but I couldn't seem to obey him. I had no strength to hold my arm up as my whole body trembled, as if in delayed outrage at what it had been put through. Keeping my hand dry was the least of my problems. He handed me a little pink soap that I'd packed in the hospital bag, in preparation for a dimly lit water birth that I'd secretly known would never happen, and as I took it I felt like laughing.

An old friend told me how he once went on a silent retreat to some spartan forest meditation centre, where he said nothing and barely ate for ten days. On the way home he dropped in on his sister. He seemed to have lost his mind a little, because the bowls of potpourri and small animal ornaments in her living room struck him as hysterically funny. Unable to sit and converse with her as he usually would, he paced around the room, pointing at her belongings and howling with laughter, until she asked him to leave. Afterwards, part of him felt horrified by his rudeness, yet also liberated. When I saw that little pink soap I felt a bit like my friend laughing at his sister's potpourri, except I had no energy to laugh. It was close to bliss, being so spent, and knowing that no-one expected me to do anything – because it was all done. There was only the sleeping baby, Paul and the midwife. And all three of them let me be.

Through the window I could see that more snow had fallen and the usual street noises were strangely hushed. Finding clean clothes in my bag, I dressed myself, awkward and dazed. The baby slept on under the warming lamp, larger, more real and more himself already. I stood and looked at him properly for the first time, standing back a little as if he was a famous artwork I was finally seeing in real life. I thought about picking him up but wasn't sure if it was allowed. It seemed a ridiculous question to ask the midwife, and I didn't know anyway if I had the strength, so I left him there.

'We'll move you to the postnatal ward soon, if you're happy to go?' said the midwife, coming over to me. 'We're all done now.'

'I guess we are,' I said, flashing back to everything that had happened here an hour or so ago. The silent huddle of medical students. The obstetrician ordering me to *Look away, look away*. The stirrups, the looming metal forceps. Even, at one point, a porter trying to bring in a breakfast trolley, and someone shouting at him to come back later. The whole humiliating, undignified, biological process had taken place in this room, with Paul, who by the looks of him right now should have been kept outside, pacing, like the old days, and my midwife, who did this every day.

'Do you – do you like your job?' I asked her.

She nodded and smiled, a little sadly. 'I always say that ninety-nine percent of the time it's the best job in the world, and one percent of the time it's the worst.' She paused, looking down, and I knew what she was referring to.

No-one spoke and I felt sudden relief as I looked at the baby, still lying in the heated crib, an angry red mark curved across his cheek. I wanted to draw him close.

Paul cleared his throat loudly, breaking the silence. 'Let's go, then, shall we?' he said briskly to the midwife.

I could tell from looking at him that he wanted to tear out the door like he sometimes did when we were at home: away from me and domesticity and thoughts of work, to his favourite old English pub on Farringdon Road where he could relax among the warmth and chat of friends and strangers. He leapt to his feet and picked up my bags.

'Yes, of course,' said the midwife. She waited for me to sit in a wheelchair, then took the sleeping baby, bundled in his blanket, and gave him to me. An unfamiliar floating anxiety faded away the moment he was back in my arms.

The midwife wheeled me slowly through the waiting room while I held my baby like a prize, and I wondered if the labour ward had been specially designed this way, to parade all the new mothers like a motivational tool past those waiting to be admitted to the next stage of the conveyor belt of a hospital birth.

A security guard checked our paperwork and then the doors to the postnatal ward swung open. A roar of noise and stifling heat hit me first, coming from what looked like endless rows of crowded bays, each one separated by a thin blue paper curtain, every bed occupied by a mother and encircled by visitors, small children running wild in the clamour. It looked like half of East London was whiling away the afternoon here in this vast barn of a room.

The midwife wheeled me to my bed and took the baby from me, placing him in a plastic cot. Climbing awkwardly onto the bed, I could feel that the shock was wearing off, and pain was right behind it, biding its time.

'This is insane. You'll never sleep here,' said Paul. 'I'm going to ask about getting you into a private room. Or should we have you both discharged and go home?'

He looked at me, waiting for me to speak. I was about to agree with him when I noticed a man coming out of a door marked *Toilet – Patients Only*, still doing up his fly, and I realised I couldn't face the outside world yet.

'I think I want to stay here,' I said. 'They still need to check the baby. But you don't need to get me my own room.'

He leaned over the cot. He looked sad, almost, but I still didn't know him well enough to interpret his expressions. Normally he was contained, and his face never betrayed emotion unwittingly. If anything, he was adept at reading other people's moods, while giving away nothing himself. But right now, he looked raw with feeling.

'You need to feed him,' he told me. 'He's hungry.'

'Is he? How can you tell?' Looking at the baby, I saw that he was writhing in discomfort and moving his head from side to side, his mouth open. Did that mean he was hungry?

'I can't, really. But you should try.'

I picked him up and tried to feed him, feeling guilty that I hadn't noticed his distress, as Paul disappeared in the direction of the nurses' station. While he was gone I focused on feeding the baby, positioning him as the midwife had shown me just after the birth. It seemed to work. As his jaw moved his eyes closed and he became motionless against me. After a few minutes Paul returned.

'Okay. You're moving to a side room now. I had to pay for it, but at least you'll get some sleep.'

'You didn't have to do that, Paul. I'm fine where I am.'

Surely there was safety in numbers, and at least here I was surrounded by other mothers. And maybe once all the visitors left it would feel less frenetic. But Paul shook his head.

'I really do think it's better for you to have a private room. It's no trouble, Simone. It all feels a bit much out here.'

'Okay.'

'Come with me.'

'Let me try to feed him a bit more first. I think it's working.' And it was, somehow. I could feel his timid mouth moving sweetly against me, and the noise and chaos of the ward receded as I stared down at him, mesmerised.

Soon he was asleep again, and I got off the bed slowly, feeling swollen and weary, holding onto the plastic trolley for support. Once we had shut the door and settled into the new room, Paul seemed to relax a little, and I suddenly remembered I hadn't told my parents.

I messaged them, attaching a photo of the sleeping baby, and felt guilty for not calling sooner. Although they'd never said anything, I could sense from their measured tone in emails and phone calls that I'd disappointed them by moving to London to launch my illustrious career and instead getting pregnant with a man I'd only just met. Although it was after midnight in Perth my phone lit up almost instantly, but I wasn't ready to answer my mum's questions about the birth or anything else, so I put it screen-down on the table, telling myself I'd call her back in the morning, once I'd pulled myself together.

As it darkened outside, a porter arrived with food, and I fell upon the lukewarm chicken with shiny gravy, mashed potato and limp grey broccoli as if it was the most delectable meal I had ever been presented with. While I ate, Paul held his son. It suited him. He was unmistakably the baby's father, and as he watched me eating, encouraging me to finish it all, I saw something new in him: a gentleness, a vulnerability, that was unlike his usual loudness and energy.

'How are you feeling?' I asked him. 'Everyone has been so focused on me and the baby, but you must be exhausted.'

Over the weekend he'd been by my side the entire time, neither of us sleeping much. We'd started off counting contractions, listing each one in a notebook. God knows where that notebook was now. Abandoned somewhere between the unmade bed and the messy kitchen and the undrained bathtub and the vomit bucket, probably. All those birth and pregnancy books I'd read and not one had bothered to mention that so-called early labour could go on for days. Once we'd got to the hospital he'd been quiet, letting the midwives and doctors take over, appearing younger and meeker than I'd ever seen him.

'Oh, I'm pretty tired. I'll be fine, though. I'll get some sleep tonight, at least.'

'It's funny, isn't it – I've been so focused on the birth, like that's the main event, I haven't really thought about what comes next.'

A silence. He looked down at the baby for a long moment, before standing up and placing him back into the cot. 'What comes next is sleep. Once you're home it will be – I don't know, crazy, probably. Try to get some rest and we'll see where we're at tomorrow.'

His phone beeped and he pulled it out of his jacket pocket and checked it, then sighed and put it away again.

'Who is it?'

'No-one. Messages from family.'

'What did your parents say?'

'They were happy. Said they'll come and see us soon.'

Through the window, the courtyard was grey and bare as the lights inside seemed to glow brighter in contrast. Across the way I could see into a room identical to mine, where an older, bearded man in a hospital gown sat facing me. A doctor stood over him, talking and gesturing while he appeared to sink further and further into himself. She glanced out the window, then walked over to it and drew the curtains shut.

'Maybe I'll get going,' said Paul. 'Sort out the apartment and do some food shopping. God, I'm tired.'

'Okay.' My belly full, I felt myself falling irresistibly into sleep, away from this day.

'Will you be alright here? It feels strange leaving you two.'

'We're fine. Honestly. Come back in the morning.'

He kissed his son's forehead and adjusted his blanket, then kissed me goodbye.

'You look beautiful as a mother,' he told me. 'I knew you would.' And then he was gone, closing the door behind him.

Finally it was just the two of us, like it had been for months. Instead of rolling and stretching in my belly, here he was in the room with me. Feeling like a small girl saying goodnight to her doll, I pulled the cot closer and stared at him for long moments, then turned off the lamp, lay down and closed my eyes in relief. Sleep. At last.

Ah-ah-ah.

A strange bird-like call was coming from the plastic cot, somewhere close to my head in the darkness. I sat up, too quickly, and felt immediately that the painkillers had worn off. I could feel a dull ache, a swollen, pulling pain from the stitches that was like sitting on a cushion of glass shards. I found the light switch as the cries got louder and more insistent, then picked up the baby and tried to feed him again. I rocked him while simultaneously trying to force my nipple into his mouth. He frantically attempted to make contact but couldn't, and soon he was screaming with frustration.

Eventually a tiny woman with a gentle face and light brown, very curly hair appeared at the door. She invited me to sit on a chair beside her, then placed a pillow in my lap and laid the baby on it, opening up his blanket so I could see his tiny nappy, his skinny little legs curled up against his body. Because it was what I'd seen mothers do with newborns, I started to rock him again.

'Don't rock him,' she said. 'You'll give him wind. If you tilt his head towards you, his mouth will open naturally.'

Her voice was low and French-accented, and somehow its calmness washed over both the baby and me, as he managed to latch on.

'If you leave the blanket open it will keep him slightly chilly and he'll stay awake for longer,' she said. 'And that way he'll get a better feed before he wears himself out.'

And, exactly as she said, he stayed awake, his spindly, purplish legs splayed on the pillow, his mouth moving rhythmically, his body relaxing into mine and then slowly into sleep as his belly – the size of a walnut, apparently – filled with milk. What had felt awkward and unachievable on my own had suddenly become possible, even easy, with the help of this anonymous curly-headed saint.

She melted away at some point, as silently as she had materialised, closing the door behind her. And then I was back in bed,
the baby beside me in his cot, and we both fell into a soundless
sleep.

2

Again the baby woke. The time was a little after four, according to my phone. I turned on the light and peered into the cot, where I found him crying and drawing his feet up to his chest. As I picked him up I smelled something strange.

Laying him on my bed, I opened his nappy and in the lamplight I could see a black substance with a greenish tinge to it. It had a strange, biological smell and an oily sheen like it came from some liquefied tree, long buried in a primordial forest. In my drowsy state I wondered if he had been somehow poisoned, until I woke up a little and realised it was meconium. The stuff was impossible to clean away, clinging to his skin like tar, so I picked him up and rinsed his skinny legs and bottom off under the hand basin, making sure the water wasn't too hot or cold.

As he hung there, limp and helpless as a skinned rabbit, I felt so sorry for him. He had no choice but to submit to me. He couldn't move, couldn't talk, couldn't do a single thing for himself. He had no language apart from wailing, and was completely dependent on my mercy. And what he didn't know, or perhaps he did, was that I was hopelessly incompetent, in no way capable of being in charge of such a fragile being. I had never even owned a kitten.

I didn't have a towel, so I dried him on the sheet, found a new-born nappy in my bag and carefully put it on him, trying not to straighten his legs, which were drawn up, frog-like, to his belly, as they would have been less than a day ago when he was still inside me. Then I attempted to feed him again, like the French angel had shown me, with his bare skin against mine and his face falling towards me on the pillow. It seemed to work.

Wrapped up again, and lying on the bed beside me, he gazed into my eyes. He seemed suddenly alert, so I put my arm around him and waited to see what he would do next. Still he looked at me and it was an eerie feeling, to know that he was staring into someone's eyes for the very first time. His pale face was a curved glowing moon in the dawn light, his dark, lashless eyes fixed on mine with an expression that seemed to mirror my fascination. Finally we were seeing each other, after all these months together. No-one had ever looked at me like that – so honest and unguarded.

Eventually his eyelids closed in slow motion. I waited, but they did not open. His face became as motionless as a photograph. Still I kept staring at him.

A mother had once said to me, *If the baby's happy, I'm happy*, and I had assumed she was stoically making the best of what looked like a pretty uneventful existence. But I had been wrong. As soon as the baby was comfortable, fed and sleeping, I felt at peace. It seemed that while he was awake I was on duty, but once he was asleep I could loosen my grip, and his hold on me relaxed. He was stable, coasting in neutral, and I had time to work out what to do next. For now, still enclosed by the hospital, by the big silent security guard at the door of the ward, by the machines and protocols and that folder of notes recording our progress, I felt no pressure. Outside I could hear the ward waking, shifting up a gear, but here in this room it was quiet.

Soon we'd have to go home. It was a place I'd never given much thought, but suddenly the prospect of living somewhere like the Barbican with a baby seemed odd. A famed modernist development rising in stained concrete from a wartime bombsite, its public areas were windswept and bleak. Even the ducks in the formal rectangular ponds looked subdued. It was a place for finance professionals and rich artists and eccentric elderly lawyers. Not babies, or their mothers.

I had moved in with Paul towards the end of last winter, after staying there more often than not and falling into a dream-filled sleep every night thanks to the underfloor heating that kept the whole apartment deliciously warm.

My real home, if you could call it that, had been a narrow Victorian townhouse in Finsbury Park, where the landlord, who lived next door, kept the heating on for exactly one hour in the morning and one more at night, never quite taking the chill out of my dark, creaky single bedroom. I'd found the place online a few weeks after I'd flounced out of Perth and realised that my salary wouldn't quite stretch to the one-bedroom flat in Borough I'd been anticipating.

It had felt a bit weird to be sleeping in a single bed again in my late twenties, but the rent was cheap and all-inclusive and my bedroom window looked out over a patchwork of back gardens with wooden sheds and purple buddleias, and a golden-haired fox sometimes lazing on the grass. These were the wild, unloved gardens of people who worked full time in the city and rarely thought about them. Each owner at some point had made their attempt at planting a tree, and so crowded along the back fence were pale birches and an apple tree that flowered extravagant pink in spring, and a lone thin pine that sharpened the air when I hung washing out there on a rare sunny day. It was a long commute after work, catching the Victoria line to Finsbury Park and then a bus up Stroud Green Road.

So somehow me and my unironed work clothes from cheap high-street shops, and a few books and toiletries, had become semi-permanent fixtures in Paul's tightly sealed Zone One apartment, where the bathroom had a long white tub with endless hot water, and a garbage chute in the kitchen wafted foul and ancient odours from the depths of the building, and a curved concrete balcony, stained by chemical rain, overlooked the office blocks of

Farringdon, which were permanently lit up, even at three in the morning.

Here in the heart of the financial district everything felt controlled and sterile. Nothing much grew apart from the unnaturally bright pansies that spilled from hanging baskets outside old pubs, and they were maintained not by the pub owners but by a private gardening company. Security guards patrolled the main roads into this maze of narrow streets, and even the walk from the Tube was fast and warm, through a sheltered underpass. At the front desk were doormen – uniformly grey-haired and closely shaved – who never acknowledged me, yet must have recognised me as they always let me walk past them and into the lift without comment.

Paul worked in the city for an American bank as an information security threat management specialist, whatever that was. He wasn't around much, but then neither was I. He left before dawn to go to the gym and then to the office, and didn't return until eight or nine at night. He made money, though. Enough to take me to dinner on a Friday night at Le Café du Marché, or to bring me home Swiss chocolates or roses or tickets to Paris on the Eurostar for a weekend. Compared to me, on my entry-level salary as an editorial assistant at a lifestyle magazine in Mayfair, he was rich.

Even when he wasn't at the office, he was often out, or away on business trips, and I would sometimes wonder, as I opened the door to the empty apartment, whether this was actually what I wanted. He had chosen me, really, casually asking for my phone number at the end of a work colleague's birthday party. Her boyfriend had been to uni with him in Bristol, and a week later he'd called me up and invited me to *supper* at his apartment.

His cooking that night had been careless but somehow impressive – asparagus, pasta with fresh clams, still in their greyish shells, and a block of dark chocolate for pudding, as he called it – and his apartment was sparsely furnished with the obligatory Barcelona chair, a soft white leather couch, a shabby Persian rug.

We shared a bottle of champagne and I stumbled out, sometime around midnight, suspecting that he would be happy if I stayed but wouldn't really care if I left, either. To me he seemed like a rich kid who had been given everything he needed in life, and while he was always kind to me, I was wary of getting too attached to someone so comfortable. I didn't want to get too used to his apartment, or the ease with which he could throw his credit card at problems. Those expressionless and clean-cut white men who guarded the lobby would have seen plenty of young women heading up to his apartment. I didn't want to start thinking I mattered.

But then, one Friday night at Le Café du Marché, he surprised me. I mentioned how exhausting it was travelling up to Finsbury Park after work, when I wasn't staying over, and how packed the Victoria line was in the mornings. As Paul started on his *côte de boeuf*, he appeared to be thinking.

'Why don't you live with me?' he said, as casually as suggesting we stop by Waitrose on the way home. 'You don't have much stuff, do you? And most of it's at my place now anyway. Maybe you can help out a bit with bills, but you don't need to pay me rent. You don't even need to pay for bills, actually.'

'Really?' More than half of my pay was tucked into an envelope for my landlord each month.

He smiled at me. 'Yeah. I don't mind. You're here most of the time anyway. I mean, all that rent you're paying. Keep it for yourself. Or spend it on me.' He poured himself another glass of Beaujolais.

'But we barely know each other. Doesn't it seem a bit early to be living together?'

He looked at me fondly. 'Not really.'

'And what will your parents say? I've never even met them.'

'They will think you're wonderful. A gift from a benign god. You're sweet, hard-working, clever. Trust me, you'll make them very happy.'

I didn't know what to say. On the one hand, I barely knew him. But I liked him. He was good company. Funny. Passionate, when the mood took him. Sometimes he went a bit quiet, and a few times he'd neglect to answer his phone and I'd go home alone, wondering if I'd misunderstood our plans to meet up that night. He'd always ring the next day, sleepy and apologetic, and I'd let it go.

It was too soon to be living together. But my commute would be so much faster, so much less hideous. His apartment was warm. And it would be a relief to live with only one other person, and not in a shared house, always competing for limited fridge space and hot water. We weren't that close, it was true. But maybe I could fall in love with him over time. Maybe I did love him?

'You really don't mind?'

In the dimly lit room he had looked so solid, his white shirt sleeves rolled up, his dark blond hair gleaming in the candlelight as he sliced his rare steak with an unhurried certainty that seemed to come from knowing there would always be more food. And that he could pay for any number of equally fine dinners in any London restaurant, pulling out two or three rumpled pink fifty-pound notes and tossing them onto the silver tray so they fanned out slightly, before the waiter came to take them away.

He shook his head, his eyes on mine.

'Okay.' I lifted my glass of wine and clinked it against his. 'Thank you.'

And just like that, I moved in with him. The following Saturday I hired a white van and packed it with my collection of mismatched suitcases and plastic bags, and soon my room in Finsbury Park was empty and I told the indifferent landlord I wouldn't be leaving another envelope of cash in the fridge for him on the first working day of the month.

Paul seemed happy enough to have me there, when he rolled in late at night from work or the gym or the pub and sidled up to me, warming his cold face against mine. But it was lonely sometimes, up in that tower block, without the chatter and slamming doors of a shared house, let alone a Sunday-night roast dinner at my parents' house or a long morning at the beach with friends. At least until I was pregnant, and had a baby tucked in my belly for company.

He didn't need me and I didn't really need him, either, when it came right down to it. It was, for me, a place to pass the tail end of winter; for him, a warm body in his bed, someone to come home to so he didn't have to go looking.

It wasn't really fair to bring a baby into our precarious arrangement, I realised now, looking down at my newborn's solemn face. A pregnancy was not part of the plan, and when I broke the news to Paul I expected a throat-clearing, followed by the tactful mention of some private clinic in Surrey where the matter could be quietly taken care of. Not that I would have gone, because when I saw those two strong pink lines on the supermarket test I felt ready, sensed that there would be no letting this one go, whatever Paul might say about it. I comforted myself with the thought that I could always slip back to Australia if he turfed me out, could send him photos and birthday cards and be a single mum back in Perth. It wasn't exactly how I'd pictured motherhood, but I'd seen friends make a success of it, and maybe I'd meet someone else eventually.

But Paul surprised me. 'I want you to have it,' he said, and as I stared at him, thinking of how to reply, he appeared to be holding his breath. 'I've wanted a baby for years.'

'Really? But we've only been together a few months.'

'That's how it happens sometimes. Doesn't mean it can't work. I'll look after you,' he said, taking my hand and kissing it. 'I'll look after both of you.'

And he did, coming along to the twelve-week scan and appearing humbled and a little intimidated, as I was, by the great thundering machine of NHS healthcare. He even suggested getting married, sometime in the future, and I said, 'Maybe.'

And when the baby was born and the doctor handed him to Paul, he spoke to the little mewling newborn so softly that I knew he had fallen in love with him, that he would always be around for him, even if we weren't quite together in the way that other parents seemed to be.

The baby startled suddenly in his sleep and I picked him up. Maybe it will work, I thought as I held him close, the weight of him against me an oddly familiar comfort when everything else felt so strange.

A voice called from somewhere outside, 'Breakfast, ladies! Come and get it.'

'Seriously?' I muttered to myself. 'Don't they know what we've been through?'

But I was too ravenous to stage much of a protest, so I got out of bed and shuffled towards the smell of coffee, leaving the baby alone for the first time.

As I stepped into the bare light of the early morning, the postnatal ward looked dingy and overcrowded: a modern, women-only version of a Dickensian workhouse where exhausted new mothers in crumpled gowns lined up for Nescafé and high-fibre cereal instead of gruel.

I thought back to my giddy departure at Perth airport almost two years ago, slinging my passport with its embossed UK Ancestry visa at the border official, boarding the Tube at Heathrow with sparkling visions of career success, cocktail bars, every hair day a good one. The unkind morning light of this ward had not featured in those daydreams. As I stirred sugar into my coffee I looked down at my bare feet, and noticed that one of my toenails, which I'd painted just before the birth, had been inexplicably scrubbed clean of polish. When did that happen? *Why* did that happen?

The hospital, which had felt soft-edged and safe in the hours before dawn, now felt sinister and bureaucratic. Whatever hormonal cocktail had buoyed me through pregnancy and labour, giving me endless reserves of energy and high spirits, now seemed to be departing my cells with efficient haste. Hot, urgent tears welled up in my eyes as I got back into bed and lifted the sleeping baby onto my lap. I wanted to go home. More specifically, I wanted to have a home to go to. Paul's apartment didn't feel like a place that belonged to me. It was his, not mine.

As the morning went on, people came and went: a nurse to give the baby an injection, a doctor to check on the baby and me. In between visits, I tried to call Paul, but he didn't answer. A midwife appeared and took my observations, then looked at my drugs chart and said, 'Oh, we've only given you Panadol. That's a bit mean, isn't it? Let me write you up for something stronger.'

'Thanks.'

'Is your partner coming in soon?'

'I think so. He isn't answering the phone right now. He might still be sleeping.'

'Are you okay?' She sat down beside me but said nothing, leaving a practised silence for me to fill.

'Oh, I feel a little bit stunned by it all, I guess.'

'Is there anything you want to bring up about the birth, before you go home? Anything you want to ask about?'

I thought for a moment, wondering how I could tactfully explain how barbaric it had all seemed without offending her.

'I had very low expectations of childbirth ...' I began, *but that was absolutely horrendous*, I readied myself to say. I was surprised when she laughed and touched my hand.

'Oh, bless you. Most women who come in here have such high expectations for their birth experience. We always say, the longer the birth plan, the greater the likelihood of an emergency C-section. They get stressed when it goes off-plan, the baby gets distressed, and off they go to the theatre.'

'Well, I really didn't expect much. I mean, I didn't see how it could go well, given what actually has to physically – you know – happen. But it was kind of so much worse than I'd expected. And I guess I was surprised that there were so many people in the room.'

She picked up my notes, read through them. 'Ah, yes. Instrumental delivery. And you had very high blood pressure. You would have a lot of doctors for a high-risk delivery like that. Two for the baby, one for the birth, one for you. Plus two midwives.'

'I didn't realise it was a high-risk delivery.'

'A lot of them are. Birth is a risky event. But you were in the right place. Do you have any family here, or just your partner?'

'Not really. They're in Perth. I think they'll come over in the summer, when things have settled down a bit.'

'And your partner? He's supportive?'

'He's great. He's really happy, I think.'

'You think?' She tilted her head.

'He seems happier than me.'

'Well, he didn't just deliver a baby. You're allowed to feel a bit shell-shocked. It would be strange if you didn't.'

'I know. One more thing – what happened to my toenail?' I showed her my foot, with its four perfectly manicured pink nails and one scrubbed clean.

'We take the nail polish off if it looks like it might go to a C-section. Your nails turn blue if you're oxygen-compromised.'

'Oh, right.' I suddenly thought back to all my glossy pregnancy books, with their photos of serene women and illustrated cross-sections of babies gliding smoothly from 'birth canals'. When I got home I was going to take every single one of them to the charity shop. Or chuck them in the bin, and spare some other woman the nonsense.

We sat quietly for a moment, and I was about to mention the feeling of panic, the fact that I hadn't really slept and didn't know what I was supposed to be doing with the baby, but just as I opened my mouth Paul burst in, looking larger than life, well-rested and eager, bringing with him the cold air and hustle of the outside world.

'Hello. How's the little man?' He leaned over the cot and picked up the baby, who had been lying quietly, eyes open, as I talked with the midwife.

'How are you doing, Simone? Should we get going? I want to take him home.'

'Do we need to go now?' I asked the midwife.

She looked conflicted. 'You can go now, if you feel up to it.'

I really don't, I wanted to say. But I also knew how busy London hospitals were, how there were never enough beds for everyone that needed one. If I left, someone else would be in this room within half an hour. Yet part of me wanted to stay here, to put off the moment I had to go home and face up to my new existence instead of being a passive patient.

'I think you should come home now,' said Paul. 'We'll be fine. We've got everything we need and you can get some proper sleep in your own bed.'

He started packing my bag, throwing my phone and water bottle into it, gathering up the baby's nappies and wipes from the table.

Soon we were ready, and I put on my coat. The midwife had gone to see another woman, and I was suddenly returning to the real world. The security guard checked our form and the ID wristband on the baby and opened the locked door of the postnatal ward, and then I was back in the lift that I had whimpered in two days earlier with a contraction, my face pressed to the wall, telling myself, *Soon this will all be over.*

'You okay?' said Paul as we stood in the hospital entrance, waiting for the rain to stop, while the woman at the reception desk cooed over my sleeping newborn, tucked into his car seat.

'I'm fine.' I scanned the car park for hazards, half-expecting someone from the hospital to stop us. It seemed absurd that I was allowed to shuffle out of here with a day-old infant.

'You sure? I feel like I had a smiling girlfriend two days ago and I've walked out with a stranger.'

I looked at him blankly. 'I'm fine. Just tired.'

He stared at me for a long moment.

'I guess I'm surprised that they let us go,' I said. 'I mean, neither of us knows what we're doing. Well, I certainly don't.'

He smiled, looking relieved. 'You'll be fine, Simone. Really, how hard can it be? Feed, sleep, change nappies.' He picked up the car seat. 'Okay, it's easing off. Let's race out now.'

Once in the car, I tucked a blanket over the baby, making sure his head looked comfortable. I'd read somewhere you weren't meant to leave babies in car seats for long as they could suffocate, and the rush hour was still on.

Paul drove with his usual pushiness through the streets, braking hard and accelerating harder. I gritted my teeth. He didn't like me commenting on his driving, but sometimes, behind the wheel, he was a different person, engaging in petty warfare with every other driver, swearing and blaring his horn and fuming to himself. Usually I could ignore it, but not today.

'Can you please stop that?' I finally said.

'Stop what?'

'Driving like that. So aggressive. And swearing at everyone.'

'I always drive like this. It's London. This is how you drive.' He looked at me in apparent disbelief.

'But with the baby here, I think you need to slow down a bit. Not get so angry.'

He sat back and took a deep breath. His driving slowed, and he looked a little contrite. 'You're right. I'm sorry, Simone.'

As we drove past Old Street and turned off towards the Barbican I felt my mood shift. By the time we made it through the reception I was almost in tears. It hit me that life as I'd known it was over and I would never adjust to this. Everything I'd had – sleep, work, freedom, a body free of injury and pain – was gone without warning. What had been an exciting checklist, another rung on the ladder of being an adult – getting ready for the baby – was now a life sentence.

As I sat down on the couch and picked up the baby, who was waking up and crying with hunger, I had a sudden memory of last year, in early spring, when I'd just arrived in London and was staying at a flat in Kennington with an old school friend, Michelle.

I had gone out in the morning, the sun shining, wearing a t-shirt and jeans, buoyed by the pale blue sky and the tall mauve tulips growing in the park. But as the day went on the temperature dropped, until I was colder than I had ever been in my life. A bone-deep, aching cold that made me long for a hot bath and then a warm bed.

When I got back to Michelle's flat, I realised I was locked out, and when I called her she was stuck on a slow-moving bus from Brixton. The entire front of the old Georgian building was covered in scaffolding, but I could see that her third-floor living room window was slightly open. So I climbed up the builder's ladder, planning to walk along the timber planks and enter through the window.

But I went too far up the ladder, all the way to the top of the building, and suddenly I was looking out over the rooftop and across south London. There was no more ladder, nothing to do except contain my fear and try not to panic or look down and see how far I might fall, or how precarious my hold was on the paint-spattered metal. Slowly I edged down, reminding myself that the builders did this every day, that if I kept going I would soon be safe.

This was the exact same feeling of panic, of vertigo. Of suddenly finding myself doing something I was in no way qualified for, and that was nothing like I had expected. There was no more ladder. This was it.

3

As the weak winter daylight outside faded away and the office buildings glowed in the dusk, me and the baby – and I needed to stop calling him that, we had to think of a name – lay together on the bed, him wrapped in my grey cardigan, a tidy little bundle, beside me. Paul had made me food and tea and I could hear the TV in the living room.

Sometime later, I opened my eyes to darkness. The bundle was motionless beside me, sinister and quiet. Half-asleep and panicking, I yanked it towards me, thinking that the cardigan had slipped over the tiny nostrils and mouth and suffocated him. But he was breathing. Still, a moment of inattention, a deep sleep, a fall, could be catastrophic.

The clock beside me read 11.10 pm and as I lay there, it felt like a dark sheet had slid off a movie screen in my mind and a scratchy film began playing of all the dangers that now surrounded us, which I half-remembered from news stories and the lives of people around me – former neighbours, cousins of friends.

He was a baby, but he was also a light, delicate object. How easy it would be to slip and drop him from one of the Barbican's walkways, or over a stairwell, or for his pram to roll in front of a Tube train, or for a blanket to cover his airway in his sleep. For some innocuous rash or cough to turn deadly. To leave him on a bus, or out in the rain. For someone to steal him away from me. And then to be forever living in the aftermath, imagining all the things I would never know about him. The scenes rolled in front of my eyes, each one making me hold my breath and squeeze my eyes shut. These were cut with out-of-body moments from the labour ward and all those blank bodies in uniforms surrounding me, and even though I was still so tired I resisted sleep, because I felt as if the only way I could keep us both safe was by watching him.

Every hour or so he would stir in his sleep and begin to fret beside me, wanting to be fed. Feeding him was starting to hurt, his dry, peeling hands scratching me, his mouth on my raw skin, his little face banging against me as he failed to latch on and I started to sweat with panic. At some point, I must have fallen asleep, but then the city started to wake up, with the thump and crash of the slow-moving garbage trucks and the hum of traffic dragging me back to myself and the restless baby beside me.

By morning, my head felt like it was wrapped in a fog-coloured blanket. My eyes were gritty, my body dragged. The apartment felt different, too, cold and bleak. In the last days of pregnancy, after I'd gone on maternity leave, it had felt like a peaceful little nest high above the city. I watched movies and walked in the Barbican's residents-only garden, the trees still holding a few papery apricot-coloured leaves and the baby warm in my belly, and slept through the short afternoons until night fell. Through those last days of pottering and folding baby clothes and imagining what lay ahead of me, he'd been an invisible presence who demanded nothing, and the prospect of meeting him or her had made me almost faint with happiness.

And now he was here, and I was constantly vigilant, wondering what he'd require next, and how I might deliver it. A *little stranger*, as the Victorians had called newborns, and he was. A small, howling stranger, so different from that lovely, unseen creature in my belly. It felt like he'd barely slept since the birth, and as a result neither had I. How long would this go on for?

Around noon, the doorbell rang. Paul was in the hallway and I expected him to deal with it, but I heard him shut himself into the spare room. The bell rang again, this time a little longer, as if someone was pressing down hard with a finger. I got up slowly and made my way to the front door. Two women stood there, dressed in puffer jackets and boots. They smiled at me warmly, and I remembered reading something in my NHS Red Book about home visits after the birth.

'We're from the hospital. We've come to check on you.'

They came into my bedroom and weighed the baby, holding him up in a little calico sling attached to metal scales. He slumped in the cream fabric, dangling in the air like the stork was delivering him. The clear winter light crossed his sleepy face and I wanted to hold him close.

If I focused on him and nothing else, I felt euphoric, admiring that perfect skin, his soft and compact body warm with life, his clenched fists and his rich baby smell that I suddenly wanted to bury my face in. His eyes were starting to sprout lashes, I saw, when the midwife handed him back to me.

In the hallway, I heard Paul's phone ring and him stepping out of the spare room to answer it.

'She's with the midwives at the moment.'

A pause. I listened, wondering if it was Paul's parents calling to arrange a visit. The door closed and I couldn't hear anything more.

The midwife was looking at me. 'How are you going, generally?'

Her voice was so gentle that my eyes filled with tears. 'Okay.'

'Day three. Totally normal to be crying,' she said cheerfully, and I felt a bit happier, even as I tried to wipe away tears with my sleeve. She pulled out a box of tissues from her bag and offered me one.

'And it looks like you have a supportive partner? Is he off work for now?'

'Yes, he's got three weeks off. He's been great.' I dabbed my eyes. Of course he was supportive. But neither of us had known what we were getting into, what it meant to have a child. And what had been so casual between us now felt precarious, the responsibility of the baby hanging like a heavy, priceless ornament on a spindly Christmas tree. I struggled to remember why we'd done this, what the thought process had been. How I'd even gotten pregnant.

It had been, most likely, one night when I'd gone out in Soho with my work colleagues. We went to Black's, a club that our magazine's art director belonged to, crowding into a basement room of timber-panelled dark grey walls and creaky tables, with glass jars of fresh spring flowers providing the only spots of colour in the gloom. I sat with my colleagues late into the evening, emptying bottles of red wine as people's legs passed by on the pavement outside. And then someone from home appeared, a boy from my high school history class who now lived in Notting Hill. I'd been quite drunk, chatting to him about London, and then Paul was somehow beside me –

'Any more questions? Is the feeding going okay?'

I looked at the midwife in confusion, because for a long moment I'd been back in that blurry Soho basement. There was something about that night I'd forgotten, something important.

'Not really. It's starting to hurt.' *And it feels like it's all I do*, I wanted to add. *And I haven't had more than two hours of unbroken sleep since I went into labour.*

'It's often like that at the start. But let me help you.'

The midwives stayed for a while, helping me feed the baby, who seemed to sense their authority and calmed himself enough to fill his belly and then fall asleep in my arms.

After writing some notes in a folder and handing me more brochures on local support groups, they prepared to leave.

'Call if you need us.'

A week passed, and then it was Christmas. We marked the day with a couple of festive ready meals heated up and eaten in bed.

The baby – we had named him Thomas, after Paul's grandfather, but I still thought of him as 'the baby' – alternated between a still, almost breathless sleep and what appeared to be pure, unfiltered rage. His whole head flushed a deep pink and his mouth grew huge, his eyes locked on mine. Was he terrified, dying in agony, or simply hungry? I never knew. The sight of him in that state left me drained, yet wired. Afterwards, I'd pace around the apartment, trying to get back to neutral. Or I'd lie beside him, wanting to sleep, but knowing that as soon as I did he would wake me again. Sleep had become something unpredictable that fell upon me, wiped me out like a heavy grey wave, then dumped me on the shore, wide-awake again, at three in the morning or five in the afternoon, alert and terrified.

One dawn, when he was maybe two weeks old, I had a magical thought. As I lay beside him watching objects in the room slowly become visible, knowing there was no point in closing my eyes, it suddenly came to me: I didn't need to sleep. How had I never realised that before?

When my mother called I told her everything was going fine, not wanting to worry her. I posted photos of the baby to Facebook, and liked every comment from friends and relatives back home. And when people dropped over to hold the baby and give us gifts of teddy bears and tiny shoes, I smiled and talked and accepted the tea and the cakes they'd brought with them, feeling oddly light and detached, like they were very far away. Of course sometimes I'd drop into sleep, unexpectedly, but mostly I didn't bother.

'He loves you so much,' Paul kept telling me.

'Really? How can you tell?'

'He just does. He needs you.'

And he did seem to. Curling into my belly, asleep, I could see how he'd lain inside me. It was as if everything else – the whole messy world – had vanished, and now there was only me and him, existing in some strange, lamp-lit world of blankets and toast crumbs and the remote control.

Paul seemed very far away – he was the sound of dishes being washed in the kitchen, or a sleeping presence beside me during the wakeful nights. The orderly progression of working weeks followed by trying to pack as much enjoyment and sleep as possible into the weekends was gone. A constant checklist ticked over feverishly in my head – *change nappy feed baby buy food coffee water feed baby nappy bath shower dress*. It all blurred, the need to both look after him and keep him safe. He was surrounded by peril, requiring me to be completely present, listening for the stirrings from the bassinet where he never slept for long, summoning me at any time of day or night, while Paul hovered in the background.

Sleep when the baby sleeps, said the pristine, bossy baby books that I'd read before he was born, and I had planned to do exactly that. But what I hadn't realised then was that the unpredictable hours when the baby slept were the only times I had to myself. Why would I miss them by sleeping? Instead I wandered from room to room, staring out of the windows at the office workers busy at their desks, thinking of all the things I should be doing, but usually ending up slumped on the couch, watching a hospital emergency documentary on TV, which in its messiness and panic and general grimness suited my mood perfectly.

The baby himself was the only thing that seemed to make sense. While my thoughts wandered down dark corridors and my body felt pinned down with pain and exhaustion and baby weight, there was still the quiet pleasure of wrapping him up, tucking away his tiny-boned hands and long, mottled feet. Some dim, primitive corner of my brain revelled in attending to his small and perfect body.

And then, at the end of week three, as Paul was getting ready for his first day back at work, his phone rang. He looked at the screen, got up and walked to the spare room, quietly closing the door behind him. He was in there for a long time. And then he was sitting down beside me.

'So that was Rachel on the phone. Do you remember her? My cousin?'

'No. Not really.'

'She was at Lucy's wedding. Tall? Dark hair?'

'Oh. Sort of.'

'She wanted to know if she could come and stay. She's been away for six months on some forest herbs research thing in Brazil and is hoping to get some work in London.'

Every word in that sentence made my head pound, but I didn't want to be rude about his cousin, so I kept my voice steady.

'But does she really want to stay here? It's chaos at the moment. No-one is sleeping.'

The thought of anyone seeing me in this state did not appeal. I seemed to be devolving into a near-mute, soft-edged nocturnal creature, blinking at bright light and incapable of wit or decision-making or even basic small talk. I could chat on the phone and appear normal when I needed to, but the prospect of never being able to drop that facade was daunting.

'She said she wants to help you.'

That swayed me. Paul handled some tasks with surprising competence, changing nappies, bathing him, dressing him with sure fingers. But whenever the baby cried, he handed him straight back to me, often disappearing into the bathroom or spare bedroom as if he couldn't tolerate the noise, and he was going back to his normal life today. Having someone around might be nice, even if I didn't know her that well.

'Rachel. I'm trying to remember her ...'

As I stared down at my newborn, I pieced together my first impression of Paul's cousin. We'd only met once, at Paul's sister's wedding last May – a gathering of impeccably dressed people with refined accents, endless gin and tonic flowing, the hum of serious hunting talk and light banter filling the spring air. The ceremony was held on Paul's family estate in Dorset, a rambling sixteenth-century manor with some beautiful ancient name and surprisingly unrenovated interiors, a dog lolling on every shabby couch and faded Persian rug. The actual service was held at a small chapel on the property, the evening reception in a vast white marquee in a back paddock. There was a lot of food – prawns, roast beef, Eton mess and cheese – and a subdued atmosphere that was at odds with other weddings I'd been to back home. As an Australian, and the only foreigner, I was treated as something of a novelty, and no one seemed to quite know what to say to me, although his mother, Penelope, made a special effort to introduce me to everyone. Paul and I were given an attic bedroom to share with thick plaster walls and a huge bed covered in a heavy red quilt, matted in dog hair.

Rachel was a bridesmaid, and when we arrived she walked up to Paul and looked me up and down while he made introductions. Something – some mood I didn't understand – was right there between them. She was willowy, but tall, much taller than me, with a pale oval face and dark hair, and she had a way of looking down at me that seemed to shut me out.

'This is Simone,' he said, smiling at me encouragingly. 'Rachel. My cousin.'

'Lovely to meet you, Simone,' she said. 'We've heard about you. You're from Australia, right?'

'That's right. From Perth.'

'Never made it to Perth,' she said, as if to herself. 'Now, can I get you a drink?'

Paul went on to get horrendously drunk, drinking with Rachel and their old friends, and eventually I left him to it.

Feeling dizzy and nauseous with morning sickness, it had been a relief to give in, to not even try to keep up with him and his family. Leaving the marquee glowing white in the darkness of the field, I'd made my way back to the house and fallen asleep in the attic room around midnight, and woken at six, alone. He appeared an hour or so later, and was sweet to me, almost apologetic. A few hours later he packed up the car and I drove us back to London straight after breakfast, and I hadn't given his cousin another thought until now.

'You can say no, of course. I said I'd check with you first.'

'Okay. It's fine.'

'Really?'

'Well, maybe she can sit up with him sometimes, in the mornings. And do some cooking, if she wants.'

'You can honestly say no. She can easily find somewhere else.'

But he looked at me as if the decision was mine alone to make. I thought of them at the wedding, how close they'd seemed. What could I say? It was his apartment. She was his cousin. If he felt obligated to put her up it wasn't my place to refuse, and anyway, I didn't have the energy. I closed my eyes, wanting the conversation to end.

'Yeah, it's fine, I guess. When does she want to come?'

He sighed. 'Well, that's the tricky thing. She gets here tomorrow. We'll have to organise the spare room a bit, make up the bed. I can do it now.'

'Don't worry, I'll do it. You need to get to work.'

'Okay. You're a star. Thanks, Simone.' He kissed me, rubbing his face against mine for a moment and I wished he could stay for longer.

As he stepped out the door, closing it behind him, I envied him for his ability to slip so easily back into the world, back into his work, despite the fact that he'd become a parent only three blurred weeks ago.

The bed in the spare room was a double, with a new mattress and a huge, downy quilt. I had thought about making it into the baby's bedroom eventually, if Paul didn't mind, as it was larger than his study and next to the bedroom we shared. Unfolding a white cover from the linen cupboard, I wrestled it over the quilt. Then I found two pillows, stretched a fitted sheet over the mattress, and dusted the furniture with a damp towel.

Once the bedroom was ready I gave the baby a bath. He was relaxed in my hands, the weight and shape of him already so familiar that it was like washing myself.

My phone, when I checked it, was full of messages, along with my inbox. Cards and flowers from work colleagues and friends and family back home still crowded the bedside table, but were starting to get lost among the milk-stained muslins and half-full water glasses. This was the new normal, I realised, at home all day with a tiny wordless human my only company. I picked up the cards and read through them. Flowery and pastel-coloured, they referred to a *safe delivery* and a *healthy beautiful baby* and *enjoying these precious days*.

Reading them, I felt like a captain on a lonely ship, far out at sea, receiving well-meaning messages from shore. None of the friends I'd made here had babies yet, and I didn't know where to find the women who did.

'Maybe it would be good to have some company,' I said aloud to the empty room. The baby stared at something I couldn't see, and made no sound.

That night, I lay awake as Paul fell easily into sleep and the baby stirred and began to fret beside me. I fed him and tried to settle him but still he cried. I rocked him and tried to put him down in his bassinet, again and again, but every time he woke up and wouldn't stop screaming until I held him again. Still Paul slept on, so I carried the baby out to the living room, where two walls of glass let the city in: offices to my right, a tower block of council flats straight ahead, across the road.

There, a single light shone. It was three am. The light glowed yellow against the darkness, cosy and intimate, and I stared at it as I held the baby, rocking him against my chest while he howled.

It was probably some young couple in there, home after a house party or a night out in Shoreditch. They would have been talking nonsense, the bloke getting hotter and funnier with every loose glass of vodka and soda. The two of them drawing closer, their friends glancing over every now and then but leaving them to it. Heading out together after some effortlessly negotiated agreement when it was clear where things were going. Still talking all the way down the middle of luxuriously deserted London streets. Silent dwellings all around, and only the two of them out in the night. Maybe a lone insomniac watching from a window as they finally kissed on the footpath. Stumbling up a flight of stairs, into a bedroom. Out of clothes, the alcohol easing everything, and then finally to bed, skin against skin. Drunk enough for it to be uninhibited, not so drunk that it would feel like a mistake in the morning. I could see all of it in that lit window, that yellow light.

Fools. Completely oblivious to what might lie ahead. Up in the night, holding some small screaming creature speaking a language you should understand, but don't. Silently panicking and sleep deprived and broken. Hormones all over the place. In no fit state, physically or mentally, for an easy drunken night like that ever again. The whole world dark and lonely and somehow skewed. And definitely no vodka.

When morning came I dressed the baby in a newborn nappy, then a white bodysuit and finally the cardigan Paul's mother had knitted him, a tiny pale blue thing of tightly packed wool, as if each stitch had been pulled hard. He looked compressed in it, the dense wool like armour against the cold, his face the brightest, freshest thing in the whole world. I was so tired now I couldn't see beyond him, beyond his little body. It had all vanished.

Sometime around five in the morning I had finally given up on the bassinet. He hated it, woke instantly when he was in it and cried like some pitiful animal abandoned in a forest. So by dawn he was in bed beside me, instantly asleep. I woke a couple of hours later, still on my side, curled around him, one arm below his wrapped legs, the other supporting my head, cold and stiff from being so still.

After his bath, my head foggy from deep sleep, I had breakfast and fed him and put him down for a nap, and as I was about to have a shower, the doorbell rang.

It was Rachel. She was wearing a thick, smokey layer of makeup on her eyes, with some glitter mixed in, and a tightly fitted, dark maroon dress, the kind of thing I would love to own, that I would have loved wearing before I had a baby. No coat, which was odd. Beside her stood a brown leather suitcase, worn but expensive looking.

I was still heavy from the pregnancy, and wearing billowy clothes that enabled me to breastfeed. I cared, but I didn't care.

She didn't quite meet my eyes as she said hello, looking beyond me, into the apartment. Before I could invite her in, she picked up her bag and slipped past me, heading for the lounge room as if she had been here before, and knew the apartment well.

'How are you getting along?' she asked over her shoulder.

'Not too bad.'

'Can I have the baby?'

Was that a weird question? Three weeks in, and I was so tired, I was finding it hard to have even the simplest conversations without getting confused. But I knew one thing: the baby was still and quiet in my bed, and she wasn't going to disturb that.

'He's sleeping at the moment.'

'Oh, that's okay. I might go and look at him.'

She walked away from me, down the long corridor to our bedroom, and I found myself following her uncertainly as she opened the door and stepped into the dark mess of our clothes, our unmade bed, the intimate smell of our shared sleep and, in the squalid lamplight, because I hadn't bothered to open the blinds yet, the shameful sight of our pink flannel sheet stained with milk and even some dried blood.

I didn't want her in the room, but how could I say it without sounding rude? She didn't seem to register my embarrassment as she sat down on the bed, and I tried not to think about her journey here, probably sitting on some filthy Tube seat.

The baby lay with his arms flung above his head in an attitude of complete abandon, his chest moving very slightly as she leaned closer and started stroking his head, right at the fontanelle where I knew there was no bone protecting the brain, only a layer of skin. I had only touched it once myself, by accident, and recoiled from the feeling of the ridged bone giving way to soft skin and nothing else between it and the baby's brain, but she stroked it, again and again, her hand trembling slightly, and I had to bunch my hands into fists to stop myself from clobbering her.

Just as I was about to say something, she stopped.

'He's so beautiful, Simone. Do you mind if I pick him up?'

Yes, I wanted to say, but she was already reaching for him, not waiting for my response.

He startled in his sleep when she lifted him, the falling-from-a-tree Moro reflex that the baby books told me he would soon lose, and I had to fight down an urge to take him from her. She was Paul's cousin, related to him by blood, I reminded myself. It was only normal that she would want to hold him. He wasn't mine, I had to get used to sharing him. I was probably being precious, and possibly unhinged. Except that he *was* mine, in some indefinable way. He wouldn't always be mine, but right now he was. A few weeks ago he'd been living inside me, and there was something painfully raw about him that compelled me to keep him close, against my skin and away from other people's.

As he woke and started to writhe in her arms, clearly unhappy, I wanted to ask for him back, but I forced myself to wait for her to offer. I always used to hand babies back when they got restless; there was nothing worse than holding someone else's howling baby. Yet Rachel seemed oblivious. She held him up, laughed at his little cries, put him over her shoulder and patted his back in a way I already knew he hated.

'Let's go for a walk,' she said to him in a baby voice, and took him into the kitchen, where she stood for a while in front of our calendar, which had all of our doctor's appointments scribbled on it.

'Now let's go this way,' she said to the baby, kissing the side of his face again and again. Her silver jewellery clinked and I could smell her woody perfume as I followed her helplessly through the apartment and the baby's cries got louder and more urgent.

'Um, Rachel? I think he might need a feed.'

She stopped walking, and I thought I saw annoyance in her face. 'Does he? Are you sure you don't want me to distract him for a bit, give you a break?'

Give him to me now.

'That's okay. He's hungry. He's probably still a bit tired, too.' I held out my hands. 'Thanks.'

She gave him back with a sigh and averted eyes, and his crying began to lessen, but still, I felt distress in his rigid body. I carried him to the living room, holding him close against me, trying to soothe him, but also myself. He was safe. I was safe. *This will all be okay*, I told myself, like my mother used to say to me when I was a child.

Rachel sat down beside me and stared, looking confused and mildly disgusted, as I attempted to feed him.

'Does it feel weird?'

'Not really.'

'Does it hurt?'

'A bit, at first. It's getting easier.'

'I heard of a woman who used to turn up at her son's school to feed him on his lunch break. He was *six*.'

'Really?'

'I thought that was disgusting.'

'Well, the World Health Organization says you should breastfeed until two?' I told her, stumbling over the words and ending with an involuntary question mark. Which defeated the slim authority of something I half-remembered reading online.

She looked dismissive and slightly irritated. '*Do they?* And didn't they also say bacon causes cancer or something like that? Anyway, those guidelines are more for people in really poor countries, not here.' She paused for a moment. 'So how's Paul going? Is he a very hands-on dad?'

'Yeah, he's great,' I replied automatically. He had been helpful, during his brief paternity leave, but now that he'd gone back to work the baby would be with me for most of the time.

'Because he did tend to disappear a bit, when we were younger.'

'Oh, did he?'

'He's quite traditional, I suppose. Like his father.'

'Is he?' Where was this going?

'Yes. That's partly why I thought I'd come for a bit, to help you out. Make sure no-one is getting too tired. Is Paul tired?'

'I guess so. We're both tired.'

Her gaze was fixed on the baby, who turned away and screwed up his face in frustration, trying to latch on, and I began to sweat, knowing I had less than a minute to get him feeding before he became inconsolable.

'It's so hard, at the very start. The baby needs you so much, but it will get better, you know.'

Oh, how would you *know?* I wanted to snap. It was as if I was on the first chapter of a lengthy and unfamiliar book with very small print that required all my concentration to decipher and Rachel was standing over my shoulder, commenting on the plot, analysing my reactions. All I wanted was to carry on learning, to absorb any information I could from the signals the baby gave me. Nothing was particularly important right now except this new person I needed to understand.

'This is hopeless,' I said, getting awkwardly to my feet. 'I think I'm going to have to lie down. Sometimes it works better if I go into a dark room.'

'Wow, so primal.' She said it jokingly, but her expression was distant, almost solemn.

Lying in bed, the baby finally settled enough to feed. His jaw moved in a blissful rhythm and his eyes half-closed as his body relaxed against mine.

A short story came back to me that I'd read online somewhere, about a Chinese woman who sits out an entire month in her bed with her newborn as the women of her family bring her warming soups of ginger and chicken and ginseng. How lovely it sounded now, to have women take care of me, bring me nourishing food so I didn't have to shuffle to the kitchen for another muesli bar and a cup of tea. Maybe I could somehow encourage Rachel to be that kind of house guest, to convey to her what I needed, because she probably had no idea. Tactfully, I could suggest that she did some cooking, and then maybe I wouldn't feel resentful of her presence.

Footsteps down the hallway, and a single knock as she simultaneously pushed open the door.

'Can I quickly use your laptop, Simone? I have one tiny email to send to a friend. My phone is out of charge and I can't get into my email account without a code or something.' She nodded quickly at me, impatient for a response.

'Uh ... okay.'

I didn't want her going into my email account, but the baby was finally settled, and that was all I really cared about. And it seemed rude to say no, now that she had offered the simplest solution, which was that she used my laptop. I told her my password and heard the familiar creak of my desk chair as she settled into it, and suddenly the flat didn't feel big enough for the three of us. Today, as soon as I could, I'd go out. It was time.

4

By the time I was ready to go out, an hour had passed. I arranged the baby in his pram, made him snug beneath the soft zippered cocoon with a bonnet on and his hands tucked away, as he fell into what I thought of as his dead sleep, his face still and perfectly symmetrical. Again I noticed how self-possessed he was. It was in his face, his aura.

I knocked on the closed door of Rachel's room but there was no answer. Perhaps she was sleeping. I scribbled a note for her – *Gone for a walk, back later* – and left. The baby stayed asleep through the elevator ride, and out into the cold morning air, and I felt myself relax as I pushed the pram. This wasn't so hard.

I walked on, up City Road and past the hectic Old Street roundabout and along the narrow footpaths of Shoreditch until I reached the grey church at the start of Hackney Road. From there, I threaded my way through Columbia Road and then to Bethnal Green Road with its rows of fried chicken and one-pound shops, through the fragrant waft of kebabs and curry, with dusty winds blowing drink cans under the wheels of buses.

The baby was stirring now, woken perhaps by the smells, and I kept walking, trying to think of somewhere I could take him and feed him quietly. Passing through the dank underpass, I was suddenly somewhere new, in that strange way that London has of linking places overland that you never realise are so close when you travel to them by Tube.

I crossed the road and turned left, remembering that there was a museum here. And suddenly it was in front of me, a grand red-brick building with three gables like a children's fairytale, enclosed by a tall, wrought-iron fence, where a single orange mitten with a white snowflake pattern had been placed on one of its black spikes, awaiting its owner's return. The red bricks glowed like roses and the patchy London lawn was dotted with snowdrops, bunched in tree shadows and around the entrance. On the wall, a mosaic plaque spelled out the words *Museum of Childhood* in dark-red tiles.

The winter solstice had passed now, so there were two minutes of extra light every day. Soon, I knew from last year, the leaves would start to form and by June would provide a wide green canopy. For now, though, it was all white sky and empty trees and the light falling straight through. January was a bare room, swept clean, that I had somehow to fill. Having nowhere else to go, I headed towards the museum entrance, thinking that the old me would have walked past this building on my way to somewhere more exciting, but now I was looking for different things – somewhere warm and quiet and free to anyone, where I could fill the baby's belly undisturbed once he woke up.

Inside was airy and softly lit, the walls painted a dusky mauve. I took the lift upstairs, to the dollhouses. I had always loved them as a child, but now their stillness disturbed me. Sealed away in antique glass display cases, with no-one playing with them, they looked creepy. My tired vision thought it saw a smile on the face of the baby doll, or a quick movement in a cluttered floral nursery. But at least it was dark up here, and I could sit quietly. The toy shop and the café were down below, busy with children, but here it was almost deserted and the baby slept on, halfway through now, I thought. Long enough left of his nap for me to sit and think. Except that a child came screaming past us, chased by his mother, and the baby startled and woke again. As I picked him up I felt the tension in his body – a bellyache, perhaps, or hunger.

He began to fret and then scream, and I noticed a woman nearby looking over, and thought maybe she was irritated by the sound. Alone within the thick concrete walls of the Barbican, the crying bothered only me. But here, suddenly, there was an audience, and all my fumbling settling techniques were on public display. I hadn't factored this in when I'd left the apartment.

Somehow, as his cries became louder, his distress infected me like a virus, rising up – a queasy blend of guilt and anxiety and the conviction that he needed to stop crying, he had to stop. Rocking him, patting his back, I felt a kind of fury at his persistence, and frustration at my inability to stop it. How long would this go on for? People nearby were glancing over now, their faces neutral but no doubt critical of my failure to look after my baby, and with their close attention I felt even more pressure to make him behave. But he didn't. Sweat began to bead under my suffocating winter clothes as my breath became shallow.

'Come *on*, go back to sleep.' I rocked him and held him closer, hoping he would drift off again. I could try feeding him, but I knew he was still tired and that might not work.

Could I put him down and run, get on a bus and become myself again? I couldn't. There was no way out of this. But if he didn't stop screaming soon, here in this public place where people were not supposed to scream, what would I do?

It was as if he was hearing my panic and fearing for his safety. As well he should be. His raw, desperate wails filled the air until there was nothing else. I felt close to snapping, to shaking him, to simply throwing him against a wall to stop the noise. And I knew that if I did that, at least for one brief, deranged moment afterwards, before my actions had sunk in, there would be a clear moment of release. Because at least he would have stopped crying. I would no longer be listening to that sound: his terrible unhappiness, and my failure to relieve it.

'Do you need some help? Do you want me to take him for you, for a moment?'

A soft, friendly voice, speaking low enough that no-one but me could hear. A kind-faced woman was standing in front of me, holding out her hands. I shook my head at her.

'He won't settle. He's so loud. And I know he wants to go back to sleep.'

'Please. Let me have a try?'

I looked at her, into her dark eyes. Like the baby, I was relying on instinct, steered by it, operating on some kind of Stone Age perception of the world. Reduced to an infantile state myself, trying to relate to this tiny being: *Night. Day. Eat. Sleep. Loud. Quiet. Safe. Not safe.*

Safe. She's safe.

Handing the baby over, I sank back into the seat, horrified by the thoughts I'd been having. She took him with gentle, practised hands and held him against her, his head – so tiny – leaning into her chest in an obedient downward tilt, as if he was listening carefully to her. She began to sway very slightly, undeterred by his cries, her eyes half-closed, and I could see she had done this many times before, at all hours of night and day. As she rocked she smiled down towards him, tenderly and with such love, and he seemed to somehow receive it, becoming relaxed and still. And so did I.

'How old is your baby?'

'Three weeks.'

'So new. I'm amazed you've managed to get yourself out of the house.'

'Thanks. It's not as easy as it used to be, that's for sure.'

Still she held him and rocked, and I felt him falling into sleep, into complete relaxation. Eventually she laid him down in his pram, and stepped back as I drew the blanket over him.

'And there you go.'

'I feel so bad. I was getting so worked up by him crying.'

'Well, it happens. It's a terrible sound when it's your own baby, but the funny thing is, it doesn't bother anyone else nearly as much. Forgive yourself and move on. That was always what I used to tell myself.'

We looked at the baby. He was so perfectly fitted into his pram, into his sleep, that light head with its downy golden hair fine and smooth along the soft scalp and ridged fontanelle.

Back home, when Rachel had stroked his head constantly, I had felt like snatching her hand away and roaring in her face. But this lady simply looked at him, along with me, and I felt understood, not overpowered. After a minute or so she wandered away, and I stared into space, not thinking of anything in particular. Leaning my head back, I even dozed a little.

After a while he woke up, hungry, and I picked him up and fed him. The woman reappeared with a glass of water. 'I thought you might like this. I used to get so thirsty when I fed my babies.' She smiled, tidying up some toys and placing them back into a basket. 'And is the feeding going okay?'

'Sort of. Getting easier.'

'Someone described it to me as a relationship, once. I found that quite helpful. You kind of learn how to do it together.'

'I hadn't thought of it like that, but it's true. It's a bit weird, getting used to it. And we've got someone staying with us at the moment who thinks it's disgusting.'

She laughed. 'Well. *Disgusting* is a pretty strong word, isn't it? A bit over the top, actually. I mean, the head of a charity stealing donations and spending it on … I don't know, a private pony collection. That's disgusting, isn't it?'

I laughed along with her. 'It is. Especially ponies. I've always thought there's something a bit warped about them.'

We sat for a quiet moment, and for the first time in ages I felt somewhat normal, almost myself again.

'So, this visitor. Will they be staying long?'

'I don't know. It's my boyfriend's cousin; she's come to London to find work. And it's his apartment, so it's sort of up to him. I don't really have my own place at the moment.'

'Ah.'

'It didn't bother me before I had the baby. I mean, I never even thought about it. And it's not like I'm actually homeless. But I guess now I should be a bit more responsible.'

I thought of the woman I saw sometimes, sitting outside the Barbican Tube station with straggly blond hair and a gaunt, spotted face, watched over by a man who always stood close by, yet appeared not to know her. My situation wasn't as dire as hers, of course. But with a baby I was dependent on Paul in a way I hadn't been beforehand. How had I not considered that?

'But you can live there, obviously?'

'Oh, of course. But it doesn't feel like my home, in a way. I only noticed now that I've brought the baby there. It feels precarious. I only got to London two years ago and now I'm a mother.'

She looked confused and I realised I was rambling. 'Can you talk to your partner?'

'Yeah. I can. I will do, when I see him.'

'And your parents – where do they live? Somewhere in the Antipodes by the sounds of it?'

I smiled. 'Antipodes' was something that especially polite British people said when they didn't want to offend you by assuming you were Australian when you were actually from New Zealand.

'Oh, my mum lives in Perth. She'll come in the summer. My dad I'll see when I get back.'

'Oh.'

We sat quietly for another moment. I wondered if I'd said too much, and made her uncomfortable. But she just smiled and stood up.

'Would you like a cup of tea? My office is downstairs, and I'm going there now. Tea always helps – you'd know that after two years of living here. I'm Jennifer, by the way.'

'I'm Simone. And this is Thomas.'

I felt curious about her, and it was that, more than the offer of tea, that made me say yes. She was dressed in a long skirt and a warm-looking soot-coloured jumper. Around her neck was a fine silver necklace, and on her feet, polished leather ankle boots. She didn't seem to be wearing any makeup, and her hair was white, yet she looked attractive, well cared for and sharply intelligent, a wry, expectant look on her face as she waited for me to gather up my things and follow her. For some reason I felt drawn to her, like she was standing in a warm patch of sunlight in a dark room. I was curious to see where she worked, and I also felt drawn to her motherliness, as if it was something I could somehow absorb. And the way she talked – so open and honest – I hadn't talked like that with someone for a long time.

She led me back downstairs and to the far end of the museum, where a heavy green door opened into a warren of rooms, dimly lit and stale smelling. As she fumbled with her key before a locked door I leaned against the wall and closed my eyes. In my pelvis was a heavy, dragging feeling, with pain creeping up behind it, digging in.

It was quieter here, in the bowels of the museum. It was like being deep in the belly of childhood itself, where rooms were sometimes scary for no good reason – a dark timber wardrobe hanging open a few centimetres would be enough to terrify me in an unfamiliar house – and sometimes safe havens, like my old bedroom at home in Perth, with its faded cotton sheets on the single bed and a fan spinning the air, the dusk light as furry as the wings of moths and the garden outside full of velvety damp flowers and warm dirt sprinkled with water from an old green hose as I drifted towards sleep …

'Are you alright?'

Opening my eyes, I saw that the woman was looking at me.

No.

'I'm fine, a bit tired. I feel like I could fall asleep on my feet.'

'Come inside and sit down for a while, and we'll get some good strong tea into you.' She smiled. 'You should actually be home in bed, you know.'

A desk lamp was the only source of light, casting a glow on the room's soft surfaces, and looking around I instantly knew that as a child I would have felt safe here, as I peered at every one of her abstract, shadowy pictures and looked through the children's books that were piled up on the coffee table. Most of all, I would have loved the deep pink roses, spilling out of a glass vase on her bookshelf. Outside, on the window ledge, was another plant in a terracotta pot, a mass of dark shiny leaves and pale green flowers.

'Hellebores,' she said, seeing me staring at them. 'Winter roses.'

'So this is your office?' I asked her. 'It's lovely.'

'Oh, I've been here for years,' she replied.

She offered me a seat in a comfortable-looking leather armchair. I sat down and looked at her again, and she looked back at me, and for a moment we didn't speak.

'They gave me this room to work on the museum's records – really, though, I've been here so long they don't seem to remember me half the time.'

She looked at me as if waiting for me to speak but I felt so tired, I didn't know what to say. Alongside me, the baby slept on in his pram as if finally soothed.

'So where did you walk from?'

'The Barbican.'

'Oh my goodness. That's quite a walk with a three-week-old baby.' She sounded surprised.

'It was. Once I got going it felt good to be out in the world again. The Barbican isn't the most baby-friendly place.'

'No, it most definitely is not.' She laughed. 'Do you think you'll go home for a bit? It's a long way back to Australia with a baby I suppose, but easier now than when he's a toddler.'

'I hadn't thought of that. But maybe.' My mum had suggested the same thing and I'd dismissed the idea as impossible, thinking there was no way I could face that long-haul flight. But now, having ventured out on my own for the first time, it seemed less daunting. I would love to show my parents the baby, to be back in that easy, familiar world for a few weeks. To take him to the beach and dangle his feet in the water, then watch him fall asleep under an umbrella to the sound of waves.

'To be honest, I don't think it matters where you are when your baby is small and portable. At the moment, you're his home. He doesn't need much else. And I always found London a wonderful playground for my children, once they were a bit bigger. Especially in summer when you can get out more.'

'How many children do you have?'

'Two daughters. They both stayed in London, which is nice. One is a milliner and the other is an accountant.'

The kettle boiled, and she brought me tea in a wide blue-and-white mug. She moved very slowly and as she handed me the mug I noticed how pale her hands were, the skin completely without colour, and how she lowered herself into her seat with great care.

We kept talking, about children and books and London and the museum, until I noticed that outside it was getting dark, and I could hear the strangled roar of buses gearing up for the evening commute. 'Gosh, it's late. I should head off.'

'Are you alright to get home? Would you like to call a cab, perhaps?'

'It's okay. My bus leaves from Bethnal Green Road.'

She took my cup and waited as I put my coat on, then held the door open for me and accompanied me back out to the museum.

'So were you working, before the baby?' she said as we walked together to the exit.

'Yes. At a magazine called *Dove Grey* as an editorial assistant. Sort of a lifestyle magazine, I guess. Quite serious about it all. Can't really imagine getting back to it now.'

'So many opportunities here in London for that kind of work, I suppose.'

'Oh, there are. But to go from that to this,' I pointed at the pram, its dense presence, the stillness that was ready to break at any moment of night or day, and require my immediate attention.

'Well, I feel like I've gone from doing my old job to being an astronaut. It's so different.'

'It changes your life, doesn't it?' she smiled. 'But it's worth it.'

'It will be worth it. Once I get some sleep and work out a few things.'

She laughed. 'You will.'

5

As I left the museum gardens and stepped back into the street, I picked up on that familiar, hectic edge of thousands of people heading to their separate homes, exhausted from a day of scanning groceries or bellies, selling insurance or teaching children, wanting only to unlock the door to their own little private corner of the city and close it behind them. Usually I'd be a part of it, forging my own path on Tubes and elevators after a day under fluorescent lights in a sealed office, my eyes gritty from looking at a screen all day. But now I was out of step, getting in people's way with my pram as they ploughed forward, hungry and impatient at the prospect of home. Everyone looked pale under the streetlights, rushing into the warmly lit entrances to the Tube, or along the footpaths like fugitives in search of a hiding place. The dress shops along Bethnal Green Road were closing, but the fried chicken and kebab shops were busy and Tesco glowed blue and red in the gloom, its checkouts jammed with people.

I headed under the viaduct to the nearest bus stop, where I stood next to two kids, earphones in and hands busy with boxes of fried chicken, and a woman with a young boy on a balance bike. We squashed in when the bus arrived, my pram awkward and noticeable in the crowd.

'Get out of the way.'

I looked around and saw an angry man staring down the mother and her boy from the bus stop. The boy's balance bike seemed to be leaning against the man's leg.

·'Move the bike, you stupid, selfish bitch.'

The boy's eyes widened as another drunk-looking man leaned towards him, holding out a spindly hand to lead him away, but instead terrifying him with his yellow leer.

The mother said nothing back to the angry man. She can't, I realised, because she has a small child with her. She can't allow it to escalate because while she could get away on her own, if she needed to, with a child it would be much harder, and she would be putting him in danger. No-one said anything, including me, as she did her best to move away from the man and reassure the boy. I thought of the phrase *women and children*, used so often in war reporting, and suddenly I understood what it meant. Women and children are weak and vulnerable. At this moment, on a London bus, it means this mother cops a bit of verbal abuse from a stranger and no-one stands up for her. Elsewhere, it could mean anything at all. Yet another thing I'd been mostly oblivious to in my former life.

The baby started to wake up and then cry, and I pulled him out of the pram and onto my lap. He was hungry, his mouth wide-open, and I knew what needed to happen to stop him. I closed my eyes and took a deep breath. Was I actually about to do this? I didn't sunbathe topless, I didn't walk around changing rooms naked, I didn't even wear low-cut tops. But if it would stop the screaming, I would do it. My old self looked on, fascinated and mortified, as my new maternal self unbuttoned my coat and, as discreetly as possible, pulled out a veiny, rock-hard breast on a London bus. It was done, and somehow the world went on.

Except that it didn't work. I felt, rather than saw, every drawn, blank face on the bus turning towards me curiously as he tried to latch on, becoming increasingly vocal about his distress. My vision closed in and I thought suddenly of the birth, of being surrounded by silent faceless strangers.

'Maybe try the other side?' said a woman beside me, quietly, in an accent that was Spanish, or perhaps Italian.

I tried. It still didn't work.

The bus was hot, packed with bundled-up bodies heading home and the kind of silence I had always enjoyed in London, being among people but quiet and still. But tonight it was unbearable as the baby fretted against me, and although no-one had said a word apart from the woman who was trying to help me, I felt like I had to leave, like me and the baby were too loud, too needy, too exposed.

'I think I'm going to get off,' I whispered to her, panicking, buttoning myself and ringing the bell and pushing past her, past the small child on the balance bike whose mother had her arm around him.

'Your baby doesn't like the Number Eight bus,' observed the drunk man, giving me a sympathetic smile.

'Looks that way,' I said. You can't ignore drunks on a confined bus but, like toddlers, you shouldn't encourage them either. At the bus stop I pulled the pram awkwardly down into the street, with the baby in my arm.

'I reckon he's well within his rights!' yelled the man, as the door closed behind me. 'There's always been something deeply fucked up about the Number Eight bus!' He sounded outraged.

My breathing slowed. The bus rumbled away towards Liverpool Street Station, leaving us alone in the kind, spacious darkness, away from the emergency that wasn't, in fact, an emergency except in my noisy brain. Away from people and bright lights and panic was a bench, close to the bus stop but in a pocket of darkness. Settling into the hidden quiet, it was easy to feed the baby and I sat for as long as I could with him tucked under my coat, compact and warm against my bare skin. I stared across the road and through the window of a Japanese restaurant I'd been to once with Paul. My belly rumbled. I kept the baby in my coat, supported by my left arm, as I threw my bag into the pram and headed in the direction of home.

Paul always declared the Barbican an architectural masterpiece, and spoke of its 'brutalism' in hushed tones. Built in the 1960s on a vast bombsite close to Liverpool Street Station and the border of the East End, it was some kind of idealistic postwar attempt to create a self-contained community of terrace houses and tower blocks, sealed and comfortable and built of solid concrete. I'd never admit it, but privately I thought of it as cold and institutional, a kind of failed utopia, and tonight I felt a sense of foreboding as I neared the estate.

Paul's apartment was in one of the three huge towers that blocked out the light and loomed over pedestrians scurrying past. Between the towers were low-rise apartments, which enclosed a huge court-yard of paved terraces, rectangular lakes, a gated garden and a playground, built around remnants of the Roman wall that once ringed the city. Long walkways with obscure yellow signposting all pointed to a cultural centre at the heart of the estate, where elderly residents dozed over small glasses of sherry on the red leather couches in the vast foyer, and outsiders arrived breathless and late for concerts or films after scurrying down the endless windy walkways. At night-time, the streets around the Barbican were eerily deserted for central London, and as I hurried down the darkness of Chiswell Street and into the dimly lit reception I felt, as always, something at my back. Imaginary, I hoped, but never quite knew for sure.

As I burst into our apartment, I smelled food and heard voices in the living room. Rachel was in the kitchen, pouring red wine straight from an open bottle into something bubbling away on the stove, a full glass in her other hand. Voices in the living room fell quiet as I closed the door behind me.

'Oh, you're back!' said Rachel. 'We didn't know where you'd got to. Paul's been calling you. George and Penny are here to meet the baby.' She was talking very fast, and gulped down her wine once she'd finished speaking.

Paul's parents. Wheeling the pram into the living room, I said hello as they stood up, then leaned into the pram where the baby lay.

'You've been out for a while. Where did you get to?' said his mother, a slender, quiet woman with dark hair and a nervous manner.

'I went for a walk and then got a bit stuck in traffic on the way home. I didn't know you and George were coming over tonight. Sorry.'

'Oh, it's alright. We were just a little worried.'

She looked at the baby with a strange expression, I thought. Somewhere between love and trepidation. Maybe, like me, she was wondering what kind of parents we would make, what kind of a team.

'Well, he's absolutely perfect,' said Paul's dad briskly, giving me a gentle pat on the back. 'And how are you? Should you be out so late?'

'I kind of lost track of time,' I said. 'Where's Paul?' And then suddenly he was behind me.

'I've been here waiting. We all have. Where were you, Simone?' he asked. 'I tried calling but you left your phone at home.'

'Oh, did I? Sorry. I told Rachel I was going for a quick walk, but then I somehow ended up at the Childhood Museum in Bethnal Green.'

'Really? What a funny place to go. I don't think I've been there since primary school,' said Rachel. 'I remember it being kind of spooky, all those old toys and creepy masks and things.'

'Well, I liked it,' I said.

Paul looked pale as he took my coat. 'Sit down, Simone. You need to rest.'

So I sat, taking in the warmth and the conversation flowing around me and wondering how soon I could politely steal away with the baby to bed. Paul, who looked to be on his second or third glass of wine, lifted the baby out of the pram and passed him around until he ended up with Paul's father, where he lay against his broad chest looking utterly at peace. Paul's father seemed tense, though, and I wondered if he looked down on me, for getting pregnant so quickly and trapping his son.

Penny sat beside me with a big Liberty shopping bag, and began unpacking things for me to look at – a soft grey blanket of Welsh wool, a tiny yellow sleepsuit, handmade leather baby shoes and finally a voucher from John Lewis, in a cream envelope, for a thousand pounds.

I looked at her. 'This is too much – I can't take this.'

'Of course you can.' She shook her head quickly. 'It makes it easier for us. I didn't really know what you needed, and then I thought, well, this way you can decide for yourself.'

Paul wasn't keen on baby shops, so collecting everything we might need in the months leading up to the birth had fallen to me. I'd bought a second-hand pram and a cot off Gumtree, and found most of the clothes in cheap high-street shops, as I hadn't liked to ask Paul to contribute when he was already giving me somewhere to live and covering bills. Now, though, I started thinking about what I could do with so much money. Buy a better pram, for a start. And get a few things for the baby's room, once Rachel moved on and I could set it up.

'Thank you. This will be really helpful,' I said quietly.

'Not at all. A girl should always have money. Especially when she's the mother of my grandchild!' she laughed.

'Such beautiful things,' said Rachel, appearing beside me and picking up the miniature leather shoes. 'So sweet. Tiny.'

Penny seemed to freeze for a moment as she held them up, resting them on the palm of her hand, and I felt suddenly embarrassed at being showered with all these expensive gifts when Paul's parents barely knew me.

We'd first met last spring, when they were in London for the weekend and had come by to leave some shopping at the apartment while they'd met friends for lunch. Paul was out when the doorbell rang, followed almost instantly by a key digging into the lock. And then a neat woman with a dark bob, dressed all in black with a long silver necklace and chunky rings on her fingers, was standing in the kitchen.

'Oh! Hello!' She practically fell over herself in her rush to shake my hand. 'I'm Penny. Paul's mother. And you?'

'I'm Simone.'

'Ah, yes, Simone. You're coming to the wedding, aren't you? Paul mentioned it last week when I spoke to him, that he was bringing a friend.'

I nodded, smiling, and wondered if she knew that I – Paul's *friend* – had moved in with him. Somehow, I'd managed to ignore the fact that he had a family, a whole network here in London and beyond. He was skilled at keeping everything separate, I realised. Discreet. Maybe it was a British thing.

'Paul said he was on his way – oh, I think I can hear him. Hellooooo!' She gave him a kiss as he walked in, pulling off his bike helmet.

'You've met Simone?' he asked, smiling at her.

'I have.' She had looked approvingly at me, and so did he, until I got embarrassed and put the kettle on for something to do.

'Lovely,' she'd said. 'Just lovely.'

'You still with us, Simone?' said Paul now, interrupting my thoughts and pulling me back into the room where his parents now smiled at me, the mother of their first grandchild.

'Yes. Sorry.' I rubbed my face, trying to wake up a bit.

A little later, Rachel called us to the dining table and served up a rich beef stew with buttery mashed potatoes and green beans, heaping my plate lavishly and fussing over me.

'Here you go, Simone, have lots. I thought the iron might be good for you.'

'Thanks, Rachel.' I was ravenous. 'It looks really good.'

As Paul and his father fell into a conversation about Paul's work, his mother leaned over and said quietly, 'And how was the birth, Simone?'

'Oh, it was … Well, it all went fine, I guess, in the end. But it was – you know – a bit of a shock.'

She nodded. 'I know. It is. No-one warns you. They can't,

really. We were going to come sooner, but we thought we'd give you a few weeks to get settled. Are your parents coming over? Your mum, I mean?'

'Oh, maybe. We're still working it out. She's thinking of coming in the spring, or I was thinking today I might fly home to see them.'

'Oh, right.' She looked worried and glanced over at Paul, and I realised I should probably talk to him before dreaming up plans to leave the country with our son. 'Well, they will have a lovely time if they come to London in spring. And you have some good help here with Rachel in the meantime.'

'It was lucky timing, I guess, that I was moving to London,' said Rachel, before I had a chance to speak. 'It's only to help out for a bit, until Simone finds her feet.' There was something disdainful in her tone, and I sat up straighter, trying to look more alert than I felt.

'I've been managing okay,' I said, as neutrally as possible.

'Of course! Of *course* you have,' Rachel said, with insincere enthusiasm.

'Do you want to go to bed, Simone?' Paul asked. 'You look exhausted.'

'Thanks, Paul.'

Rachel raised her eyebrows and looked at Paul's parents, as if to say, *Oh dear, Paul's in trouble*.

'I don't mean you look bad, but maybe you should get some rest.'

'We should be off anyway,' said Paul's mother, putting her knife and fork together on her half-eaten meal. 'We're booked to stay at the Thistle tonight. We can walk there from here, and then we're up to Scotland first thing in the morning on the train, to visit the Crawfords for a week. We might try to pop past on the way back and bring you some food.'

'That would be lovely, Penny. Thanks for coming,' I said, as warmly as I could. The atmosphere was so strained, so odd, it was all I could do to act normal. But it was probably me that was out of step. They all seemed fine, although no-one was quite meeting anyone's eyes.

They got to their feet and we had a long, awkward goodbye at the front door, with everyone dithering over whether to hug or kiss or both, and lots of hand touching and assurances about future visits and phone calls and family gatherings. As they finally stepped out the door, Paul's mother looked at me and said, 'Anyway, I'm so glad you have Rachel here. I can see she's taking such good care of you, cooking and so on. She was always like that, the little nurse of the family.' She reached out and squeezed Rachel's hand one last time.

Again, Rachel caught my eye and smiled. Something lurked there, some story. The door closed.

Dazed, I made my way to our bedroom. As I walked past the spare room I saw Rachel had already made herself at home, her clothes all over the chair and the bed, the table covered in perfume, makeup, books and papers. Her brown leather suitcase was nowhere to be seen and I wondered how it had held so much.

Later, as Paul and I lay in bed, the baby asleep between us, I asked him to tell me more about Rachel, keeping my voice to a whisper.

He sighed.

'Well, what do you want to know? She's my cousin,' he said. 'But she was more like a sibling in some ways, when we were growing up. Our mothers are sisters, so we saw a lot of her when we were little. Rachel went to boarding school and she used to come and stay with us sometimes in the holidays because her mother was often away. And then when she was older she ended up living with us, for a while.'

'Where was her Dad?'

'Oh, he was out of the picture by then. Her mum remarried and ended up in Nigeria for a while, and she preferred coming to our house, I think.'

'How long is she staying here for? Has she said?'

'I don't think she'll stay long with us. She's been drifting around for years. She's a bit like her mum in that respect – always at some mystical sound healing ceremony in California or some self-discovery retreat in Borneo. She'll come out with some pretty strange theories, but they're mostly harmless.' He yawned. 'I'm exhausted, Simone.'

The baby stirred a little and I could hear the bath running, the smell of my bath oil drifting in under the door. I knew I should let Paul sleep but I needed to know more.

'And she's planning to work here?'

'I think so. She was a nurse, but then she was studying herbal medicine or something and now she wants to look for a job. She mentioned some clinic in Hampstead she's been in touch with. You know what it's like when you first get here.'

I thought back to arriving at Heathrow almost two years ago, carrying a suitcase and a couple of phone numbers and no warm clothes. Catching the Tube for the first time and a child playing next to me with some loud, annoying toy. I was practically crying from exhaustion, and then I met the eye of a young bloke who gave me an encouraging smile as if to say, *Hang in there*. London had always enchanted me like that – those sudden human connections that happened when strangers were crammed up against each other, even if they never saw each other again. But there were bad moments, too. Going to a café and having my wallet stolen so expertly from my bag, which I had left at my feet, that I never even saw the person, let alone noticed their hands taking my money – ninety pounds, although I'd had another four hundred, most of my savings, tucked away in the very bottom of the bag, and they hadn't found that. Paul had been so welcoming to me, and had made my life so much easier. Perhaps it was only fair that he looked after his cousin, too.

'It is hard when you first get here. It's good that she has somewhere to stay.'

He sighed. 'We've always helped Rachel. Her mother was pretty distracted so my parents took her in. All you can do is humour her. Don't get into any heavy discussions about anything. That's what I do.'

He put an arm around me, drawing me closer to his warm-bread smell. I felt like I hadn't seen him for days, like I'd been missing him, even though he'd been here all along.

'Okay. I'll try that.'

'She'll probably only stay for a few days while she works out what she's doing. She's that kind of person: one minute she's here, the next minute she's working in a tapas bar in Barcelona or something. She moves around.'

'Okay.'

'I'll send her to the shops, keep her busy, get her to do some cooking. She wants to help. She said to me tonight that I should say thank you from her. For letting her be here, helping you.'

'Oh, did she? That's nice, I guess. She doesn't have to thank me, though.' I kissed him. 'Night.'

Despite the long walk, as soon as I heard Paul's breathing change from wakeful to slow and steady, I became alert, my thoughts stumbling between my new life and my old.

I felt uneasy about Rachel. It wasn't something I could be as rational about as he was; it was a gut feeling more than anything. I wondered what my mother would advise me to do in this situation and realised I had no idea. Mum wasn't one for confrontation. She seemed to come from a gentler world where you faced down any hint of interpersonal tension with a benign comment about the cooler weather we'd been having or that nice tree over there. Maybe that was the smart approach. Maybe I should try to get along with Rachel, to be pleasant, to pay less attention. And wait for the situation to resolve itself without me having to do anything. After all, she hadn't actually done anything wrong. It was more about me being tired and oversensitive and paranoid. She was here to help, according to Paul. All she wanted was to help.

The baby woke, and I fed him until he rolled away from me, milk-drunk. Feeding him made me drowsy and I rolled towards sleep with blissful ease.

When I opened my eyes again it was to the sound of smashing glass. Something being pounded with efficient, furious force. A destructive, mindless din. I struggled to think while my body remained deeply relaxed, then adrenaline flooded my brain and my muscles tensed. I reached for the baby and found him there beside me, the soft, cotton-covered hump of his back curved away from me, moving up and down with his breath. What was that noise? Were we being invaded? Had someone found their way into the flat? Whoever it was, they were fast and strong and methodical.

I shook myself awake. The sound had stopped. Beside me, the baby was asleep but Paul wasn't there. The light in the room was subtly different, the grey of dawn, and I realised I'd been having a nightmare. But my heart was still thudding, and my breath was fast from the terror of the sound, and from the certainty that some force had found its way into the apartment and was wrecking it with efficient strength. I heard quieter noises, muffled sounds of something moving, and then Paul appeared in the doorway. As he slipped into bed I turned towards him.

'What was that noise?'

'Oh – you're awake?'

'Did you hear it?'

'Hear what?'

'That banging. It sounded like the whole building was shaking.'

'No. You must have been dreaming,' he told me, pulling me close to him so I could smell his skin, its familiar scent. I breathed in, trying to ease myself back into sleep. The minutes slipped by as I lay there, trying not to look at the cold numbers on the digital clock as they flicked silently into early morning.

On my bedside table lay a baby book I'd bought from Foyles a few months earlier. Maybe reading would help. Getting up as lightly as possible from the bed, I went out to the living room and settled on the couch, then looked through the contents page to see where to begin. A chapter titled 'Your Head' stood out, and as I read I could hear the author's voice, as if she was speaking directly to me: *When you have a child, you need to decide what you want to give him or her from your own history, and what you want to make new.*

I closed my eyes, and I was back home in Perth, where I had everything I needed and more – two loving parents at home, books, education, clean air and water – and yet I'd been so restless to see new things. As a teenager I used to sit in my room for hours, mostly reading novels set in faraway places or plotting out in my diary my eventual escape to the chaos of a big city. London had called to me, like it did so many people from Perth. But it was meant to be a rite of passage – you went there for a year or two on a working visa, partied and travelled and slept with inappropriate people, then drew a firm line under the whole episode and went home. I'd certainly complicated things now. Could I legally leave the country, now I had a baby? Why had I not considered this earlier? Because I hadn't planned to have a baby with Paul. That night in Soho was the only time we slipped up. I thought about it briefly, then let my mind skip away from it.

When I found out I was pregnant I was swept up in Paul's happiness, relieved and happy that we both wanted this baby. But one evening, as I arrived home nauseous and exhausted to Paul's empty flat, I suddenly wondered if I was making a mistake.

I had called Soraya, my friend at work, and she'd been calm and matter-of-fact, as if she'd anticipated this conversation and knew exactly what to say to me. 'Look. You know you don't have to do this if you don't want to. I have the number for a very good clinic. If you need someone to hold your hand, I'll do that, and if you need money, I have that too.'

'You're right,' I said to her. 'I think you're right. I'll talk to Paul.'

'So I've been thinking,' I said to him when he arrived home, before he even got his coat off. 'Do you think we should do this?

Have this baby? I know it's a lovely idea, and maybe we could think about it in a year or two, when we know each other better, but not now. It's too soon.' My speech had been rehearsed; its logic was impeccable.

But he simply shook his head and smiled, folded me into a hug, and talked me out of it. Every time I spoke, tried to argue my case, he was talking again before I'd even finished the sentence, his voice, so low and reasonable and persistent, rolling easily over mine so that I became confused, unable to complete my own thoughts while listening to his, and feeling a rising frustration at his ability to keep talking, deflecting, when I was the one who had to actually go through with it all. Eventually, I gave in. Fell silent. All I wanted was for the conversation to end, and as I drifted off he had the last word.

'It's okay to be scared, but this is a good thing. It's going to be wonderful,' he had said. 'I know it.'

Back in the bedroom I could hear the baby stirring, and I put aside the book and got up, oddly happy to be needed by him. As I breastfed him, a sadness that was becoming more familiar descended, and I wondered if there was some innate biological wisdom to a new mother feeling a bit depressed and flat. After all, if I were happier, more like my old self, I'd probably be distracted by other things, other people, when what a tiny infant needs is a kind of benign, responsive, milk-producing mass to huddle against.

All I wanted was to be here, gazing down at the baby's face. It hadn't been a mistake. Even though what I felt for him wasn't exactly love, or what I'd previously understood as love, the prospect of being apart from him was unimaginable.

6

Again, I woke to stirring beside me in the low morning light. Paul had left early, for the gym and then work. The baby was crying and flapping so I picked him up and brought him closer, lifting my t-shirt and feeding him.

Eventually his head fell away, his mouth open, a milk bubble forming and popping at his lips as his face became still. I closed my eyes. It was a little after seven, but I didn't have to be anywhere, and thought I might get an extra hour of sleep while I could. Except that I saw a shadow under the door, and then it opened, and Rachel was standing there. 'Are you awake?' she asked, in a bright, eager voice, as if she couldn't wait to see me, to see the baby, to start this fresh new day.

I wanted to delay it as long as possible, but the longer she stood there, the more I was waking up, as the baby slept on beside me.

'I'm going to keep sleeping for a bit,' I mumbled, hoping she would get the hint. 'The baby was up a lot in the night.'

The baby was now motionless beside me, and the oxytocin or whatever it was that was released by breastfeeding was dragging me down into velvety darkness. Except I was being pulled out of it again by her voice – her soft, insistent voice.

'Do you want to come and have some breakfast?'

'No. I want to sleep. Sorry.'

Even in my drowsy state I registered that she was again doing something that seemed at once entirely reasonable and well intentioned, yet didn't recognise my needs at all. Was it deliberate, or was she incredibly laid-back and I was the unreasonable one?

She stood there for a long moment and the silence was full of some emotion – anger or something else. Her silver bangles clinked lightly as she hugged herself for a moment, then walked away, leaving my bedroom door ajar so that the light from the hallway shone in. I heard her moving about in the kitchen, first the radio coming on, and then the slamming of cupboard doors, a noisy rattling through the cutlery, and finally the smashing of something that sounded like a glass jar. The warm winter smells of coffee and toast drifted into my room, followed by Rachel's voice as she chatted on the phone to someone, the sound reaching my room very clearly, as if she was standing at the kitchen door and talking in my direction.

I was aching, a dragging muscular pull deep in my pelvis that I felt as soon as I sat up. It was silly to have walked to Bethnal Green, so soon after the birth. But I wasn't going to get back to sleep now, so I climbed carefully over the sleeping baby and went to have a shower.

The bathroom was a welcoming white-tiled cave, the hot rushing water a guilty relief because I wouldn't hear the baby cry while I was in here, breathing in the steam. Awake and blissfully alone. No-one to look after but myself. After a few minutes, though, I felt uneasy about cutting myself off from his cries, and turned off the water. Stepping out, I dried myself quickly, expecting to hear full-volume howling. But the apartment was silent. When I pushed open the door of our bedroom, the bed was empty.

Still in my towel, I went in search of the baby, nauseous with sudden anxiety. The kitchen was messy but empty. I couldn't hear Rachel, or the light clinking of her silver bangles that usually accompanied her movements around the apartment.

Something outside caught my eye, and I saw her on the balcony, holding the baby up on the thick balcony surround as if showing him the city. I moved slowly, not wanting to startle her. The surround was a metre thick, and it sloped upwards, a curved modernist sculpture of concrete, deep enough for people to sit on at parties. He couldn't fall. I knew that. Yet I also knew how defenceless he was. I'd seen it myself that first night in the hospital when he'd hung so helplessly from my hand, and I didn't want him outside, I didn't want her holding him, and I didn't want him anywhere near the edge of the building. I slid open the door, but didn't know what I should do next.

What held me back from saying something to her? Was I scared of her? There was something about her that made me wary. Maybe it was the way she looked at me, a strange mix of pity and longing. What did she want? I felt the need to tiptoe around her, or maybe it was my tiredness, or hormones, or some strange maternal instinct telling me to be very polite, to not show anger or fear. I tried to keep my voice as even as possible as I said, 'Oh, there you are. Can you bring him in? He's probably hungry.'

Don't ever touch him again, I wanted to tell her, saying each word very clearly. *Don't take him from my bed when he's sleeping.*

'Oh, is he? Sorry, he looked so lonely lying there, I couldn't resist picking him up. And then I think I woke him, so I brought him out here to see all the buildings and to show him where he was born. They love being talked to, you know.'

She came inside, settled herself down on the couch with him on her lap, facing me, her eyes fixed curiously on mine.

'Is it weird, me holding him? I mean, do you feel like snatching him off me?' She smiled, watching my face. 'Does it make you all, like, protective?'

Yes.

'Oh, no, not really,' I laughed uneasily.

She looked disappointed. 'It's okay to feel like that, you know. It's good, in fact.'

'Is it? I guess so. I should probably feed him soon.'

Still she looked at me, not making any move to give me the baby. At least she's inside now, I thought. She can't throw him over the balcony.

'I need to feed him,' I repeated, walking over to her and holding out my hands in a way that looked like I was pleading. Which was ridiculous.

After a long pause she gave him back, with a small sigh.

'What are you doing today?' she asked, as I held the baby, felt relief at the weight of his body, his head resting against my chest.

'I hadn't really thought about it. I didn't get a great night's sleep … I'll probably stay here. The health visitor is coming today.'

Uneasily, I looked at our living room. It was squalid, with unwashed cups and wine glasses on the coffee table, and random headphones, dirty socks and old newspapers littering the floor. The whole apartment looked as if someone had given it a good shake – Rachel's clothes and shoes had somehow made their way under tables and over chairs, and baby paraphernalia – wipes, sleepsuits, printed flannel blankets – cluttered every surface.

'Okay. I'll stay here too, then. Do you want some breakfast?'

'Yeah, I'm starving. That would be great.'

'I'll go to Waitrose.'

She swept out and while she was gone I got dressed. Fifteen minutes later, she returned with plastic bags filled with food – *pain au chocolat*, almond croissants, bread, raspberry jam and bacon. Then she disappeared into the kitchen and I smelled the croissants in the oven and coffee brewing and bacon frying. I was ravenous. Some combination of breastfeeding and exhaustion was making me hungry for carbs and sugar and fat, and I ate and ate while she picked at a croissant and sipped black coffee. Too late, I realised that she had barely eaten a thing. She looked pleased as she took my empty plate back to the kitchen.

'Thank you. That was amazing,' I said.

'Maybe we should go for a walk later, burn off all those carbs. You can show me around the Barbican. It's so weird here … almost deserted, like some dismal 1960s social experiment. Kind of like the apocalypse but with Ercol chairs and cheese and pineapple sticks.'

I laughed. 'It's pretty bleak, isn't it? You can see what they wanted it to be, but it didn't quite get there.'

'Paul is a convert, though?'

'He loves it. Refuses to live anywhere else, though I've some-times tried talking to him about moving out to Hackney or even Bethnal Green.'

'Really? Why won't he go?'

'He likes being right in the centre. Zone One or die. It does feel like you're right in the action here, actually living in London, I guess. And he hates catching buses.'

'And I guess this is his parents' place, which makes it easier than renting. Paul is tricky, isn't he? He's tricky,' she said, almost to herself.

'Mmm …' I said, not sure how to respond. I hadn't realised Paul's parents owned this apartment. He'd never mentioned it. I thought of all those gifts last night, the elegant shopping bags filled with delicate things wrapped in fine tissue paper.

She waited, but I didn't go on.

'So how are you feeling, now? You don't look quite as shattered as you did last night.'

'I'm okay. I guess I'm waiting for it all to feel normal again, or to go back to normal, but it's looking more and more like that isn't going to happen. Some unbroken sleep would be good.'

'No-one actually tells you how to get used to it, do they? And you're already so tired from the birth, and then have to look after a baby. It's brutal. Was it – was the hospital okay?'

As soon as she said the word I was back in that room, sur-rounded by people, trapped on the bed. I saw again the obste-trician lifting up the forceps and me trying to get away, saying *No*, and him yelling *Look away, look away*, and so I did, trying to bury myself in Paul's armpit, to escape all those nameless faces, those metal instruments. In any other context, a strange man coming into the room and doing that to someone would be considered assault. With a celebrity lawyer and a trial attracting considerable media coverage. Maybe even a true-crime documentary or memoir later on. Obviously, being childbirth, it wasn't assault, and I knew it was done for the right reasons, and that my son was delivered safely, and all that matters is a healthy baby et cetera. But however much I tried to tell myself to get over it, I still shuddered at the memory of him lifting those forceps high up in the air, and knowing exactly where they were about to go. Rationally, I think he was enthused. He loved his work, he knew that in a moment I would be holding a healthy baby, and he had a crowd of wide-eyed students about to witness him do something extraordinary. But from my point of view, it wasn't exactly ideal.

Suddenly I had to talk about it. It didn't matter who was listening. It could be a hamster or even a fencepost, for all I cared. It had to come out.

'You know, I can't quite believe how horrible the whole thing is. And so many women go through with it, and then go back and have another one. It actually makes me sad that women are going through it right now, all over the world. Some of them with no pain relief. It's barbaric. And what if their partner isn't supportive? That's a whole new world of trouble.'

She said nothing as a tear slid down my cheek, but I felt her close attention on me, the awareness that she was really listening. I wiped my eyes on the baby's muslin.

'You'll heal,' she said, very quietly, and I realised that was the one thing I'd been wanting to hear since it all happened. 'You will heal.'

Encouraged, I kept talking. 'And I guess I was surprised at the birth, you know, at how long it dragged on, how many people were in the room. It felt like maybe ten people, I couldn't count them all or really see them but it was crowded.'

'Really?' she sounded uncertain. 'Was it really that many?'

'I think so.' Now I doubted myself, and my recollection of that morning.

Unexpectedly, she laughed. 'It's funny, I sort of remember working on maternity wards when I was a student. The first-timers used to come in with a ten-page birth plan, wanting to control every single thing, when actually, the whole thing about being a parent – a mother – is that you have no control at all. We used to just laugh at them!'

I thought back, a little stung. No-one had appeared to look down on me for being a 'first-timer', as she put it. If anything, they'd seemed even kinder because they knew I'd never done it before. My birth plan was limited to a scribbled message in my maternity notes to the midwives, saying, *Whatever works*, because I knew it was out of my control, down to biology and whatever happened on the day.

But Rachel repeated it as if she was reminding herself, as if it was funny. 'We used to really laugh at them!'

She was quiet for a moment and I thought about leaving the room, because I suddenly felt sweaty, as if there was something not quite right in my belly.

'Why were there so many people in the room, anyway?' she asked.

'I don't know. The obstetrician came in – he had a whole lot of medical students with him. They didn't really do anything, just stood there.'

'Ah, medical students.' She nodded to herself. 'They're vultures. They sort of hang around the labour ward, keeping their fingers crossed that a high-risk delivery comes along. Were they men or women?'

'I don't even know. It feels weird that I can't picture their faces. That they were all there, but they never said a word.'

'Oh, the male ones are the worst. They would have had plenty to say afterwards ...'

'I feel like they should have at least checked with me, before they all came in. I feel like I should have been asked.'

'They didn't ask you?'

'Well, I think I ticked a box somewhere saying I would allow medical students to observe, but I didn't think they would all troop in for the birth. It was weird.'

'Medical students are *vultures*,' she said again. 'They would have seen you as a piece of meat, nothing more.'

I thought back to the obstetrician, a bespectacled Nigerian man with such a relaxed, open face, who had looked me in the eye and spoken to me as if we were equals, in a normal social situation, despite the fact that I was out of it on pethidine and half-dressed and barely verbal. And how he'd chatted to me afterwards, commenting that birth was not as easy as the movies made it look, and how I was going to be 'very unhappy with all of us later for causing you all this pain'. And how, looking back, what he was really saying to me was, if you are unhappy about this birth, blame me. Blame us. Don't blame your baby, and don't blame yourself.

'Well, the midwife said I was lucky to get the obstetrician I did. He doesn't normally deliver babies, apart from at the Portland. So maybe a gaggle of students was a fair price.'

'Really? I remember the students as being so insensitive. The midwives all hated them, they were such arrogant little brats.'

I suddenly realised we'd been focused on me for the whole conversation, yet I still knew so little about her. Maybe if I did it would be easier to like her.

'So did you work as a nurse for very long?'

'Not that long. Well, it felt like a lifetime, but it wasn't, really. Very grim places, hospitals. So many rules, bureaucracy. Demanding patients. It wasn't for me.'

'What made you go into it?'

'Oh, I guess I was sort of directed into it by people who were … in my life at that time. I did like it, but there was so much pain and sickness and injury. So I left after a few years.'

'Paul said you've been studying in Brazil?'

'I did. I've done all kinds of things. And then all of a sudden it was as if I was being called back here.' She trailed off, looking out the window.

'Fair enough. What is your work going to be, anyway? Paul explained it to me but I'm not sure I understood.'

She got up. 'I'm a herbalist and I'm training in naturopathy. A few different things.'

'Sounds like you'll have loads of options.' I paused for a moment. 'So … have you started looking for a job?'

'I will do. I'm getting to it. There's some other – there's stuff going on that I need to deal with first.' She looked at me strangely. 'Is that the time? I'm going to go and have a shower. I've left the kitchen in a bit of a state, is that okay?'

'Yeah sure, I'll sort it out.' The conversation had left me oddly drained, and when the bathroom door closed I sat for a moment, going over it in my head, wondering if I'd said something to annoy her. This is why people go to work, I realised. Staying at home all day wrecks your head.

The baby was asleep in my lap, so I carried him carefully to our bedroom, and went into the kitchen for a glass of water. It was chaos, with open jam jars and eggshells and dirty pans and croissant flakes and spilled coffee grounds everywhere, along with all the dishes from last night, which had been left piled next to the sink. How did she make such a mess?

My foot came down on something sharp. When I lifted it I saw a globe of blood and the sparkle of fine glass. Quickly I pulled it out with my fingernails and got on with cleaning the kitchen. The health visitor was due and I didn't want her to think I wasn't coping.

Rachel spent a long time in the bathroom and when I listened at the door I realised she was in the bath, running the water continuously. As I waited for the health visitor, I felt uneasy about something. What she said about the hospital: *They would have seen you as a piece of meat ... They're vultures ... They would have had plenty to say afterwards.*

None of it really chimed with what I had felt from the people at the hospital. Not that it really mattered, because I would never see any of them again anyway. But it bothered me. Whatever good I had felt about the birth felt oddly diminished now, as if I had misread what had happened.

The baby woke and I was feeding him when the doorbell rang, causing him to scream in outrage as I broke off his feed, put him on a rug on the floor, and went to answer the door. It was the health visitor, who introduced herself as Mary. She was a slight, middle-aged woman who stepped inside and busily started investigating, taking notes and discreetly sniffing the air, looking, I realised later, for trip hazards and evidence of smoking and co-sleeping and illicit drug use.

Eventually we sat down in the living room where she smiled in a perfunctory way and started firing questions at me, about domestic violence and bed sharing and diet, telling me I shouldn't be drinking coffee or eating garlic as they would cause colic. As she rattled on, I tried to feed the baby while answering her questions as best I could, the baby becoming increasingly distressed, and all the time she sat there watching me with what felt like deep disapproval.

'Your house is very tidy,' she said, looking around with narrowed eyes. 'How are you feeling? Okay?'

'I guess so.' I stared at her blankly. 'It's tiring, though. I'm still getting used to the broken sleep.'

'Well, we like to see a messy house, because that means you're looking after the baby, not cleaning your house and ignoring him.'

No-one told me that. It would have been easier to not clean up.

'Oh, I'm not ignoring the baby. I don't see how I could, he wakes me every two hours for a feed.'

'You're pretty lucky, living in a place like this,' she observed. 'Some of the women I visit on the council estates around here, you should see how they have to live.'

And she was right. Compared to what some women were going through, I had it so easy. This was a situation I could manage, if I could work out how. After one night of solid sleep I could map out a way forward. But when was that one night ever going to arrive?

'Okay, well, I'm going to go now. It all looks fine here, I suppose. Call your GP or us if you need anything. All the numbers are in your Red Book.'

She left in a flurry of mild disapproval, darting a final pointed glance at the tidy kitchen as she passed. Rachel was still in the bath, and I needed the toilet.

The baby started to wail, so I carried him to the bedroom, shut the door and lay down beside him, and then I wailed too.

7

My phone beeped as I was drifting off to sleep.

Hey! I'm passing by, off sick from work (not actually sick) ... Can I drop in and see you and the angelic blob?

It was Soraya. We'd met at work when we were both newly arrived in London, her because she'd fallen in love with an Englishman who was moving home from New York, and me eager to find myself a bolthole and a life in London.

Sure, me and the angelic blob are ready for you

Be there in 5

The buzzer rang. Soraya sounded frosty. 'There's a midget Satan on the front desk, wanting to get confirmation from you that I am a legitimate visitor. And would he be doing that if I were *white*? I don't think so.'

This was followed by a deafening clatter, as if she'd dropped the phone on a hard surface, and then someone picked it up and sighed deeply. A terse male voice spoke. 'Hello there. You have a ... Soraya here to visit you at the front desk.'

'Thanks, send her up.'

Soraya burst through the front door in a rush of perfume, dressed in layers of plum and grey knitwear and sporting pink streaks through her curly hair and new glasses with rims of clear emerald green.

She clutched me to her cleavage for a moment, then pushed me impatiently aside and looked beyond me to the apartment. 'Let me see him! Let me sniff his head!'

She swooped into the living room, where the baby lay on his mat, blinking up at the ceiling. Placing a hand on her chest, she looked over at me and said, 'May I?'

'Of course.'

Bending over, she scooped him up expertly and inspected him. 'My God, you really have produced the perfect Aryan child. So blonde. Although his eyes aren't ice-blue. More of a dark grey – does that mean they'll change?'

'Maybe … maybe they'll go brown?'

'He's completely adorable. So, how are you?' She looked at me curiously, perhaps wondering if I'd changed. She had no kids herself, and hadn't ever expressed much of a desire to be a mother, although she did tell me once she'd made thousands and thousands of dollars babysitting the children of her neighbours on the Upper West Side of New York, where she'd grown up with her academic parents.

'I'm okay.'

'And how's the Alpha Male coping with fatherhood?'

'He's fine,' I said. Paul and Soraya circled each other warily for some reason I had not yet worked out. I remembered how she'd offered me money for a termination and the number of a clinic when I'd rung her in a panic, convinced I was making a huge mistake. What did she think of the fact that I'd changed my mind and gone through with it? She would never bring it up, I knew that, but some small part of me wanted her to see I'd done the right thing.

She shuddered. 'Don't tell me a thing about the birth. I'd really rather not know. But how is it going generally?'

'Ah, it's going okay. We're staying at home, mostly. Trying to get some sleep. Haven't done much since we left the hospital.'

As she settled the baby on her lap, I waited for the prickliness, the desperate urge to snatch him back that I felt when Rachel held him, but it was absent. Soraya handled him carefully, but she was looking at me, seeing me, like she always had.

'Here. I brought you some gifts.' She reached into the bag beside her and handed me two packages, one containing four nursery rhyme puzzles, the other four dinosaur-shaped plastic bath toys. Soraya was someone who shopped with a mix of generosity and extreme skill, throwing things into her basket for this friend or that, a running list in her head of who had a birthday coming up, who was leaving work next week. She knew all the best sample sales, from House of Hackney to Issey Miyake, and she could speak with authority on any brand you cared to name.

'Oh, Soraya, thank you! These are great. I keep having to remind myself that he's going to change, that this newborn stage will be over and he'll start doing stuff.'

'Of course he will.' She looked at me over her glasses for a long, sober moment. 'He won't stay a blob. That's why I got you toys, Simone.'

'Thank you. And what's been happening with you?'

As she told me about work and her new boyfriend, I had a rare opportunity to study the baby properly. When he was close to me, he felt like my equal, someone who was as communicative and persuasive and powerful as any adult I dealt with. Away from me, he looked small and defenceless, and I remembered how new he was, how much easier things would feel when we were more used to each other.

Rachel appeared in the doorway and I watched the two of them size each other up. Rachel looked immaculate – dressed all in black, with perfectly blow-dried hair framing her made-up face, and long silver chains around her neck. She lifted a hand to her hair, adjusting it slightly, and her bangles clinked. My stomach tightened at the familiar sound.

'Hello,' said Soraya, in her most formal voice, and I had a sudden hysterical urge to laugh.

'Hi.'

'Soraya, this is Rachel. Paul's cousin.'

Soraya looked at me, eyebrows raised.

'Rachel has just moved to London, so she's staying here for a bit while she looks for a place to live.'

'Oh.' Soraya looked unconvinced. 'That's tricky timing, isn't it, coming here when there's a new baby?'

Rachel stiffened, and I smiled at Soraya and widened my eyes slightly. She got the message, and when she spoke again her tone was friendlier.

'And where are you looking for a flat, Rachel?'

'I don't know, really – maybe south? Brixton or Kennington or Vauxhall, around there.'

Soraya's face softened, and her formal tone loosened a little. 'Brixton is very nice. Well, not *nice*, exactly, but a good place to live. I actually have friends down there who may have a room going.'

The baby started to fuss on her lap, and she handed him back to me quickly, wiping her hands on her skirt.

'Really?' said Rachel. 'I haven't checked it out properly yet, but it sounds good, like there's a lot to do, live music, stuff like that.'

'My friends live up at Poet's Corner. It's lovely there. Although lots of prams,' said Soraya, rolling her eyes.

'What, lying around on the footpaths?' I asked.

'No, stuffed full of screaming babies. Nappy Valley, we call it. Sorry, Simone, but it's true. You're one of them now. A *mom*. You've crossed over.' She blew me a kiss and laughed. 'I still love you, but you have.'

'I have not! Don't say that.' I knew she was joking, but at the same time I recoiled at the thought of disappearing formlessly into the world of motherhood, so sanitised and sleep-deprived and dull, and leaving her behind in the real world.

'So where are the good places to go out?' said Rachel.

'Well, Brixton Academy, obviously. I was there the other night. The Ritzy Cinema, lots of restaurants, bars, the markets – depends what you're after.'

'And where do you live, Soraya?'

'I'm in Vauxhall. A place called Bonnington Square.'

'Oh, I think I read about that in a magazine. Is that the place with the garden with all the oversized tropical plants?'

'The Dan Pearson one, yes it is. And there's Bonnington's, the café. They only serve one meal a night, the same one to everyone, vegetarian. It's quite famous, in an insider's kind of way.'

'Speaking of the same meal every night, I'm going to feed the baby.' I said it jokingly, but Rachel looked at me like it wasn't funny at all, and Soraya didn't laugh. She seemed a bit distant, and if Rachel hadn't been there I could find out what she'd been up to since we last spoke a few weeks ago, let her know that even though I had a baby, she was still important to me, that nothing had really changed. But Rachel was there, and she was quietly taking over.

'I'd love to come and see that garden, and the café.'

'Oh you should. It's beautiful.'

'Really?'

'Sure.'

'Today?'

'Well, I was going to spend some time with Simone today, and give her a chance to rest.'

Rachel was scrolling through her phone. 'I'm just looking at the Ritzy. There's actually a movie I've been wanting to see that's on there. *Gravity*. It starts at two. I've kind of been cooped up here.' She glanced at me apologetically. 'Not that I mind, of course!' She showed Soraya her screen.

'Oh, that one! It looks good.'

Soraya loved movies and I thought back to the last one we'd seen together, when we'd laughed so hard the people in front of us had moved seats.

'You should go, Soraya,' I told her. 'Make the most of your day off. There's not going to be much happening here, honestly. I'll have a nap when the baby does.'

'Really? I wouldn't say no to a lazy afternoon movie.' She fake-coughed delicately, covering her mouth. 'I'm *technically* off sick from work, but a movie won't be too taxing.'

Rachel looked at me. 'Will you be okay here? Or do you want to come along with us, or …?'

Panicked thoughts crammed up against each other. Can you take a baby to a movie? Do I want to take him underground? How do I get the pram down the escalator? What if there's a bomb scare? Or someone sneezes on him?

They both looked at me, and I knew their afternoon would be far more relaxed if my needy bundle and me weren't a part of it.

'Oh, I won't. I went for a big walk yesterday so I think I'll stay home today.'

'Well, if it starts at two we should probably get going. I can text my friends about the room and maybe we can drop by there first.'

'Oh – that would be *amazing*. Thanks Soraya!'

It wouldn't actually be *amazing*, I thought to myself bitchily. Helpful, yes. A good use of time. But amazing was a bit of a stretch.

They were both looking at me oddly. Had I said that aloud? What was wrong with me? Soraya had come to visit, brought me thoughtful gifts, and I was fuming and jealous and miserable.

Rachel was still playing with her phone. 'It says there's a good cocktail bar near there. The Rum Kitchen? Have you been?'

Soraya glanced at her screen. 'I have. There's a better one close by. We can go there after.' She rolled her eyes at me. 'London newcomers, right? Always trying to tell you where you should go. You can leave the cocktail bars to me, sweetie.'

'Okay, Soraya.' Rachel smiled at me. 'Will you be okay here, Mummy?'

I had struggled to get used to this in the hospital, when midwives would say, *And what does Mum think?* and I'd look around, wondering why they thought my mother was with me, before realising they were referring to me, that I was the mum. It was fair enough, easier than memorising every patient's name, but coming from Rachel it sounded a little patronising.

'I'll be fine.'

'Are you sure?'

'Yes, honestly, I'll probably have a sleep,' I said, imagining cool, sour cocktails and smoothly melting ice cubes and sitting back in a dim, restful theatre on the red velvet seats of the Ritzy with nothing more to do except watch scenes appear in front of me.

After they left, as I fed the baby again, I thought back to when Soraya and I first worked together at *Dove Grey,* before she was headhunted and took up a role as features editor on a rival magazine. She was the chief subeditor, and I was the lowly editorial assistant, and one Saturday she came over and we went out for lunch, and then she invited me to a party, some friend of an acquaintance of hers, and I said yes. And then I remembered I had left my new gold skirt at work, and I really wanted to wear it, so Soraya suggested we drop past the office on the way to collect it.

When we got there the security guard recognised Soraya, of course, because she knew everyone, and we made our way to the office, a huge basement space of low, sagging ceilings and fabric-covered partitions, always strewn with half-eaten packets of Hobnobs and straggly indoor plants drying out in the overheated air.

Just as we were about to enter, we heard someone thundering towards us, down the overpass. Clutching each other, we turned towards the sound.

It was the security guard. 'Stop! I just remembered – it's been sprayed in there for pests. No-one is meant to enter for twenty-four hours.'

I gasped with more drama than, in retrospect, the situation warranted.

'What do you need in there?'

'A skirt.'

The guard looked at us blankly. It sounded ridiculous. But we'd come all this way and my beautiful gold skirt was right there. I could see the navy paper shopping bag on my chair. And I really wanted to wear it that night.

Soraya saw my face, took a huge breath of air and blocked her nose, and before the guard could stop her, thundered into the office and retrieved my bag.

She exhaled and handed me the loot.

'Sorry, Max,' she said to the guard, who looked like he was trying not to laugh. 'I'll buy you a coffee on Monday.'

And then we went to the party, and shared a bottle of wine, and I woke up to her dressed in my beach towel and frying eggs in my flat-share kitchen, making it feel like home for the first time since I'd moved in, three weeks earlier, in a minicab with my suitcase and a clutch of bulging plastic bags.

Rachel was out for the rest of the day, and as if disturbed by the sudden quiet, the baby began to howl up and down the walls. By five we were barricaded in our bedroom, the curtains drawn and the lights low, the relentless noise making my head pound, pinning me to the bed as my eyes roamed around every dusty corner of the room, where discarded clothes and damp towels lurked and multiplied. I tried calling Paul a few times to ask if he could by any chance come home early, but his line rang out. The pale yellow roses sent by my work colleagues seemed to tremble with the volume of the crying, and dropped their cupped petals onto the bedside table until every stem was bare. Eventually, in an effort to steer the day into happier territory, I retreated to the bathroom, scrubbed the tub and ran a warm bath.

The sound of the water and the steamy warmth seemed to soothe the baby, so I fed him sitting cross-legged on the floor, then undressed him while he was drowsy and full, wrapped him in a towel and undressed myself, then picked him up and carefully lowered myself into the water. His umbilical cord still looked raw against his poddy belly. But he lay limp on my chest, no longer crying, and as I relaxed and closed my eyes our shared agitation seemed to fall away.

It was so quiet, with only the pipes of the building murmuring through the walls, and I began to soften and drift, thinking of sleep, of owls and dark caves and everything drowsy and still.

And then I was wide-awake, adrenaline pumping, and lifting us both out of the tub, appalled at my own carelessness. A new image to add to my night-time horror screening: waking up in a lukewarm bath with the baby slipped under the water. He cried as the cold air hit his body, but I wrapped him in a clean towel, then dressed him in a tiny nappy and a grey sleep suit and breathed him in for a moment, thankful for his body, as healthy and active as a beehive beneath that poreless skin, before taking us both to bed.

We were still there as night fell, when Paul's key rattled in the lock. I heard him on the phone, then a soft knock at the door and he came into the bedroom with bowls of Thai food, warm and salty and delicious, and we ate it together in bed, watching a movie on his laptop, exactly as we used to, but with the baby safe between us.

8

The baby woke through the night and each time I fed him and fell straight back into blankness, clutching at sleep like it was a blanket that might be pulled away without warning, leaving me cold and exposed.

At some point Paul wandered off to sleep elsewhere – apparently one of his work colleagues with children had advised him that there was no point everyone being tired – and I lay there, listening as a key fumbled at the door for a long time, and someone stumbled in. The bathroom light went on outside my door, and I heard Rachel, swearing and exclaiming loudly. Eventually, I got up and went to the open bathroom door, blinking at the bright whiteness. She was standing in front of the mirror, teetering slightly on her heeled boots and supporting herself with one hand on the basin. With the other, she appeared to be pinching her squinting, red eye, again and again.

'Fucking hell! Come on! *Fuck!*'

The cold tiled room was sharp with the smell of alcohol.

I blinked. 'What are you doing?'

'Oh, Simone! You scared the crap out of me. Trying to get my stupid contacts out. We ended up at the Notting Hill Arts Club.'

'But you were going to Brixton?'

'It's a long story. I can't get them out. If I go to sleep with them on I'll wake up and my eyes will be glued shut.'

Her eyes, so red, met mine in the mirror. My Isabel Marant silk scarf, the one Paul had given me on one of our early dates, was wrapped around her neck, but I noticed for the first time how bedraggled she was, with her scuffed boots and a hole in her shirt. She looked like a neglected teenager, although she was in her twenties like me.

'Are they still in? Maybe they fell out.' I said.

She rested a finger on her left eyeball and moved it slightly, then did the same to the right eye. 'Oh yeah, that's it. I was thinking I couldn't see straight because I'm so drunk but maybe everything's blurred because they actually fell out hours ago. Probably on the dance floor. It got pretty loose.'

'Okay, well, I'll leave you to it.'

'Night.'

Three am. I lay in an agitated half-sleep, waiting for the baby's cry, but for once he slept on, and the longer I lay there the more anxious I felt, every bad thing that might happen to him queuing up at the bottom of the bed to present itself to me in vivid detail. Sliding under the bathwater. Falling out a window. Dying in his sleep. Forgetting to breathe. Some virus slipping into our house and stealing him away in a few panicked hours as we dithered too long over calling an ambulance and he succumbed, the exact chilling Victorian word the midwife had used in a hushed tone as she told me about his immunisation schedule. Terrible things happened to small people. I had always known this, but now there was the possibility that a terrible thing might happen to this particular small person, and as his protector, I was the only one who could prevent it. He slept on beside me, breathing open-mouthed, unaware of his many ends being played out in the head beside him.

Around four, for a bit of much-needed variety, the birth reel started up again. It played on repeat, like a visceral horror movie I'd once seen projected onto a living-room wall at a Halloween party once, except with me as the main character.

Rachel's words about her time in hospitals had stayed with me. Had I misinterpreted the kindness of the doctors and midwives? Hade I done it all wrong? Why did I even care? Nothing would change the events of that night. So why did that movie reel keep playing?

What I wanted was for the baby to wake, so I could feed him and then fall asleep for a few hours, knowing I wouldn't be woken. Finally he obliged, and I drifted off for a while, before I woke up to Paul, looking well-slept and alert in his ironed shirt, placing a cup of tea on my bedside table and whispering that the baby was awake beside me and wearing a clean nappy.

Around noon, the baby and I were both dressed and fed. Today, we would again attempt to re-enter the world. I quietly closed the door of the apartment, where Rachel slept on in the spare room, and took the lift down to the lobby. The man at the desk didn't acknowledge me as I passed. As a mother, a pram pusher, I was now invisible. Strangely liberated. And lucky. For everything I might have lost – freedom, sleep, work – I had gained even more in the form of my son. Of course I had. The bad thoughts that came in the night were afraid of clear morning light, and fell silent. All we needed to do was work out how to make it all come together, somehow. And fill the hours.

We drifted through Liverpool Street Station, office workers stepping nimbly around the pram as we made our slow, lumbering way through the main concourse towards Bishopsgate, dwarfed by this brightly lit portal into world trade and international banking. Women passed in their work clothes, chatting to each other or on their phones, looking polished and rushed and always focusing on something in the distance – a train, a meeting, a deadline. I used to be like that, but now it was as if my vision had narrowed down to the perfect skin, the soft eyes, the hungry mouth of the baby. Nothing needed my attention apart from him.

A very glamorous editor in heels and red lipstick had noticed my pregnant belly at a book launch and taken me aside and said to me, very earnestly, 'In a few months time, this tiny, magical being will come into your life and he will live with you, in your house. It's the most wonderful thing.'

Looking at him now, I saw what she meant. The baby was still and somehow very grave in his sleep, and I realised he *was* a magical being, and he had come to live with me, and eventually it would all make sense, once he became accustomed to being here and I became a more competent mother.

Just then I sensed, rather than saw, Paul walking alongside a slender woman I didn't recognise, both of them carrying bags of what might be their lunch. He looked at me as he passed and his face instantly lost its formal public expression and relaxed into the face he only gave to me, his eyes on mine intimate and kind.

'Simone! What are you doing here?'

'Oh, hi! We're out getting some daylight.'

'Look, Imogen. This is my baby!' They peered together into the darkness of the pram as I looked her over. She was so pretty, so young, it was almost laughable – dressed in a cream silky blouse and pale pink skirt, with immaculate makeup and huge eyes. *Your basic nightmare*, as we would have called her back in Australia.

Her phone rang and she answered it, staring at me with the curious gaze of a child.

'Hi. Oh, yes, I rang you before. Do you realise it's a onesie party on Saturday night? As in, we have to wear onesies?'

My eyes met Paul's and both of us managed not to laugh.

'Mmmm. Look, we can talk about it later, I'm with my boss and his partner.'

'Do you have time – oh,' he looked at his watch. 'Sorry. We've got a meeting in fifteen minutes and we're just coming back from one. Do you want me to lift the pram up the steps up for you? Where are you going?'

'It's okay. I'm going to wander for a bit and then head home.'

Up on Bishopsgate, the pavements were hectic with suited men and women in dark coats, but as soon as I crossed the road and turned down Brushfield Street towards Spitalfields and the ghostly white church, the air seemed to change.

Along Brick Lane, past the curry houses and burger bars and vintage clothes shops and the bowling alley, to the bagel shop, where I stopped for a salt beef bagel and a cup of tea in a styrofoam cup as the baby slept on, and then down Bethnal Green Road, towards the Museum of Childhood again. Fuelled by food and the optimism of being out in the world, I sat in the sunshine of the museum's garden, where garish yellow and purple crocuses struggled through the bare muddy ground. The baby woke and looked up at me from the pram with his mouth opening and closing in a way that I knew signalled hunger, so I lifted him out to feed him, smiling at the small, appreciative sounds he made, like a wine connoisseur tasting a particularly good harvest. Zipped into a snowsuit, his head enclosed in a fleece-lined hood, he was a warm bundle against the cold air.

'Mind if I sit down?'

A man, middle-aged, white, thin and tough, stood over me. He didn't bother waiting for my reply before he joined me on the bench.

'Name's Brett. Who are you?'

Why did he need my name? Not wanting to provoke him, I offered it politely. His face had a hungry look, with pale, staring blue eyes, his skin cured to leather, probably by cheap alcohol and a life outside, until it stretched across his protruding cheekbones.

'Nice to meet you, Simone.' Now he extended a thin, yellowed hand with long, black-rimmed nails. It took all of my social conditioning to offer my own and shake his, and not wipe my hand on my coat immediately afterwards.

'What's your name again?'

'Simone.'

'And what's my name again?'

'Your name is Brett.' I kept my voice neutral. Was he saying that to remind himself of a fake name, or to unsettle me? Or both?

'And what are you up to today, Simone?' His voice was slightly slower than normal, without inflection.

'Nothing much. Out for a walk, you know.' I scanned the museum gardens but they were empty. 'What are you up to?' I went on, gaining some time to plan my exit. I prised the baby off my breast, as discreetly as I could, turning away from him and buttoning my coat up to the neck.

'Well, I've been away but I'm back now, so I'm here hanging out. A bit of a drink, a bit of a wander. A lot of people won't talk to me, Simone. Snobs, you know?'

'Really?'

'You don't seem like a snob, though. You seem like a good girl.'

Never meet their eye was a policy that had mostly kept me safe in London, but this one had caught me unguarded, and there was no-one nearby to rescue me. He was after something; I could see that in his eyes, which were fixed on me with a combination of desperation and cunning.

'I – uh,' holding the baby with one hand, I flicked up the brake of the pram and stood in one swift movement. 'I think I'm going to get going now.'

Pushing the pram with one hand, I moved away from him, not looking back, towards the museum, where there would be people and security guards.

'Am I annoying you?' he called after me, but the social obligation to talk, to shake hands, was successfully broken, and I was putting distance between us, no longer looking at him, no longer touching his skin, no longer answering his questions, and thinking how annoying it was that, even after having a baby, I still hadn't managed to escape that particular breed of weird, persistent men who bothered women they didn't know in public places. I would've thought that with motherhood, at least I'd be done with them.

9

Inside the dark museum, I felt safe, protected by the protocols of a public space and the security guard at the door. Through the door I could see Brett, sitting there, bolt upright, staring at nothing. He looked sad, and not the slightest bit threatening. But you never knew. Probably he did need help, a sympathetic ear, but from health professionals, not me. I tried not to feel guilty or to blame myself for the interaction, which had played out in various ways since I was a child. Why couldn't a woman sit in a park, on her own, without some man bothering her, thinking he could ask her questions, and tell her things, and comment on her appearance or demand that she smile, or cheer up, or give an account of herself? And what kind of parenting would produce a man like that? Another thought for three am.

The baby stared up at me, drowsy and currently not needing anything, but that wouldn't last. I already had a little man right here, waking me up and wanting things from me. Why should I put up with adults I didn't even know demanding my attention too? There was a certain quality I'd seen in mothers, a kind of don't-fuck-with-me diamond fury, and suddenly it was mine, too. It settled in me and warmed me from within.

I walked across the white floor, tiled in a black-and-white fish-scale pattern, and peered at a small sign informing me that women prisoners in Woking Gaol had made the tiles in the 1860s. And wasn't there something so sad about that, the thought of women working on the floors of a childhood museum they would never see for themselves, or take their children to? My eyes prickled with tears. Why was everything so poignant, all of a sudden? A moment ago I'd been furious. The pamphlet the health visitor had left behind referred sweetly to *baby blues* and *hormonal changes*, but this felt like more than the blues. It was as if all the sadness of the world, all its loss and grief and misery, was passing through my veins like a churning polluted stream. I wiped away my tears impatiently as I packed the baby back into the pram. I was being ridiculous. How could I save those women prisoners? I couldn't even get myself to sleep anymore.

Like a nocturnal animal with painfully sensitive eyes, I gravitated towards the first floor, where the lighting was low, the carpet dark and felt-like, the walls painted a soft dusky purple. There I found toys and square red and yellow cushions scattered across the floor, and when I looked into the pram the baby's dark grey eyes met mine in solemn silence. As I brought him out, he took in the colours, blinking in the dimness as I walked around, looking at the displays.

Eventually, at the furthest corner of the gallery, we came across a village of dollhouses, dozens of them, in a tightly grouped huddle on a hillside of plain white crates, each one lit from within as if it were the middle of the night. There was something quiet and welcoming about them. I thought back to the other night when I'd been alone with the baby and had looked out at that one lit window, imagining some young couple behind it. That night, I'd felt alone. But looking at all of these houses, this closely gathered night village, it occurred to me that perhaps it had been a mother in that lit room, someone like me, alone with her wakeful baby. Every night, a whole scattered village of parents across London kept vigil with their wakeful children. Sitting in steamy bathrooms with a coughing baby. Walking the floor, heating up a bottle or rocking a fretful newborn, awaiting some unknown point in the night when sleep would descend.

This dark village reminded me of the Nocturnal House at the zoo back home, where they kept the native marsupials and nightjars and owls. The subdued, furry night-time feel of it. How as soon as you entered you felt more alert, but also quieter, protected by the dark.

On my lap, the baby stared at the houses, blinking and mesmerised. And then I became aware of someone standing beside me. Looking up, I saw it was Jennifer again.

'It's a new world for him, isn't it? All so fascinating.'

The baby looked up at her, startled then interested, staring at her face and moving his head at the sound of her necklace of pale-green glass beads clinking against each other as she sat down beside him. I turned him towards her and she played with him, meeting his eyes, stroking his nose. As she entertained him I zoned out, glad to have a moment to myself, staring at the village again.

'They were donated by the artist Rachel Whiteread. She used to come here as a child, and always loved looking at our dollhouses. She collected these ones over twenty years, and then she gave them all to us.'

'I'd like to crawl into one and go to sleep.' I pointed out a Tudor house with yellow-lit windows. 'That one.'

She laughed. 'And how are you doing? Apart from tired, obviously.'

'Oh, not so bad. Still getting used to it all, I guess, but we are slowly finding our way, and he's a good baby, he really is.'

'You're doing wonderfully well to get out of the house with a newborn. Isn't she?' she said to the baby. 'And have you thought about joining a mothers group? I always found them quite nice, somewhere to go where you didn't feel you had to apologise for your baby crying or making a fuss.'

'No, but I will. I've been meaning to look into that.'

She was right, of course. I stared at the village of dollhouses. Somewhere out there in the city were women who probably felt like I did. It was a matter of working out where they might be, where they gathered to be with others of their kind.

'It's a bit like a new job – you have to get to know your colleagues.' She laughed. 'Well, we've been busy here. Children in and out all day. So loud, I've had a headache, but that's a children's museum for you.'

She got up again, slowly, and stared down at the baby. 'He's beautiful. So happy to be here, existing in this very moment.' She shook her head and was quiet for a moment. 'I need to remind myself of that, sometimes. Anyway, I'm going to go and have a cup of tea. Do you want one?'

'Oh, I would love that. Thank you.'

I followed her downstairs, past the French bridal doll in a greyish wedding dress, the African helicopter toy crafted from tin cans and the Venetian puppets in their faded silk costumes.

We went through the double doors and back to her small square room, with its artwork and a new arrangement of fresh flowers on the desk – dark pink with jagged petals, mixed with little yellow-and-white daisies and leafy stems, all arranged in very pure-looking water in a glass vase. I wondered, did she buy them at some florist somewhere, and walk here with the blooms wrapped in brown paper and bundled in her arm the way I hold the baby? Why was I so fascinated by her? Maybe because I discovered her here, maybe because of the way she looked at me, mock-stern, eyes twinkling. Or perhaps it was the intuitive feeling that she might hold the answers to getting on with this new life.

We chatted for a while, about news and the museum and London, while she made tea, then handed me a cup and sat down at her desk.

'And how is it all going at home? Is your house guest still there?'

It was as if she was reading my mind. There was something about her that was very direct. In that clear, pale skin and those small, bright eyes was someone I didn't know, but I could talk to.

'Rachel. Yes, she's still there. She was out last night. My friend came to visit, to see the baby, and the two of them ended up going out until two in the morning.'

'Hmm.' It was a small sound, but sympathetic. 'And meanwhile you're at home with the baby.'

'Yeah.' I sipped my tea. 'I mean, it's fine. But I feel like my old life has gone and I don't know what my new one is yet.'

'They're hard, those early days. I've been where you are, with a newborn. I remember it well. Lots of women have. But they don't always talk about it.'

'Why doesn't anyone talk about it? Why doesn't anyone *warn* you?'

'I don't know. Too tired, perhaps. Too unsure of what's actually wrong. Worried about getting it wrong, when it's meant to come so naturally. And when you see someone pregnant, you don't want to scare them. I see lots of new mothers in here. So I offer a cup of tea and a chat. It's nothing, really. I enjoy it. And I love seeing babies.'

I wanted to tell her more about Rachel, about the uneasy feeling between us, how I didn't quite know how to be myself around her, how it felt like there was something going on in the apartment that I knew nothing about, and how I was worried that actually, I was going crazy, through lack of sleep and wildly out-of-whack hormones.

'Paul, my boyfriend, is at work a lot. I think maybe he feels the pressure of having a family to support, all of a sudden. He only took two weeks off and then he vanished. I thought he'd be around a bit more, I guess.'

'And who is this Rachel again? His cousin, is that right?'

'Yes. She moved to London and she's staying with us until she gets settled. It's fine, but she doesn't really get it, I guess. She doesn't have kids herself, so it's a bit hard for her to understand what we're going through, suddenly having this newborn.'

'Will she be staying with you for long?'

'I'm not sure. She didn't really tell us she was coming and she hasn't told us when she'll go. But it's weird, she wakes me up and doesn't understand that I'm tired and she's meant to be helping – she said she'd cook and clean and stuff – but she hasn't done anything much.'

'Do you think maybe she's a bit jealous?'

'Of what?'

'Of you.'

For a moment I didn't know what to say. Then I laughed.

'No! Not at all. Why would she be jealous of *me*? She's got *freedom*, she's got a career to get started, she's got the whole of London to go out and discover. Why would she be jealous of *this*?'

I gestured at myself, with my scraped-back hair and postnatal bulk, the weight of the pram I needed to drag everywhere. Or did she mean the baby? But that was ridiculous. The baby was mine, he was a part of me. Being jealous of the baby made about as much sense as her coveting my earlobes or feeling bitter about my appendix.

'Maybe it hasn't been as exciting as she thought it would be, coming here? Maybe what she actually wants is a baby herself. I'm not saying I know for sure. But I do know that in life you need to get used to the fact that people will be jealous of what you've got and what they don't, whatever that might be. Because jealousy is a big emotion, worse than envy.'

'Really?'

'Oh, yes. Envy is feeling upset about what someone else has. Jealousy is wanting to take it from them.'

I looked at the baby. If she was right, if part of being jealous was wanting to take from someone what made you feel that way, I needed to be careful. The thought made me feel weirdly threatened, like I needed to dull myself, mute whatever it was that was making Rachel jealous, to stop it bothering her. To be like a chameleon blending in with the branch behind it, fading to brown.

'So how do I manage it? How do I get used to someone feeling jealous of me? Although I'm not sure that she is.'

'To deal with someone's jealousy, you need to understand that it's their issue. It's so much about *them*, and not about you, that there's actually nothing you can do about it.'

'Oh.'

We sat again in silence. The day was sunny now, all unbroken blue light. The trees were still bare, although I could see, faintly, buds appearing like messy little packages at the ends of branches.

We stared at the baby, on my lap, and it reminded me of gazing at a fire or a flickering candle. He was beginning to wake up more, looking around, taking up more space. But right now, he was sleeping, and it was a serious sleep, like he was contemplating global matters behind those closed eyes.

'Has she been looking for somewhere to live? Or a job?'

'I don't really know. The thing is, she has been helpful in some ways. She cooked a big dinner the other night, when Paul's parents came to visit. But in a way, I don't know what she's actually doing here.'

She was quiet for a moment. 'But maybe it wouldn't matter what she did. Maybe you need to be alone for a while with your baby, getting used to things?'

'Yeah, there's that. Part of me thinks, why am I complaining? I had a baby that was born healthy. She's helping. What's the problem?'

'Well, however good you have it, it's still a huge adjustment. Recovering from childbirth, however that happens, getting used to less sleep, all the hormonal changes. It's huge. I remember it myself, and it was decades ago now!'

'There's all that too. I guess I get annoyed at myself for being disappointed by the birth. I keep going back to it. And I didn't even expect it to go that well. I mean, there are definitely a few design flaws in the whole thing. But why am I still thinking about it all the time? The baby was healthy, why am I still dwelling on the birth?'

She smiled. 'Do you think that because you've got a healthy baby, nothing of what you went through matters?'

'I don't know.'

'I mean, it's a bit like saying, well, you had a car crash on Tuesday that left you badly injured, but then you won the lotto later on that day, so why are you still lying down and trying to recover?'

'Is it?'

'Yes, I think so. What happened to you in childbirth does matter. And it's understandable that you're upset. It takes time to get over it. We used to have days in hospital to recover. You can be out now in six hours.' She shook her head. 'Honestly. If men had to give birth I imagine things would be *somewhat* different.'

I watched her sorting through papers, discarding some into the metal bin under her desk, hole-punching and filing others, smoothing each filed page with her hand. Watching people handle paperwork or leaf through books had always mesmerised me, and I felt myself collapsing deeper into her soft leather armchair as the baby rested on my lap. She appeared to be packing up, to have filled some boxes, I noticed. And there seemed to be fewer paintings on the walls today than there had been last time.

'Are you leaving here soon?'

'Oh, getting organised, putting things in order. A bit of early spring cleaning ...' She smiled at me. 'Everything will be easier when spring comes and you can walk in the park.'

'Thank you. For letting me ramble on.'

'You're welcome. I still remember the women who talked to me when I had a new baby. It helped me to know it wasn't going to be such a shock forever.'

In the cold winter light, she looked older, and somehow smaller than the last time I was here. She looked like my grandmother, I realised, all her colours suddenly muted, her body taking up less room than before, the furniture appearing to grow larger around her.

Don't go, I found myself wanting to say, but I didn't.

Sleep deprivation had such strange side effects. One was that I had no sense of what to say anymore. Not that I was ever especially skilled at making that judgement beforehand, but now it was like I couldn't manage subtlety, I couldn't do humour or irony. I could ask and answer basic questions, and that was about it.

As I said goodbye, settling the baby in the pram, she was still sitting there, smiling at me, her room a warm pool of light that I closed the door on reluctantly before stepping into the dark, chilly corridor.

I wish I knew what Rachel was doing here, I thought again, as I manoeuvred the pram out onto the street. She said she wanted to help, yet she wasn't helping much. I pictured her appearing at the door at dawn and taking the baby away until morning so I could sleep, but I didn't see that happening, nor did I want it to. I wanted to learn how to look after the baby myself; it was my job, it was what I'd signed up for. No-one could do it for me, let alone someone who was out drinking until three in the morning.

And meanwhile, I seemed to be existing on toast and lukewarm sugary tea, up half the night, too tired to do anything during the day except half-finish cleaning up the kitchen or think vaguely about what to have for dinner. And Paul never seemed to be around anymore.

Was this what it was like, being a mother? The closing down of anything that was once enjoyable – going to bed after a long day at work, getting up full of energy after a rejuvenating eight hours of sleep, reading a paper, eating a plate of good food?

At the traffic lights, a long-haired elderly woman stood waiting, her arms wrapped around the traffic pole like a pale and delicate climbing plant. She looked down at the baby, who twinkled his eyes back at her, and the two of them seemed to communicate in some pre-verbal way, cooing and blinking at each other.

'It's a real achievement to have such a contented baby,' she told me, and was gone.

10

A few days later, after another pre-dawn wake up, I decided to try a mothers group, as Jennifer had suggested. The address in one of the midwives' brochures led me to a small, yellow brick building I'd only ever rushed past in my old life, on the way to the Tube or the pub or the movies. Inside, an A4 photocopy pinned up next to the reception provided the room number of Tiny Toes Mothers Group, and I sped up as we were running late, recognising the room by the row of prams parked outside it.

Through the glass panel in the door, I saw a circle of women seated on yellow square cushions, all with babies slumped in their laps or feeding or making light dents in their own cushions in the midst of the gathering. I found a cushion and sat down awkwardly, wondering if the baby would somehow sense that he was among his people for the first time.

'Hello,' said the one woman without a baby, who stood out with her clear voice and perfectly braided hair and well-rested, made-up face. 'Welcome. I'm Diane. How old is your baby?'

'Four weeks,' I said, and all the other women, whose babies looked a little older and who seemed so much more senior and knowledgeable than I would ever be, murmured their congratulations and looked lovingly at him as I settled him in my lap.

That hour at Tiny Toes was the easiest I'd spent awake since the baby was born. Diane guided us cheerfully through a few nursery rhymes and talked about breastfeeding and offered her help to anyone who needed it. The babies were all weirdly content, sleeping or feeding while the mothers talked about their births freely. The sight of a lone man, bobbing his head at the fishbowl window before disappearing, intensified the feeling of being in a protected bubble, so different to being out in London with a pram.

'Where did you have your baby?' I asked the woman next to me.

'Homerton. It was – well, I won't forget the experience, put it that way.'

'Yeah. I know what you mean,' I replied, stroking my baby's cheek, wondering if she wanted to say more.

'I had a room overlooking the car park ... and I remember seeing my boyfriend getting our suitcase out of the car and somehow losing control of the birthing ball. It went bouncing away from him across the car park and he was kind of chasing it, looking all panicky. I laughed so hard I threw up and my waters broke, pretty much simultaneously.' She looked at me and shook her head slowly. 'And it only deteriorated from there. How about you? Homerton too?'

'Yep. It was a long labour ... better once I got some pain relief.'

'Lucky you.'

'You didn't?'

'Nope. They kept saying that if I could make it past the next bit I'd be okay and then eventually they said it was too late and I had to go without.'

'That's terrible.'

'It was. I got my revenge though. Screamed the place down. The midwife threatened to leave me to it at one point.'

'My God.'

'I don't think she meant it, but I was out of control.' She looked regretful.

'Well, I think you're amazing for getting through. It was so much harder than I expected. It's all harder.'

'I know.' She stared at her baby, a big boy with gentle, happy eyes, gurgling up at her. 'You have some pretty dark moments.'

Were you *allowed* to say that? Maybe you were. She'd said it, and she'd been in this strange new world longer than me. We sat together, all of us, and I realised there was a community here that I had never before been aware of. We might not have been the liveliest company, all of us a bit tired and broken, and not up to much in the way of witty conversation, but there was a connection between us, and a secret happiness, too.

As I opened the door of the apartment and stepped into the hallway, I saw Paul and Rachel sitting at the dining-room table. Rachel was leaning towards him, her dark hair covering the side of her face so I couldn't see her expression, the lamp above illuminating them like they were on stage, performing a scene of two people having an intense conversation.

As I shut the door behind me she pulled away from the table, sat back in her chair and glanced over at me with a guilty, almost frightened expression, as if I had interrupted something private or illicit.

The baby began to howl and I waited a moment, hoping Paul would respond to him, but he got up and left the room.

'How are you, Rachel?' I asked, and for some reason my voice quavered.

She didn't look at me, just rubbed her neck slightly as if thinking about something. 'I think I'm going to travel down to Bristol. On Wednesday.' She spoke very carefully, still not meeting my eyes. From the set of her face she appeared to be holding something back from me.

'What are you doing down there? Seeing friends?' I asked, somehow resurrecting my former social skills.

'Staying with a friend for a couple of nights – she's just got back from a year in the States and we have a lot to talk about. I'll be back on the weekend.'

'Oh, okay. Well, maybe that's a good idea. Give you a chance to have a break from all this baby stuff. It's probably not much fun for you.' My voice came out nervous and appeasing.

She said nothing, but I sensed her full attention on me as she continued stroking her neck, her silver bangles clinking against each other.

Uneasy, I opened the fridge. There appeared to be nothing planned for dinner, so I got a packet of pasta and a tin of tomatoes from the cupboard.

'I guess I'll make some dinner.'

'Yeah.' Her voice was flat.

'Did you have any plans?'

'No.'

Why was she like this – sometimes totally normal, and other times so icy cold and unresponsive? Or was I being oversensitive?

'What are we doing for dinner? Pasta?' said Paul behind me, his voice husky and tired. I turned around, trying to gauge his mood, but he was shifting things around in the fridge and I couldn't see his face.

'I guess so. There's nothing else to eat.'

'You sit down. I'll cook,' he said, so I joined Rachel at the table.

'So, Simone, I was thinking maybe tomorrow we could go out, have a look around London,' said Rachel, her tone suddenly friendly and normal again. 'Maybe you could go to a movie, if you like, and I could stay with the baby.'

A movie. A dark cinema. Nothing except me and the story, not even having to read words on a page. My beloved movie stars, with their charismatic, expressive faces, so easy to stare at. Slowly building tension. Atmospheric rooms. American landscapes.

'That would be really nice, to go to a movie again,' I said, smiling at her but feeling a little off kilter at her sudden change of tone.

'Maybe we could go to Marylebone as well? In the morning?'

'To *Marylebone*? What for?'

'To have a look around the shops. I need to get some more makeup and some winter clothes. Maybe try on some boots.'

What for? I wanted to ask again, but it would seem rude. Looking at her eager face, I didn't have the energy to argue. 'Sounds great. Let's do it.'

We'd need to get a Tube there, and I didn't know if I could face it. Catching a bus to Angel and going to a movie was one thing, but burrowing down into the Underground and travelling through its busy centre was something else entirely. The prospect of being out all day in London daunted me: close tunnels with blank-faced commuters, the icy winter air hitting your tired face when you come up from the tunnel, weaving through it all with my red sleepless eyes and my heavy dragging body and the baby such a delicate package that it required its own wheeled carriage; a baby who had no need for coffee, no need to be outside, no need to eat authentic Texan barbecue ribs or to try on expensive velvety winter clothes or to gaze into a Rothko. Nothing in this whole vast noisy city was of the slightest interest to him for more than ten minutes before he became overstimulated and started to flap. Which meant that, sadly, nothing in it was of much use to me either. And that was depressing, in a way.

London had always felt to me like a magical toyshop, glowing a deep golden yellow from the street, mysterious and piled with riches. But now, with the baby, it felt like the lights had gone out. Suddenly the shutters had been drawn down, and it had closed for the season. It would reopen, one day, perhaps, but right now the owners were on sabbatical.

I sat back in my chair, feeling my attention start to drift as Rachel chattered on about the shops she wanted to visit, the things she wanted to buy. Did I even need to be here in this rushed, temperamental, expensive place anymore? I'd assumed that after the baby was born I would go back to work and continue my life here, but now I wasn't sure. The baby seemed unsuited to city life. He needed somewhere quiet and unpolluted and friendly, like Perth.

I pictured my childhood there: rainy afternoons in winter warming myself next to my grandmother's Metters stove, balmy nights outside playing hide-and-seek with a torch, rinsing off under a beach shower, tearing around on my bike in my heavy-duty Saturday clothes, exploring the building sites and wetlands around our house. I'd always assumed my kids, if I had any, would be born there, that they would have a childhood like mine. But I also knew that thought had never crossed Paul's mind, that he had assumed I'd settle here, now we had a baby together. I understood better my parents' cautious reaction to the news of my pregnancy. London was impressive, but it wasn't nurturing, or a place that loved its inhabitants nearly as much as they loved it.

So many people had lived here over the centuries. They had led their small or big lives here, and the city, with its trade and banks and vast art galleries and elegant royal parks and hard pavements, outlasted every single one of them.

'Are you still with us, Simone?' said Paul. He was draining the pasta that I'd forgotten about.

I looked up. 'Huh? Oh, sorry. I think I went off into some weird half-sleep. Do you need a hand?'

'That's okay. It's ready if you want to eat.'

Paul set a big pot of pasta on the table then dumped a tangle of spaghetti onto my plate, then Rachel's and his. He sat down and started eating, fast and focused, as if he'd been starved for days. Rachel stared at him, her expression oddly resentful as she took a tiny forkful and twirled it around on her spoon.

'Did you see that story in the paper about the woman who jumped off a balcony in South London holding her baby, Simone?' she said suddenly, turning her attention to me.

'No. But that's terrible. Did they die?'

'The baby did. The woman didn't. She'll go to jail, once she gets out of hospital, I suspect. The law is pretty tough on that kind of thing.' Her eyes were shining.

'Poor baby,' I said, my eyes prickling suddenly with tears. 'Poor mother, too.'

'Poor mother? Really? Why would you say that, Simone?' Rachel tilted her head at me.

'Because I can see how it could happen. No support, maybe. No money. No sleep, definitely. Mental health problems. Or maybe too young to cope with the responsibility.'

Paul stopped eating and looked out the window, in the direction of the Golden Lane Estate where I sometimes saw the lit window of my fellow night villager. Rachel, meanwhile, continued staring at me in disbelief.

'So you'd forgive her, let her off the hook? For killing her own baby?'

'When something like that happens, it's the system that's failed, not the mother,' I said, suddenly beyond caring what she thought of me. 'I can imagine someone getting that desperate. Not having sleep does strange things to you.' I jammed some pasta into my mouth, propping my head up with my hand, too tired to continue my line of thought.

Paul and Rachel sat in silence, and when I looked up again, she was staring at him in a meaningful way, as if I'd proved some shameful point about myself, while he kept his eyes on his half-empty plate, not looking at either of us. Was she signalling to him that she thought I was a danger to the baby? There was something confrontational about her. It was as if she had come here on false pretences. She'd said she was here to help, but it was more than that; it was as if she had come here to settle some score, or make me look bad, or ruin what we had together. Or was I imagining it all?

Things hung in the air, and for some reason I bit my lip hard. The sharp pain of my tooth cutting through and the metallic taste of blood filling my mouth distracted me from the suffocating tension in the room. She was really starting to get to me.

Later, I lay beside Paul in bed, who seemed distracted as he flicked through an old *Guardian* newspaper that had somehow made its way into our bedroom.

'What's the matter? You're so quiet,' I finally asked him. He had a tendency to stew, and while usually I'd leave him to it, right now I felt like we needed to communicate with each other.

'Nothing. I'm fine.'

'Is it me?'

'No. It's not you.' He kept his eyes on some news story about a new solar bridge at Blackfriars, and I had no idea what he was thinking. You can sleep with someone, share a living space with them, even have a baby with them, and still they have a whole interior life you know nothing about.

'Is it something going on at work? Or having Rachel here?'

'No. Nothing's going on,' he said quickly. 'Is it okay for you, having her here? You see her more than I do. Have you been talking to her much?'

'Well, not really. I was out today though. What were you talking to her about when I came in earlier?'

'Oh, nothing much.'

'Really? It looked like I interrupted something. She kind of jumped when I opened the door.'

He finally looked up from his newspaper and met my eyes. 'She … was telling me that she's a bit worried that you don't want her here. She said she wants to help you but she doesn't know how.' He looked miserable, more miserable than the situation warranted, I thought. 'Would you mind if she took the baby out sometimes, on her own?'

I looked at the baby, asleep beside me in his cot, close enough to touch. 'She can't take him out on her own. He's too little.' I closed my eyes for a moment. Summoned up some patience. I thought he would nod in agreement at this, but he only looked more upset.

'Is there anything she could do to help you? I feel like I need to come up with some ideas. Or, if you like, I can always ask her to find somewhere else to stay when she gets back from Bristol.'

'Well, what would be helpful would be if she got up a little earlier sometimes and sat with the baby so I could sleep. Or went out herself so I could sit on the couch in my undies and watch total crap on TV without an audience. Or cooked dinner. It's a bit tiring, having someone here all the time, having to keep quiet in the mornings while she sleeps, having to wait for her to finish in the bathroom, having to think about food ...' I trailed off, realising I was starting to rant, and she was his family, after all. Next to her, I was a relative newcomer.

'Well, she did cook the other night, didn't she?'

'Yeah, she did. And it was good. But that was one dinner.'

'Fair enough. I could probably do some more of that too.'

'Yeah, you could. When are you taking some more time off? I'm with the baby all day while you're at work. I don't know what to do with myself.'

'I have asked about taking some more time off. I thought maybe we could go stay at my parents' for a bit, and give you some rest.' He turned towards me and stroked my face. 'How are you feeling, generally? Maybe you should do something for yourself. You've been through a huge change. Maybe it would help to go and get some new clothes, whatever you want.'

'Some clothes that fit, you mean. Some mum clothes. Topped off with a mum bob, I suppose.'

'No. Not topped off with a mum bob.' He looked confused. 'What the hell's a mum bob? I thought you might like some new clothes, something for you. After everything you've been through it might be good to focus on yourself for a change. Take my card. Buy some things when you're out with Rachel tomorrow.'

A long pause. He was probably right.

'Maybe. I'll think about it. It feels a bit weird, though, spending your money.'

'I don't care. It's yours too. Spend as much as you want. I'll get you your own bank card, if you like. Or put money into your account.'

'Okay.' I was drifting irresistibly into sleep, unable to continue the conversation. Paul said nothing beside me. I switched off the bedside light and moved into my pre-baby sleep ritual, turning over to face the window and shifting so that my back was pressed slightly against Paul's warmth. The darkness was kind to my tired eyes, and I had one long, complicated yawn and stretched out my legs, one after the other, to the very bottom of the bed, then flipped the quilt so one foot poked out slightly for temperature control. *Sleep*. Beautiful, deep, restorative sleep.

And then, of course, the baby woke. His cry was low but insistent, and I felt a sudden despair at my inability to escape, to rest and have time alone. When would I get my nights back? When would I fall asleep knowing I wouldn't be woken?

'For God's sake.' I turned on the lamp and reached for the baby, who was lying in a cot bolted to my side of the bed, with one side missing so I could find him easily in the dark.

My frustration dissolved at the sight of him, at his smooth skin, his perfectly proportioned body, so neat in its little grey flannel sleepsuit, his eyes meeting mine and his body light enough to move towards me with one hand as I rolled on my side and pushed up my t-shirt. He latched on easily and I could feel he was getting a good feed, his eyes only half-open as he slowly drank himself into a milk coma.

'That was something Rachel mentioned,' Paul said. 'She was thinking, if you weren't breastfeeding all the time, she could give him formula. So could I. To make it easier for you to get some rest.'

How could he not see that breastfeeding was the one thing that was going well in all this? The one thing my body had managed to do like it was supposed to.

'It's hard to think about that right now,' I said. 'I've only just managed to get it working, I don't want to mess it up. And I'd have to go out and buy all the bottles and stuff.'

'Maybe you could express some milk and I could feed him, and you could get some sleep? It might help with my bonding?'

Oh, give me a break, I thought, knowing I was being unfair but unable to stop myself.

'So you want me to go out and buy a pump? And then sit and pump milk?' I started to raise my voice and the baby startled, so I made myself whisper. That was the other problem with house guests and babies: you could never have a good yelling match and then move on.

'I'm already feeding him every two or three hours, and through the night. I don't really want to sit and express milk on top of that to help with your bonding.'

'But it's a good idea. It would mean you could sleep.'

'*I want to sleep now*.'

For a long time neither of us said a word. Wide-awake again, I was furious. At my inability to articulate what was so hard about this new life, at his inability to understand how my life was transformed while his went on largely unchanged.

'Sorry,' he said at last, his voice polite and formal in the still room, and I thought to myself, with queasy certainty, *We're not going to get through this*.

11

Morning, some time before dawn. Paul had left the bed during the night to sleep on the couch and I could hear him snoring away. Deep in the kind of unbroken, luxurious slumber that I longed for.

Already I had learned not to look at the clock, because it was too demoralising if it wasn't even midnight when the baby first woke for a feed and I would know there were hours of confused darkness ahead of me to get through until daylight and coffee and some semblance of ordinary life. The baby was beside me, his arms wide in complete abandon, his mouth slightly open. Now that I was awake he had finally decided to rest.

It had been a night of constant feeding, with him refusing to lie in his cot, not settling until he was right beside me. Every time I fell back to sleep, I'd be woken again, twenty minutes later, by him crying and clawing at me, insatiable, always wanting more. Maybe I was dehydrated and he wasn't getting enough fluids. Maybe he was *boosting my supply* or having a *developmental leap*, as the baby books called it.

I felt like I was looking at everything through blurry glass. If I could only get enough sleep, I could probably work out what was going on, but the broken nights seemed to be a permanent state now, and I had no idea how to change that, how to be focused and optimistic and alert enough to make the first step into competent parenting.

The memory of the midwife making Paul a bed and encouraging us both to get some rest now made sense. She knew that sleep was over for us. It was something that I'd only realised a few nights later, after I had tucked the baby into his bassinet, thinking how intense the last few days had been and how much I was looking forward to a good night's rest. And then, after about thirty seconds of soothing darkness, the baby had woken up and howled and hadn't let up for three hours.

Eventually, I got up and made some toast and some strong black coffee and sat staring out the window, feeling as grey and polluted and drab as the ragged pigeons that clustered along the window ledges of the Golden Lane estate, avoiding the metal spikes that had been nailed there to discourage them.

I heard the baby cry out in the bedroom. He might be stirring in his sleep, only to settle himself again, so I left him alone, hoping for fifteen minutes to have a shower, or sit and stare out the window for a bit longer.

Rachel's door creaked open and she went in to him, and I heard her chatting to him, waking him up fully. She brought him out to me.

'Look who's here!'

I smiled, trying not to show my annoyance. 'Hello.'

He did look beautiful, drowsy and blinking in the grey morning light.

'Here you go.' She dumped him in my lap and he slumped against me as if he was equally disenchanted at the arrival of yet another day. Was he understimulated? Did I need to do more with him?

She went to the window. 'The sun is shining!' She smiled, looking out onto the mirrored office windows and satellite dishes of the council estate like it was some hilltop Provençal village in late summer. 'Finally shining! Let's go out!'

English people seemed to have a very different idea of what constituted a sunny day, I'd observed. It was a weak, hazy sunshine, with no stamina, and it would be gone in an hour or two, replaced by freezing cold darkness and, by the look of the dark grey sky behind it, icy sleet. The thought made me want to curl back up into bed, between my warm, slightly milk-stained sheets.

'Really? It might be sunny but it's still cold out there. And I got so little sleep last night. I don't feel up to it, to be honest.'

'Oh come *on*. Let's go out. It's my last day in London for a bit. And we'll see a movie.'

If I could get to a dark cinema it would be okay. I'd feed the baby to sleep and keep him lying on me and maybe have a little nap in the warm theatre.

'It's sunny, we can't not go.'

'Okay. I'll see what movies are on.'

Rachel rushed off to the shower and I contemplated the baby and thought about how much easier this day would be if I could share it with this child's other parent.

As Paul was heading off to work, he'd mentioned he had a drinks function after work, some networking event, and I thought, *How convenient*. Not only did he get to network and drink wine and eat rare beef canapés and pâté and cheese and lots of fiddly things that were far better than anything I would eat today, and do all that informal networking that would ultimately see him earn more and work longer hours and be more powerful than me, he also got to come home tonight, cheerful and slightly pissed and safely past the baby's bedtime, same as all the other blokes. And they all knew that they were propping each other up. They knew it wasn't fair. But they also suspected, correctly, that looking after a baby was monotonous, and it was comparatively easy sitting in a meeting with a nice coffee or going to a work function and trading banter. And that is why women turned to valium in the 1960s and to SSRIs today. Because it made it easier for us to keep smiling and to keep doing and to not feel quite so very, very angry, because despite everything, nothing had changed. We got to work, yes, but we still had to do everything else.

Not that I had much to complain about compared to some women, I reminded myself. And, yes, he did make dinner last night. But still. God, I was fuming. Ten minutes into my day and I felt ready to murder someone, namely Paul, who was probably sitting at his desk, beavering away, completely oblivious.

I looked down at the baby, lying still and content in my lap, then lifted him up and smelled his neck, felt his breath and his tiny wet mouth against my neck, such sweet air coming from his perfect, healthy, unpolluted lungs.

Rachel opened the bathroom door in a cloud of steam and the scent of the expensive shampoo the beauty editor had given me before I'd left work.

'Come on! Go have a shower!'

'Okay.'

The problem wasn't the baby. The problem was all the crap that came with it.

Out on the street, Rachel said, 'I'll take you to lunch! You've been so good, letting me come and stay. Let me buy you lunch.'

'Where should we go?' I was thinking we would head to some café nearby, maybe in Exmouth Market, but she had set her heart on Mrs H, a place in Notting Hill that she had read about in *Metro*.

We walked to the Tube station and carefully carried the pram down to the platform. We stood all the way to Edgware Road, where we had to change to get onto a Circle line train to Notting Hill Gate.

The café Rachel had chosen was crowded, and when we sat down in a cramped booth seat the couple at the table next to us – young, childless, artfully dressed – looked startled, and then annoyed. I lifted the baby onto my lap and in doing so caused his sock-clad foot to swipe a spoon off the table and onto the polished concrete floor with an echoing clatter.

The couple now looked extremely annoyed. Sighing heavily, the woman picked up her spoon and cleared her throat at me.

Oh, *grow up*. It was a baby, for Christ's sake – a human, only slightly less socialised than those two. It would pay their pension one day, if they were lucky enough to live that long. And at least they'd had a full night's sleep. Did I used to get this annoyed by babies? Possibly, but that was beside the point.

'Do you want to share a sandwich?' said Rachel, looking at the menu.

'What – why?'

'I don't know. I'm not that hungry.'

I didn't feel like sharing a sandwich. What I wanted was something hot and nourishing and filling, followed by six coffees. I was depleted and thirsty and starving and already the baby was starting to fuss against me, meaning he was going to want a feed soon, which would leave me even more hungry and thirsty. If I'd known we were going to come all this way to share a sandwich I would have stayed in bed.

'Oh, I'll order something,' I said. 'I'm quite hungry, I don't think half a sandwich is going to cut it. I can pay. You don't have to buy me lunch.'

'Are you sure?' She looked worried.

'Yes. That's fine. It's kind of expensive here, I can pay for myself.'

'Okay. Thanks.'

'No worries.' I smiled, telling myself that I couldn't get enraged at people for wanting to share a sandwich just because I was tired. At least she was trying.

The baby was fussing on my lap and the couple beside me stopped talking and eyed us with something approaching horror. As I tried to calm him down they kept looking at me, as if staring into the abyss at their own possible future as tired and dishevelled parents. Or was it my hectic imagination again? Either way, I needed to feed the baby.

I reached inside my top and unclipped my bra, which was starting to feel warm and wet, moving the baby into a position that would enable him to latch on and also keep me covered. It wasn't easy, but I managed it, pulling up my shirt and wincing at the baby's frantic mouth bumping up against my raw skin.

And all of a sudden, the café became very quiet. The woman was now looking at me like I'd slapped her, and the man looked disgusted. But the baby was oblivious, hungrily feeding, although the milk wasn't flowing as fast as it could because I was tensing at how painful it was. Still, he persisted, and I forced myself to relax, breathing as deeply as I could and ignoring muttered comments now issuing from the next table about how it wasn't really the time or place, and wasn't it also a bit of a hygiene risk?

I don't particularly want to be doing this either, I wanted to snap at them. But when a baby's hungry, he's hungry. There is nothing I can do to change that, and if they had to listen to his hungry cry for more than thirty seconds they'd be trying to jam a nipple into his mouth themselves. If anything, they should be thankful someone fed them back in the day, and they could now sit here in a fancy café being completely outraged as a result.

I stared at the woman with my eyebrows raised, and then at the bloke, who went bright red and looked away quickly. *Sometimes the abyss looks back, pal.* I suppressed a laugh at my own silly joke and Rachel gave me a puzzled expression.

'Sorry,' she said to them, tilting her head apologetically. 'It's not ideal, but when they're hungry, you have to feed them.'

I stared at her in disbelief. 'What did you say that for?' I asked her.

'I was trying to explain to them that you can't help it,' she whispered. 'They seem a bit funny about you ... feeding at the table.'

'I'm sure they'll get over it eventually.'

The couple said nothing, and I felt oddly ashamed. I thought back to my Australian childhood and how common it had been back then. Was it less acceptable here? Was it actually considered unhygienic to breastfeed in public? I should have stayed home, or found the bathroom.

A man about the same age as me walked past our table with a tray of coffee and walnut cakes for the elaborate centre display and gave me a small, understanding smile and a tiny nod. Judging by the dark circles under his eyes he had a baby at home, too.

I smiled back at him, and as the baby settled against me, falling into sleep, I didn't care when the woman gave me another dirty look and said, loudly, 'Shall we go to Barcelona this summer? Just, you know, to chill?'

My food arrived at the exact moment the baby required an immediate nappy change. Rachel offered to do it and, because I was hungry, I hesitated.

'Honestly, it's fine. You've got soup, it'll go cold. Let me do it.'

I found her a nappy and a packet of wipes and the change mat, and she took the baby from me and vanished towards the back of the restaurant.

The soup was good – dark brown lentils and bacon, salty and hot with lots of bread. I ate as fast as I could, knowing that once the baby was back I would have to hold him.

But ten minutes later, as I was finishing, Rachel still hadn't returned. The room was suddenly too loud around me. I felt my heart start to race as I got up, light and panicky, almost knocking the phone of the judgemental woman off the table next to me.

The restaurant was in one of those creaky Victorian buildings with basement toilets at the bottom of a narrow, badly lit staircase. The air was warm and smelled like old sewerage pipes and I didn't want him down here. I never should have let her take him. The women's toilets were cold and empty. Where were they? Looking down the hallway, I saw another door with a baby change sign on it.

'Rachel?' I knocked loudly, but heard nothing. The door was locked, but I could hear running water through the door. I banged louder against the scratched wood. Finally, I heard fumbling and the door creaked open. Rachel peered out at me, breathing heavily, the baby in her arms. Was she crying?

'Sorry,' she said. 'That took a while.'

'Are you okay?' I asked her.

'I'm fine.'

The baby looked at me from her arms. Whatever had happened, he wouldn't be able to tell me. But he didn't seem upset.

'Here.' I held out my arms. 'Can I have him back?'

'Sure.' She handed him back to me and walked away, back up the stairs to our table. Following close behind her, I noticed that her hands were trembling.

As we paid, I could see the rain starting to fall outside. Once we stepped into the street, it pelted straight onto my hair because I'd forgotten my hat, and trickled, icy cold, down my neck and into my collar. It was not soft London rain, but heavy and penetrating, and I was worried about the baby's pram and how waterproof it was. He would be startled by cold water, and by the sound of the rain hitting the plastic cover.

'Do you mind if we go and look in a few shops?' Rachel asked. 'I haven't been shopping like this in months.'

'Okay. But weren't we going to see a movie? There's one at the Gate starting in twenty minutes.'

'Oh, I forgot we were going to see a movie. Maybe not. I don't think we'll make it. Sorry. Another time, perhaps.'

So instead we wandered through expensive shops selling forty-pound mugs and French cosmetics and Italian glassware. Each time we left the perfumed warmth of one, we had to step out again into the darkening day, where crowds of people swarmed and coughed and shoved each other, stepping neatly around my pram, as we went from hot to cold to hot again.

After a couple of hours I said to Rachel, 'Should we get a bus home soon? I don't think I can face the Tube again.'

'Okay.'

Rachel didn't know where to go, so I checked a street map at the bus stop and worked out the bus stop we needed to be at, which turned out to be on the other side of the road and up a little, back in the direction we'd come from.

Once we were on, we found a seat up the back. I sat and shivered in my rain-soaked coat. In the seat in front of us, a man was hacking into a tissue, leaning his head against the window. Across the aisle, a teenage boy was whispering something into the ear of the schoolgirl sitting next to him, who appeared too frightened to move. The air was close and I worried about the baby getting sick.

Rachel looked over at me, and in her eyes I thought I saw a glimmer of impatience. 'You're not *that* tired, are you?' she said sweetly.

It appeared that what she wanted me to say was that I was fine, that the shopping journey wasn't too much, that it had been, in fact, a really good idea. But I couldn't.

'I'm really tired,' I told her flatly, and she said nothing. She looked closed off, staring out the window, not talking to me.

The bus felt dark and nightmarish, but the baby was asleep, so I closed my eyes too and we didn't speak again as we made our slow, jolting way home.

12

One clammy hour and another bus later we arrived, pushing the pram from the station, through the brightly lit underpass and into the dim foyer of Cromwell Tower. The grey man nodded at Rachel.

Inside the apartment, I took my coat off and drank some water – it was strange how in such freezing cold you could get so thirsty – and ran the baby a bath. My feet were damp and aching, my throat was sore and I was shivering, but once I was sitting on the tiled floor of the steamy bathroom with the sound of the water running, nothing seemed so bad.

I took the baby's nappy off so he could kick around without it, and he squealed happily, his bright eyes meeting mine, with what looked like the very start of a smile. He was so perfectly formed, with his spindly legs and his soft belly and the long feet that still had such strong reflexes, I only needed to touch them with the tip of my finger for the miniature toes to curl up tightly. He seemed spellbound by the sound of the bathwater, the smells and the warmth and the softness of the towel and the freedom of not being swaddled in an uncomfortable papery nappy. I sat and absorbed his contentment, revelling in the way that a day that had seemed so long and exhausting had now arrived at this peaceful point.

I thought of something Jennifer had said, as we had both gazed at him in the Museum of Childhood lying in his pram and staring up at us with an expression of pure contentment: *He's beautiful. So happy to be here, existing in this very moment.*

She was right. There was absolutely nothing wrong with this moment. The running water, the feel of his skin, his face. As I sat there, staring down at him and stroking his wrinkled pink feet, I became aware of Rachel standing in the doorway. She came in and scooped up his little body from the towel, then took him over to the mirror, looking at the reflection as she held his face against hers. My hands tingled with the urge to take him off her, to rescue him from whatever she was thinking about.

I thought back to how she'd disappeared with him for so long at the café, long enough for me to start to panic. And that she had offered to change his nappy. It was probably my tiredness, this seeing danger everywhere. I got up and took him from her without saying anything, and she watched as I put him back on the towel and tested the bathwater.

'That was so weird today, when I was in the toilet with him,' she said, as if reading my thoughts. 'Someone came and knocked on the door. They stood there for ages, wanting to make sure I was okay. No idea what they thought was going on.'

She studied me for a long moment, her small blue eyes un-blinking. She looked tired. Exhausted, actually. Whatever she was doing, it seemed to enervate her.

'Really?'

She sat down on the closed toilet lid and continued to study me. It was uncomfortable, the way she lurked, studying me, as if waiting for something more, so to avoid her gaze I poured some bath oil into the water.

'Yeah. I finally opened the door and said I was busy and there were two more toilets they could be using instead of banging on the door of mine.' She laughed. 'It was one of the waiters. He looked so cross.'

I looked down at the baby's face. He was so far away from being able to take care of himself. So many years until he could even cross a road unharmed, let alone know when someone didn't have his best interests at heart. Maybe it was impossible to ever know. What if he'd been harmed already and I didn't realise? It was hard to imagine anyone wanting to hurt him, but what was she trying to tell me? It was as if she were testing me, seeing what she could get away with, and what she couldn't.

'So, why *were* you in there for so long?' I finally asked, after a long, measured silence in which it felt like she hardly blinked.

Instantly she was alert, sitting up straighter, still giving me her complete attention but in a way that seemed more eager, not so apathetic. 'What do you mean?'

I sighed. Sometimes she appeared so slow to understand. Knowing I wouldn't get anywhere, that I was sure to lose, yet suddenly angry, I answered back.

'I mean, why were you in the toilet for so long with my baby? What were you doing? I was wondering myself. I probably should have come looking for you, but I kept expecting you to come back.'

In slow motion her expression changed, her mouth opening slightly and her eyes widening to a look of confused sadness.

'I don't really know,' she said eventually, in a small, careful voice. 'Maybe … you seemed like you weren't that alert, and I thought I'd give you a break, let you eat in peace. You need to look after yourself. He is completely dependent on you, you know.'

'Do you think I don't know that, Rachel? Do you actually think that has never crossed my mind?' I tried to keep my voice calm, but I could feel anger starting to flood my vision.

'What I mean is, it's important to listen to your instincts.'

She stared at me for a long moment and I felt like an infuriating schoolgirl being told off by a teacher.

'I know that too. All I ever do is listen to my instincts.'

'Oh, Simone. Why are you like this?'

I couldn't keep up with her. 'Like what?'

'So suspicious. I mean, what are you trying to say to me?' She stared off into the distance, shaking her head in despair. 'I am trying to help. You asked me to take him, don't you remember? You wanted to eat. You *asked* me to help you, Simone.'

Had I? She sounded so sure, but I didn't remember asking her. And even if I had, why was she gone so long? Every moment I said nothing weakened my position further.

'I don't remember asking you.' Did it even matter? All I wanted was to bathe the baby and go to bed.

'I want to help you. Help you with the baby. He's family, and so are you now.' I looked at her again and she wasn't looking at me, but at the baby, who was lying very still on the towel, as if listening to our voices.

My head ached as I realised she'd drawn me into a conversation that would lead nowhere useful, and might even be reported back to Paul as evidence of my hostility towards her. My throat was burning and my muscles were aching as if I hadn't used them for days. I could feel a cough building in my chest.

And then she was crying. 'I don't know what I've done. I'm really trying here.' She cried for a little longer as I stared at her, then seemed to pull herself together. 'I'm on your side, you know.'

I didn't have an answer for that. The conversation had somehow turned into a confrontation I had no energy for. The bath was deep enough so I turned off the tap and undressed the baby completely, then lifted him up and held him against me, focusing on him and nothing else.

Rachel sat, sniffing every so often, waiting for me to say more, but I couldn't come up with an appropriate way to smooth things over. It was beyond me. The only thing I wanted was sleep – long hours of deep slumber in some remote mountain cave, piled with old, soft blankets, far from the world.

After a few moments she got up and walked out, and then I heard her on the phone, talking quietly. I leaned over the water, breathing in the steam for a moment. The water was warm and deep and smelled of lavender, and when I lowered the baby into it he looked thrilled, not quite smiling, but alert, with his mouth open in an expression of comical wonder as I sailed his little body through the water, from one end of the white porcelain tub to the other, which to him must have felt like a long way. His fringe was pushed back, as if he was tearing along a river on a jet ski, and his eyes were wide. His expression had a new quality, of shocked delight in bodily sensation that I hadn't seen before, and I gazed at his face as I rocked him back and forth through the deep water.

He had so much to look forward to, and it was my responsibility to look after him, to listen to my instincts and keep him safe from harm, so he could grow up and do it all. No more letting him out of my sight. No more letting Rachel help, and allowing her to take him away to dark dingy toilets because I was too tired or hungry to do it myself. I leaned my head on the rim of the bath, still supporting him with my hands, thinking that the small room must be very steamy, because it was suddenly so much harder to breathe.

When I came out of the bathroom with the baby wrapped in a towel, I saw that Rachel was getting ready to go out, putting on my scarf and fiddling with her phone at the front door.

'You off out?'

'I gave Soraya a ring. I felt like catching up with someone for a drink and a chat.'

Soraya was my friend, and the thought of them going out together made me feel left out. I knew it was silly, though, because Soraya was far more sociable than me, always making new friends and trying new places, and it never usually bothered me.

'Does she want to come over here?'

She smiled tightly and shook her head. 'I don't think so. We both want to go out, maybe grab a glass of wine or something to eat. I am craving a rare steak. Is Smiths of Smithfield open tonight? Or that gastropub on City Road?'

'They would both be open. If you want steak I'd say Smiths is your best bet, though.'

'Okay. Well. Have a good rest. I'm going to Bristol in the morning, so I might not see you.' She wasn't making eye contact, and

I felt like I needed to somehow repair things between us before she left.

'Well, have fun. Say hi to Soraya for me. When are you back from Bristol?'

'Not sure yet. See you.'

She gave me a wary look before turning away from me and leaving, and I wondered what she was going to say to Soraya about how things were going here.

Paul was still out at his work function, so I went to bed, the baby beside me, feeding himself to sleep as I tried to stay still, my throat so raw it made me wince to swallow.

Paul arrived home sometime later, and I heard him showering and then cooking something in the kitchen before the TV went on and then off again.

I was dozing in a feverish haze, the baby beside me for once lying quiet and untroubled, like the baby I'd imagined before I had a real one. Paul slid into the bed carefully, trying not to wake me.

'Hi. I'm awake.'

'Oh, hi! How are you?' He sounded friendly, from too much wine or simply because he was happy to see me, it was hard to tell.

'I'm okay.'

'How was your day out with Rachel?'

'It was alright. A bit weird. We went out for lunch and it was a bit ... I don't know. Tense, or something.'

'How come?'

Because Rachel took a really long time changing the baby's nappy? Even in my head it sounded ridiculous, so there seemed to be little point explaining it.

'Oh, I don't know. It was probably a bit ambitious.'

'That's a shame.'

'Sorry. I know you want me to try and get along with her.'

'Oh, don't worry about it, Simone. Maybe you don't get along. She'll be gone tomorrow for a bit, and we can have some time to ourselves.' He ran his hand along my leg and sat up. 'God, you're burning. I can feel the heat coming off you. Are you okay?'

'Not really. I don't feel good. We were out in the cold for hours, on buses, in and out of shops, on the Tube. There was a really sick man on the bus in front of us, coughing away. Maybe I picked something up. I've got such a sore throat, and it came on really fast, it's weird. Do we have any medicine?'

He disappeared into the bathroom, and I heard him slamming cabinets, then picking up his keys and going out. Ten minutes later he was back with a Boots bag filled with lozenges and pain-killers and throat spray. He brought me water and dosed me up on painkillers, then gave me a couple of Strepsils, leaving everything by the bed.

'Thanks.'

'Do you need anything else?'

'No. All I need is sleep.'

'Should I take the baby from you? So you don't make him sick.'

'I won't make him sick.' I knew from all my reading on an exhaustive American breastfeeding website that I'd be passing on antibodies through my milk, but I didn't have the energy to explain that to Paul. 'He'll be fine.'

The baby rested in the crook of my arm, his face completely still, and I wished he was inside me again, a foetus, safe and enclosed, where no-one could ever take him away from me or hurt him. It was too risky, I decided, having him out in the world, with me in charge.

13

In the morning Rachel was gone before I got up, and the cup of tea Paul had left by the bed was cold and metallic tasting. The queasy viral feeling was stronger and in the bathroom mirror my eyes were red and my cheeks flushed as my body tried to burn off the infection. But despite all this, the baby was deeply asleep and I was the only one home, so I had a reason to get out of bed. Without Rachel, the atmosphere felt less stifled, the air clearer, and I set about reclaiming the apartment, which had taken on the stale and dingy look of a cheap hostel. If I could restore order, somehow, it might all feel more manageable. I could smell the garbage disposal chute from the hallway, filling the air with mysterious, foul odours from deep inside the Barbican. We probably needed to call some on-site maintenance person, but I didn't know the number. I didn't know much at all about the workings of the building; it was like living in a hotel sometimes.

As I passed Rachel's room I glanced in, feeling like an intruder. She had made the bed roughly, but had left her clothes in a pile on the carpet, and books and receipts and rubbish scattered across the table. She didn't seem to have taken much with her. The room smelled like her perfume, a woody smell with a musky undertone. I yanked the window open to let in the petrol smells and cold impersonal air of the city, then stepped out quickly, closing the door behind me.

Next I went into the bathroom, pulling out all the cleaning stuff from the cupboard and scrubbing the sink and toilet before getting under a hot shower. It had been so long since I had felt properly alone. It was a shame this virus thing was slowing me down, but if I ignored it I could try to move forward, and start making sense of this new life.

Maybe I'd go out and buy some food, from the big Sainsbury's at Angel, once the baby woke up. We'd been living on toast and pasta and lukewarm tea for days. And I'd drop off a bag of clothes at the charity shop – that always made me feel virtuous – and then come home and cook something for dinner.

Getting ready took a while. Dressing myself, dressing the baby. Undressing him to change his nappy. Finding my phone, my wallet. Standing in front of the mirror and trying to make my face and hair look less deranged. Putting on a coat, packing the baby into the pram. Unpacking and feeding him. Changing his nappy again. And all the time I felt the day speeding away from me as I struggled to catch it, held hostage by this small human and his bodily functions. But I had a vision for the day – an ambitious one, perhaps, given how I was feeling – but it was a plan, a to-do list, and I was determined to tick off every item. Finally we got out the door, after what felt like hours of wandering around the apartment with the baby draped over my shoulder, trying to remember what I'd gone into a room for.

Outside, the cold air and weak sunshine, and the bus arriving less than a minute after I got to the stop, all buoyed me. On the bus I got talking to an elderly man whose dog, a solemn grey staffy called Molly, sat on the seat beside him. Despite being bundled up in a tartan coat, she shivered slightly and he kept a consoling hand on her as we chatted.

'She doesn't like the cold,' he told me. 'It makes her miserable. But she needs to go to the vet today.'

Molly looked at me with her emotional brown eyes, as if she were part of our conversation, and I marvelled at all the endless unseen, unpaid care going on around me, even in a place as frenetic as London. How lucky any creature was – staffy or newborn baby or elderly parent alike – to have someone look after them, to put a blanket on them if they were cold and worry about them in the rain. Closing my eyes, I pictured beds, flannel sheets, lamps and darkness and the quiet of everyone asleep.

'How old is your little one?' he asked.

'Almost five weeks.'

'Ah.' He nodded. 'It gets better. We had three.' He shook his head. 'You never really get on top of it, parenting. The minute you think you have everything under control, it sort of morphs into something else. Dogs are easier children.' He smiled to himself, and pulled his staffy closer.

The supermarket was chaotic, with squished blueberries spilling from plastic punnets, pillaged shelves and fluorescent lighting, bags of oranges from Spain, tired-looking asparagus from Mexico and beyond that, the sweet waft of baking bread and the humming rows of chiller cabinets. There was one thing I hadn't considered, though. It was impossible to push a pram and a trolley at once, and I needed to carry it all home on the bus, so I took a blue plastic basket instead.

What I really wanted was chicken noodle soup, with simmering yellow broth and golden speckles of oil. Jewish penicillin, as Soraya called it. A fat whole chicken was called for, but the weight of it unbalanced my basket, so I set it down on the ground and rearranged everything. Picking it up again, it hung over my arm without tilting, and I wandered ahead feeling oddly lighter. It was amazing what simply rearranging a basket could do. It was all suddenly so much easier. A woman gave me a surprised look as I turned the corner, but I ignored her and kept going.

Standing in the middle of the aisle, trying to mentally write the shopping list I'd forgotten, I recalled my last visit here, when

I was forty weeks pregnant and so delirious I had to stop and text Soraya to see what she thought of the name Elmo if it was a boy. Her reply was obscene. I laughed at the memory, feeling unexpectedly like my old self again as I dropped some spaghetti into the basket, before venturing deeper into the aisles in search of dark chocolate and coffee beans. Something was niggling me, that feeling of being in a vast supermarket and knowing you've passed the key ingredient that was the whole point of the journey. Yet at the same time, being back in Sainsbury's, doing a food shop, felt strangely easy, easier than anything had felt for a while.

Eventually I got to the checkout and unpacked my basket. And then a cold faintness hit me as I realised what I was missing.

The baby.

Where was the baby?

The baby was gone.

My mind went blank and I looked at the checkout operator for salvation. He was a young guy and he appeared to be half-asleep, barely registering my panic when I said to him, 'I've lost my baby.'

He looked back at me, blank-faced. 'Are you kidding me?'

'No!' I stared at him, willing him to help me, to set off an alarm or shut down the store and call in a SWAT team, helicopters, the army, order a total lockdown of the supermarket and surrounding streets and the entire city and all London airports. I had some dim, terrible memory of a novel that was very similar to this exact situation, a child going missing in a London supermarket, never to return.

'No,' I said again. I was frozen, unable to think or move. One thing was certain: we were both useless in an emergency.

A woman waiting in the queue behind me, in a calm voice, said, 'Retrace your steps.'

Before she had finished her sentence I was already running back through the shop, to where I'd started, in the fruit and vegetable area.

Nothing.

On to the meat aisle, where I'd rearranged my basket, and there, right beside the free-range chickens, I burst into a small crowd that had gathered around my neat little pram. Inside, the baby was awake and blinking up at the faces, looking surprisingly well cared for, given he had been abandoned in a city supermarket by his own mother. Falling upon the pram, I leaned in towards him, amazed that everything had gone from nightmarish to normal in twenty seconds, and soon he was in my arms.

A voice interrupted our reunion, which was actually just me holding him and gazing blissfully into his eyes, and after a beat or two I realised it was directed at me. I met the eyes of a woman in a Sainsbury's uniform, a walkie-talkie in one hand, looking at me with a mixture of outrage and disbelief.

'You are very, very lucky, young lady. We were minutes away from calling in Social Services. What on earth were you thinking?'

She talked loudly, as if for the benefit of the crowd that had gathered around the pram, all delighted to interrupt their tedious food shop for a bit of real-life drama unfolding right there in the chicken section. I almost laughed. Except that she'd mentioned Social Services. They had the power to take babies away from their homes, and often did.

A quiet, rational part of me took over.

'I have barely slept for weeks,' I told her.

The crowd was hushed, and I could sense, rather than see, them all waiting for her response.

She raised her eyebrows. 'Well, maybe you should be at home in bed,' she said, sounding more reasonable.

'Oh, I should definitely be in bed, but I have to eat.' Taking hold of the pram handle, I felt the baby become mine again, no longer an abandoned orphan in the custody of this woman. 'And I feel bad enough, you know,' I threw over my shoulder. She said nothing, but looked a little more understanding.

What was it with the hostility of this city? I was sure my mother had once left me at a supermarket checkout in my wicker basket and when she'd returned they'd only laughed and said they'd been wondering when she was coming back. Perhaps I looked like I wasn't coping. Or maybe it was my appearance; maybe I needed some better clothes, a smarter pram. I bet that woman would have been nicer to Paul. She would have patted his arm and assured him that he was a wonderful father and nobody's perfect. And Rachel, with her refined accent and graceful height and ballerina face, that woman would have been nicer to her, too.

The ogling crowd separated as I mowed through it, racing back to the checkout, wanting to get away from the judgement and the slim possibility of professionally sympathetic social workers materialising with their clipboards and hidden agendas. The woman who had told me to retrace my steps was still standing in line, my groceries still piled up on the conveyor belt in front of hers.

'Thank you so much. I don't know how I did that,' I said to her.

And unlike the other woman, she was matter of fact and re-assuring as she shrugged and said, 'You have your mind on other things. You're thinking about home, about getting out of here.' Her low voice, with its lilting accent, reminded me of Gloria, the unflappable Ghanaian midwife I'd seen for prenatal appointments at the GP clinic.

The checkout operator scanned my shopping without comment and I packed everything into the bottom of the pram and paid as quickly as I could, keeping my head down. I'd certainly given myself a shiny new and completely unasked-for emergency sce-nario to dwell on tonight as I tried to drift off to sleep. Someone could have kidnapped him, slipped away with him forever, sold him to child traffickers, even, while I was wandering in a fog through those long aisles. Anything could have happened. But it hadn't. Not this time.

As I passed the second-hand shop on the way to the bus stop I remembered my bag of clothes, tucked in the bottom of the pram under all my shopping, and wheeled the pram into the warm mothball fug of old clothes, passing racks crammed with nylon evening dresses, heavily discounted jeans and faded t-shirts, and baskets of vinyl belts and handbags that barricaded the jewellery-cluttered counter.

I used to love vintage shops back in Australia, where over the years I'd found embroidered Chinese silk dressing gowns and pure wool jumpers and silver-threaded Indian skirts and antique hardback books. I could spend hours rummaging in their crowded dark corners, finding treasures, trying things on, carrying it all home. London charity shops were different, though, in volume and quality, overflowing with boxes and bags of cheap, unwashed clothes, still more piled up outside, picked over by passers-by, spilling out of their black rubbish bags and across pavements.

Living here, I could see more clearly how the disposal of every throwaway thing people consumed in the course of their wasteful days was a growing problem. Even public bins seemed incrementally harder to come by, and where we lived in the financial district there were none at all – removed back when IRA bombs were a threat, Paul told me once, they never reappeared. Managing so much stuff was exhausting. If it were possible, I'd strip my life back to a single suitcase, as I had done when I'd first moved to London. A pile of identical clothes, food, a bed and nothing else. Like Obama with his blue and grey suits. Then motherhood might feel lighter, less cluttered with anxiety and pointless pressure.

I dumped the clothes on the counter with relief. I knew they preferred to look over donations before they accepted them, because all the throwaway fashion choked their single bin. And then there were all the landfill sites out in Essex, filling up. What was going to happen when we ran out of space for landfill? Looking down at the new human I'd blithely created, who was right at the start of maybe ninety years here, with no idea of the planetary shitstorm he'd arrived into, I felt a new kind of guilt for him, to add to all the rest. Who would knowingly bring a kid into this?

The woman at the counter had faded blonde hair and a carefully neutral expression as she went through the clothes: a tiny denim jacket, a green top of beaded sparkly netting, jeans. Some she kept, some she discarded with a tactful murmur of, 'No, not for us.'

She picked up a silky Chloe top, one I'd bought for fifty pounds in Selfridges with my savings when I'd first arrived in London, single and skinny and tanned from five weeks of sunbathing in San Sebastián. I'd kissed Evan from Marketing in it, I suddenly remembered, when I drank too much white wine on an empty stomach at someone's leaving party. Embarrassed, I fought the urge to snatch it off her and hide it underneath my baby.

The woman dropped it back on the counter with a tiny sniff. 'A bit worn.'

I inspected a broken nail, trying to keep my face expressionless.

She smoothed over a pink silk dress – the outfit I'd worn to Paul's sister's wedding – with a thoughtful expression on her face. 'These are clothes from another life, aren't they?'

'I suppose they are.'

The woman looked at me, then the baby. He was asleep now.

'It all comes back, you know,' she said.

'Does it?'

'Oh, yes. You get your life back to yourself again.'

I couldn't see it happening. Or perhaps it was more of an internal shift, more felt than seen. Maybe once sleep came back it would all be easier to work out, to move forward.

'Personally I think motherhood's a bit of a con,' she continued. 'I had two lots of kids, a couple in my twenties and a couple more in my forties' She shook her head in amazement. 'I don't know what I was thinking. I look at mothers now and wonder how I did that.'

'Four kids. That would have been so much work,' I said. 'I can barely manage one. But here you are, working. I think I'd be at home in bed after raising four kids.'

'Well, they're grown up now so I've got time to give back a bit. But I remember telling my husband – the second one – that I was going to leave the lot of them. Take off. And he said, "You can't take my kids." And I looked at him and said, "I wasn't planning to."' She met my eyes and I saw solidarity in them.

I had a sudden urge to open up to this woman, to explain to her everything I'd done before kids – worked, studied, earned my own money, had conversations with friends, travelled. And how suddenly, all that had vanished. Before I'd had the baby, I'd thought the birth was the main event, and that after that everything would return to normal, except with a baby that sort of hung around and needed a new nappy every now and then, but mostly slept in a cot. What I hadn't anticipated was the change in myself, how much more vulnerable I felt, and how much more dangerous the world seemed. At least in the hospital there had been a sense of urgency. People taking my blood pressure and weighing sheets to gauge blood loss and filling in forms and talking in soft, serious voices. That kind of behaviour seemed to match, precisely, my internal sense of panic and impending doom. Out here, though, it was lonely. It was like I'd arrived in a new country and wasn't going home, with that exact same feeling of queasy disorientation. Surrounded by people, yet alone, because no-one spoke your language. Maybe all mothers felt the way I did, sometimes. Maybe motherhood – early motherhood, at least – was pretty thankless at times.

'I bet you never take your free time for granted now, though?' I said. 'You know, lying in bed, having a nice cup of tea, no-one needing you to get up in the middle of the night and change their nappy.'

She laughed. 'Never. Never ever *ever*.'

I looked down at the pile of clothes and saw a shirt in there that I used to love, black voile with a beautiful floral print on it. I pulled it out of the pile. 'I think I'll keep this one. I might wear it again.'

'You will,' said the woman, almost singing to me in encouragement. 'Of course you will!'

On the bus the baby howled, but the driver was taking corners hard and the road was shiny with rain, so I couldn't risk picking him up. He locked eyes with me and screamed through the plastic rain cover.

This is an emergency, his eyes seemed to be saying, and I wondered if I was scarring him psychologically by refusing to pick him up. But it wasn't safe. *We have to get home*, I tried to communicate to him wordlessly through the plastic, but still he screamed, almost without pause, and soon I was crying too. Why had I thought it was a good idea to go out? I was so, so tired.

An older woman, who reminded me of that gentle first midwife at the hospital, met my eyes and smiled, but I had to look away. That dreamy euphoria of late pregnancy and the marathon energy of birth had both seeped away and now there was nothing left to draw on, until I could sleep and let the well fill up again. A tumble into blank, dreamless slumber was all I wanted; it would take me two seconds and I'd be gone, my brain putting all the files of my unconscious back in order through long hours of loose-limbed, unbroken slumber.

It was no wonder parents always looked so knackered. You were constantly on duty; you could never hit the pause button or take a few days off to get everything under control or just lie under a tree and look up. Being a mother meant remaining permanently present. Always vigilant, and somehow open to the public, too, for criticism and comment and the attention of strangers.

I wanted my old life back. It had disintegrated without warning. I'd thought I'd still be living it, but with the addition of a cute little newborn. It was a nice life, I realised now. I had enjoyed it. Being able to go to the supermarket in peace, to leave the house with one small bag and meet up with Soraya for a movie or a drink, to think about what to cook for dinner, anonymous and undisturbed and completely in charge of my own time. Now I had a brand-new life, and although I'd thought I wanted it, I missed my old self. How did this baby even happen? I tried to think back, but found that I couldn't.

14

By the time I got home, my fever was worse. Even making the soup felt too hard, so I just unpacked the shopping then took off my street clothes and went to bed with the baby. He slept neatly in the crook of my arm, his face as still and waxy as a doll's, the curve of his nose and lips still round and unformed and foetal. Breathing in his breath, following him into sleep, we captured again that hushed stillness of pregnancy.

Through the long afternoon, as the room darkened and the air got colder and my fever burned through me, we lay together. Giving in was a relief. Piles of tissues and throat lozenges were building up on the bedside table but they felt inadequate against the sickness I could feel boiling inside me, sealing my throat and filling my lungs and inching along my muscles.

Night came, and I heard Paul wandering from room to room, looking for me, until he pushed open the bedroom door and saw us lying there in the light from the hallway.

'Simone. Are you awake?'

'Sort of. I don't feel well … so hot.'

'Sorry I'm so late. Work was a nightmare. What's going on?'

'I went out to get food and then when I came back I couldn't get out of bed again. Can you bring me some water?'

He returned with a thermometer and a glass of cold water, but it tasted metallic and horrible and my throat was too sore to swallow.

'Thirty-nine degrees? You were sick last night too. Why did you have to go out today? You've probably made it worse.'

'I don't know. To get food. It feels like we haven't eaten properly for days. No-one has been cooking.'

Paul turned on the lamp. Our bedroom was stifling, the blinds down, the air stale, a balled-up nappy on the bedside table from when I had changed it a few hours ago without getting out from under the blankets. It was as if we'd reverted to survival mode. Finally, Paul seemed to register that I wasn't coping. He gave me paracetamol and took the baby from me. I heard the bath running and him splashing and singing in the echoing bathroom. Then he came into our room, dressed the baby at the end of the bed, and disappeared again.

Aching and shivery, I went out a little later, and found the baby in his bassinet on the dining room table, fascinated by the steel pendant light above his head. Paul was busy in the kitchen, chopping onions and carrots and celery and lowering chicken pieces into the pot, following a recipe on his phone, more food spilling from a Waitrose bag beside him on the bench. He had an air of competence about him, sleeves rolled up, moving easily from one task to the next, not shuffling or fading out or staring into space the way I had been for the last few days.

It's because he's well rested, I realised, feeling like I was watching a wildlife documentary. What we're observing here is the remarkable difference in basic functioning between someone who gets a full night's sleep every night – because, of course, *it's no good everyone being sleep deprived* – and someone who doesn't. The clear difference between a person who simply gets into bed, falls asleep, and wakes up to daylight, and someone – a mother, usually, or a prisoner in a torturous regime – who experiences night-time as a series of unpredictable and desperate hours stacked up against each other, with no guarantee of reliable slumber. Falling into blackness, being tipped out of it, lying in a feverish half-wakeful state while the baby goes back to sleep, knowing that at any point she will be summoned again, and so on until dawn. Repeat, repeat, repeat.

Eventually, Paul noticed my empty stare directed at him and smiled.

'Oh you're up! Come and sit on the couch, this will be ready soon.'

He served me chicken noodle soup and orange juice, then cleared it all away and replaced it with the baby, who was gnawing the air, practically begging to be fed.

Sleepily, I fed him, then settled him on my lap. For a moment, in the dim light of the living room, his mouth seemed to curve into a long, evil smile.

'Paul?'

He bustled in, a tea towel flung over his white work shirt, a harried look on his face.

'Can you take the baby tonight?' Looking down at him, the smile was still there, an exaggerated grin that came in and out of view in the dim room, or maybe it was my vision that was blurred.

'But – what about when he wakes up?'

'Bring him to me for a feed. I feel really sick … but if you take him for the night and I get some rest I should feel better … because we don't really have anyone to look after him if I get worse. Now that Rachel's gone. Hopefully some sleep will help.'

'Okay.' He looked nervous. 'I'll change the sheets on Rachel's bed.' He took the baby away again, then returned him dressed in his little blue sleeping bag with a red train embroidered across the chest.

The baby was wide-awake now, gazing up at me as he balanced on my knees. It was as if he knew he was up past his bedtime, and seeing things he wouldn't normally see, and so he was quiet and undemanding, happy to be here amid the action, such as it was. My arms were so weak and aching that even the light, puffy sleeping bag and the solid weight of his body beneath were hard to hold onto. When I coughed it was so loud it startled him, and it surprised me too – a thick, bubbling sound like my lungs were full of fluid. Once I'd started I couldn't stop, and a new expression appeared on his face as he studied me – a clear, inquiring gaze, his brow wrinkled like a tiny scientist observing some unexpected, troubling development in an ongoing experiment. His eyes had a new wisdom in them, and then, as I continued to cough, his wrinkled brow conveyed deep worry. Staring at me, really staring, in a way I'd never seen him do before. Something about his expression was unsettling. Too adult. Babies have Stone Age brains, I remembered. They screamed all night, wanting to be held or to sleep on a parent's chest, because to them there was no difference between being alone in a cot and complete abandonment in a forest full of prowling wolves. He didn't know what the sound coming from my lungs was, but some primal instinct sensed danger, a threat to the only food source he knew. And as he communicated it to me, I began to worry. It wasn't enough to keep him safe. I had to look after myself, too, because if I got sick, he was on his own. Another thing I had never considered.

'Your bed is ready,' said Paul.

I handed the baby to him, and saw something close to fear cross his face as he took him from me.

'He won't bite you, Paul,' I joked, but he didn't laugh.

I went to bed in Rachel's room and burrowed under the thick feather quilt, but the sleep I had finally been offered didn't come. The weight of all those feathers seemed to press down on me, suffocating me, the spidery printed flowers filled my eyes, and Rachel's perfume was like a presence in the bed. I turned over again and again as weird repetitive fever dreams played in my head, until Paul came in at three. He stared at his phone as I fed the baby, then took him from me and went back to bed.

It was harder to breathe now, as if my lungs were somehow packed solid and there was no room for air to enter. I longed to surrender back into sleep, but then I remembered the baby's confused stare and his grave fascination as he'd watched me cough. Too confused and uneasy to sleep, I reached for my laptop to google *difficulty breathing*. A few minutes of scrolling convinced me I was close to death, so I called the NHS helpline, talking quietly so I didn't disturb Paul and the baby. The woman listened to me for a few minutes and put me through to the ambulance service, where a man asked me loudly if I was having chest pains, then sent around a paramedic on a motorbike and said that an ambulance would be on its way as soon as possible.

Paul appeared in our doorway as I tried to find a position that would allow more air into my lungs.

'What is it?'

'An ambulance is coming.'

'Really? Why?'

'I don't know. I rang them as I couldn't breathe properly and they asked me some questions and then said they would send someone. I'm just so short of breath.'

A few minutes later the paramedic arrived, a small, muscly man with a shaved head, who began pulling things out of his bag while asking questions and looking around the bedroom.

'What's wrong?'

'I woke up and I couldn't breathe properly.'

'Got your Strepsils, I see.' He nodded over at my bedside table, and the over-the-counter painkillers Paul had got for me last night. 'And your Panadol.'

His dry tone suggested I was being a drama queen, and maybe he was right. Why was he even here? Everything was fine, apart from my breathing, and I felt ashamed for wasting taxpayer money. I wanted to explain that I'd called the NHS helpline and unwittingly set off a full-scale emergency response by saying I was having chest pains, but I didn't have the energy for it.

'Any mental health issues?'

'No.'

'Did you think of going to your GP today?'

'I didn't feel this bad earlier. I called NHS Direct and they called you.'

'They always do,' he said shortly.

He checked my heart rate, and then my oxygen.

'Your sats are very low – your oxygen levels.'

'That's why I called the NHS helpline. I woke up and I couldn't breathe properly.'

'They shouldn't be that low. I'll check again,' he said, fitting the clamp back onto my finger.

As he did that, I vomited water all over the carpet. Paul came in and put the baby on the bed so he could clean up the mess, and I saw the paramedic's expression change from mild irritation to dismay.

'How old is the baby?'

'Five weeks, almost.'

His face softened. 'Bless.'

I patted the baby back to sleep, then leaned on the bedhead, sitting up as straight as I could to let more air into my lungs. The doorbell rang again and I could hear Paul talking to the paramedics, thinking guiltily that we could have got a taxi to the hospital, except that I had been too confused and panicked to call one.

The paramedics were kind, telling me not to worry about calling them, chatting to Paul in the back of the ambulance as they drove to the hospital. They gave me oxygen and when we arrived they wheeled me straight through to a cubicle, Paul following us with the baby in his arms.

'I might draw this curtain,' the paramedic said as he prepared to leave. 'There's another ambulance coming in now and you really don't want to see what's in it.'

Through the thin curtain, we could hear the screaming and groaning of a young man's voice, cursing the staff who were yelling back at him, trying to reason with him, before another clear, carrying male voice interrupted everyone and explained to the patient that he was to be given a sedative. Soon it was quiet again, apart from the terse voices of the staff.

Despite the harsh fluorescent light of the hospital, there was a certain safety in being there, in knowing I was back in a public place, where people with professional training and clear heads could work out what needed to happen next. The baby was asleep again on the bed next to me. I was hooked up to an oxygen supply and finally I felt like I could put his worried face out of my mind. He had somehow told me to come here, and he was right. Strangely, I felt less anxious than I had in days. Was it the relief of finally giving in, handing myself over to the local authorities and admitting, *I can't do this, sorry*? Was it being given a cubicle and a hospital gown and the promise of sleep and someone else to take care of the baby? I felt almost euphoric. Paul, sitting in a chair opposite me, staring at me in disbelief, did not look euphoric. He looked like he wanted to drag us all out of here, back to Cromwell Tower. He looked like he was hoping to wake up.

15

We were in our brightly lit cubicle for what felt like hours, as
new staff arrived for the morning shift and I told the story again
and again of not being able to breathe properly to various doctors
and nurses and even a lady who came in and brought me a cup of
tea and turned the lights down. People took blood and swabbed
my throat and gave me pills to swallow and put a drip in my arm
and finally a man appeared who seemed to be in charge. He had
wire-rimmed glasses and friendly blue eyes and I recognised his
clear, authoritative voice from earlier on, when we'd arrived. As
well as the cough, I'd started vomiting again into a cardboard
bowl, and he observed this with an unfazed shake of his head,
as if it was a somewhat unfortunate development, but nothing he
couldn't handle.

A porter arrived, accompanied by an air of harried tiredness,
and I left Paul and the baby to be wheeled down a long corridor
towards the radiology room – a dark, spooky chamber where I
was positioned and then left alone while the radiographer moved
into a small elevated room somewhere behind me. I was cold
and barefoot and dressed only in a gown, now officially a patient
in a wheelchair, barely dressed because I'd had to take off my
underwire bra for the X-ray. The radiographer wheeled me outside
again, parked me in the waiting area and drew a curtain around me
while she called the porter to come and take me back to A&E. A
minute later, another uniformed person peered behind the curtain,

looked irritated to see me parked there and, with a click of her tongue, whipped the curtain open again.

Now I was in full view of the waiting room of the hospital's busy morning outpatient clinic. And then I was vomiting again into my cardboard bowl, my balled-up bra on my lap and a paper mask around my neck tangling with the oxygen tubes coming out of my nose. God knew what state my hair was in.

Back in A&E, the doctor told us he had looked at my X-ray.

'Your lungs – you can't go home with oxygen that low. We'll have to find you a bed.'

I closed my eyes in relief.

'She has to stay in? Why?' Paul seemed suddenly angry, furious even. I only ever saw him these days in the soft light of the apartment. Here, suddenly, he looked rougher. More real. Hazily I remembered seeing that same expression on his face the night he'd found me in the Soho club.

Careful, Paul, I wanted to say. *Calm down*. The simmering tension made the cubicle feel even smaller, and I thought of the hospital security guards that were no doubt only a phone call away.

The doctor gave him a fixed, practised smile. 'Because she has pneumonia. And she needs to be on oxygen and to be kept under observation.'

'I really don't feel well, Paul,' I said.

He looked at me. 'I know. You don't look well either. Your eyes are so red.'

'It looks like the flu,' said the doctor. 'But you should have been vaccinated as you were pregnant. Didn't you get a letter?'

I thought of my old house in Finsbury Park, and all the letters that used to pile up at the front door from everyone who had lived there over the years. 'I don't think so. Maybe it went to my old address. So who will look after the baby if I'm in here?'

The doctor looked troubled. 'We do need to work out what to do about the baby. I've already spoken to the postnatal ward manager to see if you and the baby can stay there, but she has said that's not possible due to the risk of flu infection. So we need to get you into a side room, we're just waiting for one to be free. Give us a little more time.'

He considered Paul for a moment. 'Is there anyone who can help you? Family, perhaps?'

You, I wanted to say to the doctor. *You're so in control, so adult. Can't we take you home?*

'I'll work something out,' Paul said.

I fed the baby, with a vague awareness that he wasn't getting much milk, probably because I hadn't been eating or drinking myself. He was totally oblivious to the fact that he was back in a hospital again, and he looked so tiny and bright and beautiful as he looked around, blinking at the doctor. Everything in the room was blurry apart from him, and as I looked at him, struggling to breathe, I felt a strange elation, as if I'd been drinking champagne instead of tap water. Was there a staff party going on outside the cubicle, I wondered, or was this what it felt like to drown?

The doctor disappeared again and the baby sank into his deep morning sleep. 'You should probably go now,' I told Paul. 'You need to buy him formula. And a bottle. I don't know what's going to happen here, but if I'm not allowed to keep him with me, he'll need milk. He'll sleep for an hour or so, you've got a bit of time.'

'But surely he should stay with you. Where do I go?' Paul looked terrified by the sudden responsibility of keeping the baby alive.

'Tesco will have some. The big one on Morning Lane. Or Boots. Honestly, go now. I'll be okay. When he wakes up he'll want it straight away.' I felt myself leaving the situation and falling irresistibly towards sleep as Paul left with the baby held against his chest, almost hidden under his jacket. It was a guilty relief to have them gone, taking with them the anxiety of the last few weeks, when I had held or carried or slept beside the baby without a break.

The harried porter returned to take me to my room. He must have been told to get me there quickly to reduce the risk of infection, because he took off down a long hallway with impressive speed, past a blur of people lying in beds parked up against the walls. He moved so fast that I got motion sickness and started vomiting again into my little cardboard bowl, which prompted him to speed up even more. We must have made quite a spectacle.

A quiet room, a bed with clean white sheets. Another doctor, another nurse. And then silence. Relieved of all duties, I plummeted instantly into a silent void of sleep. At some indefinite point I became aware of a cluster of doctors standing by my bed, their voices indistinct, their bodies a white-coated huddle that was almost indistinguishable from the wall behind them as they prodded me, asking me questions and writing down my vague answers.

The next time I woke it was dark outside, and Paul was back in the room. He was sitting next to me, and when I looked around for the baby I saw the car capsule parked by the door.

'How are you feeling?'

'Worse than childbirth.'

'Really?'

'Everything is aching.'

'I wonder where you picked it up.' He looked at me for a moment. 'Well, I got the baby formula. I had to walk out of here and down to Tesco with him wrapped up under my jacket. People were looking at me, really staring. I think they thought I'd kidnapped him or something. It was horrible.'

'Oh no. Did he take the bottle?'

'Yeah, once he got used to it he was fine. And I spoke to Rachel. She's coming back in the morning, to look after him when I'm at work.'

'She doesn't have to rush back, does she? She only left yesterday.'

'She needs to be here. I spoke to the doctor before, and he said I can't bring the baby in again for now, but if Rachel's at home I can still visit you and go to work. We can't risk him getting sick.'

'So he said the baby can't come in at all?'

'Not after tonight. I only brought him in because I didn't have anywhere to leave him. But Rachel will be back tomorrow so I can go to work. The team leader has been leaving me messages all day. Oh, I've got a bag for you. Some clothes. Your phone. It was completely dead so I charged it for you. Your Strepsils.'

I laughed under my oxygen mask.

'What?'

'Nothing. I don't know. Strepsils.'

He looked blank. 'What's so funny about that?'

'I don't know. Last night you were buying Strepsils and tonight I'm in here. It's not funny. It's just weird. I've never been sick like this before.'

He didn't seem to hear me, and his eyes were glazed as if he was caught up in some memory.

'You should have seen the way people stared at me, when I was outside, carrying the baby. I had to put him in my jacket because I didn't have the pram, and I thought someone was going to call the police.' He looked hunted, and I realised my own panic about taking the baby out, my fear that everyone was staring at me, was perhaps normal.

'People are obsessed with newborns,' I told him, lifting my mask off for a moment. 'I'll have to tell you about some of my weird encounters … once I can breathe properly. It must have some evolutionary purpose, for strangers to be so tuned in to them. They mean well.'

'I guess so. Look, I should probably head off. I don't want him to be in here for too long.' He got up, kissed my forehead, then walked to the door, lifted the baby capsule, and was gone.

Maybe it was the blank uninterrupted sleep, or the sterile whiteness of this quiet room, but something felt different. Even though my body felt like its own cells were poisoning it from within, and my lungs were twin cauldrons of infection, there was a small part of me that was alert, detached from this situation, making decisions with newfound clarity. It had started last night, with the baby's worried expression. It was the realisation that no-one was going to do this motherhood thing for me, that I was more or less on my own, and I had to start directing things, rather than allowing myself to be pulled along like some aimless jellyfish. And I had to take better care of myself, if I was going to take care of him. Maybe part of that was focusing on the small wins, and not the areas where I felt like I was failing. When I got out of here things would be different.

I closed my eyes, and when I woke up a new nurse was in the room, a dreadlocked man who introduced himself as Justice as he took my temperature.

'So you have a baby?' he asked me. 'How old is he?'

'Five weeks.'

'And is he a good baby?'

'He's getting better,' I said, remembering my new resolution to be more positive, and Justice threw back his head and laughed. After a moment I laughed too.

'You need to stay awake now,' he told me. 'You have slept all day. You need to be sleeping at night. I will make you tea and toast.'

The room was dimly lit and looked out over another bare courtyard, like the one outside the postnatal ward, equally grey and sparse. And now it was as if I hadn't had the baby at all. I'd longed for a night's sleep, and here it was, in this bare room with the snores of eight cardiac patients outside my door, but I couldn't stop thinking about him. He was so far away, high up in the concrete tower of the Barbican like some kidnapped prince in an urban fairytale, and he wouldn't know what had happened to me, and no-one would be able to tell him. All I wanted was to pick him up, to settle him across my front and feel his weight, to stroke his feet and lay my hand over the warm curve of his back, but I couldn't because he was out there in the world and I was in here, attached to this bed with tubes. Even if I tried, I didn't have the strength to get up, let alone find my way out of here.

It had always struck me as weird that in this grand sprawling city there was a small rectangular space I returned to every night to sleep, high above the rain-slicked, unpredictable streets, and that wherever Paul might have been on any particular day, he landed there, too. The Barbican may not have been homely, but it was as secure and solid as a vault. And now night had come and I wasn't tucked up in my private corner of the city, but in this vast hospital with its long corridors and unlocked doors and the unfamiliar sounds of sleeping strangers, shivering with cold and sleepless with anxiety.

My phone rang, an unfamiliar sound because I hadn't bothered to use it lately. It was Rachel.

She talked over my hello.

'Paul told me. How are you?'

'Not great. And I don't know how long I'll be in here for.'

She was silent for a moment. When she spoke again, her voice was breaking with emotion. 'Look, I'm going to come straight back and help Paul while you're away. He said he needs to keep working, so I can get dinner ready and look after the baby.'

'Paul mentioned it. It's probably a good idea.'

'And are you sure it will be okay? I will take care of the baby, don't worry about that.'

'I know you will. It's good you can come back.'

'What do they think you've got? Paul said it might be a virus.'

'I don't know. Pneumonia and some kind of flu. I'm really achey.'

'Right. Well, I'm on my way back. Paul said the baby is having bottles now, so I'll be able to help with that, and he will still go to work, and come and visit you.'

'I will try and express milk too, so he can still have that. Look, I need to go now. Speak soon, okay?'

'Get some rest. The baby will be fine, Simone. I promise you.'

16

In the morning, another doctor appeared at my bedside, with a few students wearing plastic aprons and face masks trailing her. She wasn't wearing a face mask, as if she alone was immune to illness, elevated far above the germs and viruses of mere mortals.

'So the tests have come back. Influenza and pneumonia,' she announced in a crisp Eastern European accent. 'It's a bad strain going around.'

Again I thought of the baby's face, his worried expression and wrinkled brow as I coughed. I thought of how breathless I had been, how quickly it had developed from a sore throat into something more. Somehow he had known, and communicated it to me.

'The flu can be dangerous for postpartum women and their babies. We can't let you go home until you are completely well. And you must keep a mask on every time you leave this room. This is a ward full of very sick people.'

Later, Paul visited, alone. Rachel had returned, he told me, and was looking after the baby. He seemed less tense, unpacking a brand-new breast pump and books and extra food for me, telling me proudly about his newly established bottle schedule and perfect sterilising technique. I wanted to ask him if the baby was missing me, but how could he tell?

That night, I couldn't sleep, so I asked the nurse for a sleeping pill. She had a sidekick with her, a student nurse who eyed me with suspicion as I talked to the nurse. Later, the student returned with my pill and set it down on the bedside table in its white plastic cup.

'Should you be taking these? You're a mother with a young baby,' she said, affecting a casual tone. 'And you're expressing milk. Won't this go into the baby's system?'

She seemed furious. Maybe she was right. But I remembered my decision to be less of a docile pushover, to take better care of myself. I knew that with the porters crashing around in the kitchen next door and with the heart patients snoring all night in the nearby ward, I would not get any sleep. I'd lie there and think about the baby – what was he doing, was he upset – and if I didn't sleep properly it would take me longer to get better, and get back to him.

'It won't go into the baby's system because he's not here with me, and that's *why* I can't sleep,' I replied.

'I don't know if I'd be taking anything, if I were you.'

'Well, you're *not* me,' I answered back, drawing on all the times I'd witnessed stern mothers address cheeky little girls, or been that cheeky girl getting told off myself. Mostly, as a mother I felt like a fraud. But now I felt the power of using my voice to stand up for myself.

She was silent, and I felt strangely exhilarated as I took the pill from the cup and put it in my mouth, poured some water and swallowed it, then turned my back on her.

That night I dreamed of a long hallway in some old creaky hotel, somewhere temporary and unloved, where many people had passed indifferent nights and left nothing of themselves behind. The walls were lined with lamps, but they were dim. Anyone looking at them in daylight would assume they worked, would have no reason to question their functionality, but at night, as I wandered alone down this hallway, they did nothing. They gave off no real light at all.

The next morning my door opened and there stood Rachel, look-ing immaculate in grey jeans and a blue-and-white striped shirt, a grey coat – my coat – over her arm, and my scarf wrapped around her neck. As she was about to step into the room a nurse rushed over to her and handed her a face mask.

'You need to put this on before you enter,' he told her. 'It's an infection zone.'

'Oh.' Rachel took it from him, but fumbled with it and appeared unable to work out how to wear it, so eventually he put it on for her.

She came in and shut the door behind her, then removed it immediately. 'You're not that sick anymore, are you?' She put it down on a chair, and rearranged her hair in the reflection from the window.

'I do feel better, but the doctors want me to stay in until I'm a bit better. Maybe another few days. They said they want me completely well since once I get home I'll be looking after the baby again. Where *is* the baby?'

'He's at the nurses' station. I left him there as I thought it would be safer than in here.' She looked at me blankly. 'I got the bus here. The driver was going so fast.' She shook her head, quietly fuming as her eyes met mine for a moment.

'Do you think you could bring him in? Even to the doorway?'

'I don't think so. We don't want him getting sick.' She stared at me, as if daring me to challenge her.

I had to look away at once; they were so cold, nothing in them at all that was warm or giving. My dream came back to me – *a lamp that gives off no light* was the phrase that had lingered – and I wondered if it was about Rachel. She presented herself as a saint, rushing back here, writing to Paul about how much she wanted to help me, how hard she was working, and yet alone – just the two of us – it all fell away and her lack of emotion was frightening.

She had exhausted me, worn me out, dragged me across London in the freezing winter until I'd ended up here and now she was standing over me, dismissing my situation, dismissing me. And she was looking after my baby while I was here.

You're not that sick.

You're not that tired, are you?

Or was I imagining it?

A long silence passed between us, until I spoke again.

'How *is* the baby?'

'He's fine, absolutely fine. Not upset at all. We've been having a lovely time when Paul is at work.'

She said this casually, but it hurt. Was he really fine? Did he know the difference between Rachel and me? Who could say? He was everything to me, but maybe I was nothing more than a generic, milk-dispensing blob to him. Maybe he could attach himself like that to anyone.

'Glad it's all worked out so well for you,' I said quietly, my voice trembling slightly. She didn't give any indication of having heard. Her eyes, though, were no longer meeting mine, and again I sensed her anger. She was going home to look after my baby, I reminded myself. I thought of her taking him to that bathroom, spending so long in there. I couldn't antagonise her. Not while I was in here.

'Anyway, thanks for being here, and helping out,' I said. 'It's really lucky you're here, what with Paul not having anyone to leave the baby with.'

'It's fine,' she said. 'It's not like it's particularly hard, looking after a baby.'

She always made her cattiest comments in an especially sweet tone, I realised, and it took me a moment or two to register their strangeness, because her delivery was deceptive. And then the moment when I could have questioned her, or stood my ground and disagreed, was gone. Right now, though, it wasn't a good idea to be getting into fights with her. I needed her on my side, on the baby's side.

'Oh, Rachel, before I forget … if you go next door there's a bottle of milk I expressed. Can you take it with you and give it to the baby?'

'Where is it, again, exactly?' She said this in the same confused little-girl voice she'd used when the nurse asked her to put a face mask on, as if something huge and complicated was being asked of her.

'Next door. There's a little kitchen, right next to this room. It's in the fridge. The nurse put it there for me earlier.'

I had expressed milk for an hour, staring at a few black-and-white pictures of the baby that Paul had printed out for me at work, and managed to fill the bottle almost to the top line. If she took the bottle home with her and heated it up a little before giving it to him, maybe in some way he would know I was still close, that I hadn't disappeared for good.

'Oh. Okay.' She seemed put out, like I had asked her for an enormous, unreasonable favour. 'Anyway, I guess I'll get going.'

She left, closing the door behind her. Did she think I should abandon breastfeeding altogether, rather than make her and Paul shuttle milk back to the baby? My milk supply seemed to be dwindling, without the baby there feeding through the night, so I might have to stop anyway, if I didn't get home soon.

Later, Justice came in and told me he had found the bottle in the sink, opened and lying on its side, empty.

'I don't know how it happened,' he said, apologetically. 'You'll have to make some more.'

That night after dinner I got out my pump and my photocopied pictures of the baby, and began again. I texted Paul. *I wish I could see the baby. I really miss him.*

He replied immediately. *I know, but we can't risk him getting sick. He's fine here. Rachel is taking such good care of him.* A few seconds later a photo appeared of Rachel on the couch, smiling at the camera, my baby in her arms.

Eight, nine days passed, and finally the doctors said I was well enough to go home. It had happened gradually, the shift from bedridden to feeling almost normal.

On the last night, Paul brought the baby in to see me, and I could finally feel his solid weight in my arms, sniff him, bury my face in his neck and kiss his smooth cheeks. He accepted my affection with good-natured patience, fitting himself into my arms as snugly as he could.

Justice was back for the night shift, and when he saw me saying goodbye to Paul at the door of my room he came over and took the baby out of my arms, cuddling him and delighting in him with me, while the grandfatherly coronary patients looked on from their beds. Everything felt normal again, all of a sudden.

The next day, Paul left work early and came to pick me up. Dressed in my own clothes and filled with good intentions, I took Paul's hand and left the ward.

17

As we stepped into the dark, overheated apartment, I saw Rachel's bag and my scarf on the hook by the front door.

'You're back!' Rachel came to greet us, holding the baby against her shoulder with one arm.

'I am.' I smiled at her, fighting a wave of exhaustion. 'It's so good to be home.'

Still she held onto the baby and I wanted to snatch him away, but instead made myself slow down, take off my coat, go to the bathroom, wash my hands and splash my face with warm water to get rid of the chemical film of the hospital. What exactly was I supposed to do with a baby, again?

I made myself smile again as I went back to the living room, where Paul was watching the news and Rachel was sitting on the couch, the baby in her lap. I sat down beside her and held out my arms until she gave him to me. He was heavier, and it felt strange and cumbersome, having to hold him upright. I sniffed his head and all I could smell was Rachel's perfume, which made me feel irrationally betrayed. She'd dressed him in new clothes, ones that Paul's mother had given us, and he looked different, too, bigger and sleepier and more boyish. After ten days of being mostly on my own, reading, dozing and staring out the window, I'd somehow lost the will to care for him, as if the feverish passion that had kept me needing him close at all times had been diluted by our separation. When I put him down on the couch beside me, exhausted by his weight after only a few minutes, Rachel was right there, almost as if she'd been anticipating it.

'Here, give me the baby,' she said in a brisk tone, picking him up. 'You're finding it hard, aren't you?'

That small smile again, that sweet voice, the quiet sound of those tinkling silver bangles. As she held him, I saw that she had slipped into her role as his mother in my absence. And even though I wanted to look after him, I had lost the drive. My milk supply had dwindled and my arms felt too weak to hold him for long. The nurse had warned me that it would take time to build up my muscle tone again, but I hadn't believed her until I'd done something apart from lying in bed.

Sitting on the couch, I listened as she ran him a bath and washed him and dressed him and cooked us all spaghetti for dinner, and the whole time she and Paul chatted easily, like the close cousins they were, but also like a married couple looking after a baby. The strange tension between them seemed to have loosened.

'Here, Simone, have this,' she said, handing me a mug of herbal tea. It smelled sweet, almost smoky, like roses and something else.

'What is it?'

'It will help you sleep. I can get up with the baby.'

I didn't want to miss those small night hours, though, now that I had caught up on sleep, when it was just me and him together in the darkness. Feeding him, lying with him in the quiet, stroking his forehead and revelling in the simple fact of his existence. Just the two of us, awake in the night village as the whole city slept around us.

'Have a little,' she said encouragingly, and I did, and soon afterwards I was tilting forward in my chair and sleepwalking towards my bed.

When I opened my eyes again it was dawn, and I'd somehow slept the whole night without waking. Paul dozed beside me, but as I rolled over to face the cot I sensed an absence, a lack of warmth where the baby should be. Reaching out, my hand met not the rise and fall of his back, but a cool flannel sheet. Forcing myself to wake up fully, I got out of bed, and went first to the living room. Empty. Rachel's door was closed, and I felt like an intruder as I pushed it open. On her bedside table was a half-empty bottle, and in the bed, curled up against her, was the baby, relaxed and deeply asleep, his mouth half open. The lamp by her bed was on, so I could see her clearly, lying on her side, one arm under him and the other circling his head, exactly the same way I slept with him.

He was mine. I was allowed to take him back. But I felt like I was disturbing something private. Asleep, Rachel looked defenceless; some tension that was usually there in her face was simply absent. As I moved closer I saw something on her bare inner arm, the one that was curved over the baby's head. Three words, spelled out in flowing black copperplate. I leaned in to read them, holding my breath.

Only you return

How had I never noticed her tattoo? Was it a line from a poem? Not wanting to wake her, I gathered the sleeping baby into my arms and took him back to my bed. His hair smelled of her perfume, but I'd give him a bath later and wash it away.

A few hours later, the baby woke beside me and within minutes Rachel was at the door, a bottle of formula in her hand.

'Here, Simone,' she said. 'I've warmed it up already. He's been loving it. You can see how much weight he's gained with some proper food in his belly.'

'I'm going to stay in bed with him,' I told her. 'And try and get the breastfeeding going again.' My voice wavered as I said it, knowing she found breastfeeding distasteful and would far prefer to give him a bottle.

'You need to rest, Simone. Give me the baby,' she said with brisk impatience, as if I were being childish, and wasting her time.

'He's happy here, Rachel.'

There was something like despair in her eyes as she looked

back at me, and I felt nauseous, dizzy. Why did she have that effect on me?

Eventually she walked away, had one of her long showers, and left the house.

I stayed in bed for the next two days, feeding him and, on the advice of kind anonymous women on the internet, drinking rooibos tea and eating oatmeal to boost my milk supply.

As for Paul and me, we would get through this, I reassured myself. We were going through something huge together and he had not let me down, not in any big way. Right now, he knew that I needed to focus on the baby, and he needed to support all of us and he was doing that by going to work every day. We were both doing our best and for now, that was enough.

When I felt stronger, I slipped out of the house one morning with the baby in a carrier and walked to Moorgate Station, where I caught the train to Whitechapel for Baby Rhyme Time at the library. It was way too soon for the library from the baby's point of view, I knew that, but I wanted to be around some adults, and Rhyme Time was my best bet. As I walked along the high street I saw, across the road, a familiar figure standing before the grey, stained façade of the Royal London Hospital: Jennifer. She was dressed for the street, in a long, belted coat and leather boots, dwarfed by the scale of the hospital. Behind the Victorian façade was the blue cube of the new wing, so massive it blocked the sky. A building that could swallow you up, that you might go into one unremarkable day and never come out of again.

She saw me and smiled as I crossed the road and walked towards her.

'Oh, hello, Simone!'

I always pictured her in her office, an inside person, surrounded by pictures and flowers and lamp-lit, mellow warmth. It was disconcerting to see her on the street.

'How are you?' she said. 'I was wondering about you. A woman came into the museum last week with a baby, and I'm sure it was yours. Was someone else looking after him?'

'A tall woman with dark hair?'

'Yes. I was so sure it was your baby – I recognised the pram. She said he seemed frightened, so she brought him in to settle him.'

'He was frightened?'

'No. He wasn't at all. He was asleep.' She looked puzzled. 'Are you alright?'

'I was in hospital. I had the flu and then I ended up with pneumonia.'

'That sounds terrible. What rotten luck. You look like you've lost weight.'

'I'm much better now. The woman you saw, the one who's been staying with us, she took care of him. It was lucky that she could help.'

'She did seem incredibly fond of him. Let me give you my number. If you ever need to call. Call anytime.' She pulled out a pen and a notebook and scribbled her number down.

'Thanks. I gestured to the hospital entrance, not wanting to intrude but wondering why she was there. 'And how about you? Are you alright?'

'I will be.' She smiled at me. 'I'm having a bit of treatment, but I will be.' I noticed a needle positioned in her hand, and taped into place. Seeing me looking at it, she turned her hand so that it was out of sight and asked, 'Where are you off to, anyway?'

'I thought I'd go to the library, to get out of the house. I caught the Tube here.'

An older man came out of the hospital's sliding doors, looking around until he spotted her, and she nodded at him.

'Look, I need to go back in – I'm here for an appointment and it's been a long wait, so I was getting some fresh air. Now you have a lovely day and take care, and maybe I'll see you soon at the museum.'

That evening, Paul and I cooked dinner while Rachel sat at my computer.

'Remember I was saying before you got sick that maybe we should go away for a few nights down to Dorset,' he said, 'to give you a chance to rest? Maybe we should go this weekend? Head down early Saturday morning. I've booked Monday off work.'

'That's such a great idea,' I said gratefully, thinking of sleeping in, of two long, undisturbed mornings in bed while Paul got up with the baby instead of disappearing at dawn to the gym and then the office. Walks around the estate, or into the village. Home-cooked meals in the big farmhouse kitchen, and early bedtimes in the deep black nights of the countryside. The air there was different, so rich and oxygenated you could almost chew on it. The picture in my head expanded, bucolic and golden-tinged, a chance to start again, to finally enjoy my baby and my new life. Our new life.

'Oh, Paul, do you think I could squeeze in if you're driving?' called Rachel from the next room. 'I have a few friends to catch up with down there and was thinking of heading down this weekend anyway.'

'Er … okay,' said Paul, not looking at me.

'Great. It's been so crazy here,' said Rachel. 'Do I have time for a shower before dinner?'

'Yep – it'll be ready in fifteen minutes or so.'

'Why does *she* have to come?' I asked Paul, as soon as I heard the shower running.

'Oh, I don't know. It's like her family home too. She spent all her holidays there. It would be weird, telling her she can't come.' He looked tense. 'It's only for the car ride.'

'But why? She's been here for so long already. It's too much. And why does she only ask you? She should ask both of us.'

He looked tired, and I felt bad for making things harder for him. We were both exhausted, after all, and he had to go to work every day, too.

'We won't see her, honestly. She'll go out hunting, she'll do her own stuff, in the village, at the pub. She's got lots of friends down there. You'll see less of her there than you do here.'

Before I could answer, the baby woke, and I went to pick him up.

Paul avoided my eyes as the three of us ate in silence, and when it was over I put my plate in the dishwasher and went straight to bed with the baby.

On Saturday morning, Rachel's leather bag was by the front door.

18

We arrived in Cerne Abbas around lunchtime, after a four-hour drive during which I sat in the back and watched the baby while Rachel and Paul listened to music and chatted in the front seat.

The house was quiet when we arrived, and Paul said his parents were visiting friends nearby. We weren't sleeping in the attic this time, but in a large bedroom on the first floor with green walls and tall windows looking out over the orchard. By the bed was an old wooden cradle that looked like a family heirloom.

Once I'd unpacked I went down to the kitchen, where the big Aga stove was left on constantly through the winter, emitting steady warmth. I huddled close to it, rocking the baby to sleep, while Paul went for a run and Rachel disappeared for the afternoon. Despite the Aga, the house was freezing and the baby seemed to press himself against me, his eyes huge when I looked down at him. It hadn't occurred to me that he would notice a change in location, let alone be unsettled by it, but he was.

Paul's parents arrived home a little later, and within ten minutes his mother had somehow produced a whole meal of ham and cheese and boiled potatoes and salad, with big mugs of tea and fruit cake to finish. The baby was still fretful so I paced with him in my arms, trying to soothe him, as Paul and Rachel sat at the table, eating and drinking and gossiping with Paul's parents. Afterwards, Paul and I went upstairs, the baby sleeping between us, and ending up falling asleep before Penny called us down for yet more food, a huge cast-iron pot of rabbit stew, the tiny bones unfamiliar on my plate.

I was starving and ate quickly while Paul held the baby, before giving him back to me so he could eat. I felt Penny and George watching us, observing our parenting and seeming to approve of what they saw. Paul even jumped up to change a nappy, and held the baby afterwards while I sipped strong black tea and he and his father shared another bottle of dark ale.

The first night's sleep was fretful and broken by the baby's frequent cries and Paul coming in later on, smelling of beer. He woke me up and began kissing my neck and working his hands under my clothes.

'Do you feel ready to … you know?' he murmured, kissing my ear.

'Not really,' I replied, wanting to push his hands away. Thinking, *not at all. Never again, in fact. Sorry about that.*

'Really? Come on …'

'I can't. I'm not ready yet. Soon. Just go to sleep.'

Still, he persisted, and I was relieved when the baby woke up with a cry.

'Great,' he said with a sigh, rolling away from me. I fed the baby then lay still, pretending to be asleep, as he rolled over and started snoring. For some reason I had thought a new location would make everything feel new and fresh: the word *holiday* still retained its old associations of freedom and exploration and afternoon naps, followed by relaxed evenings of food and wine and talk. But the baby was still here, needing me. I was still tired, and presumably my sleep would still be broken, and I'd still wake in the dark, except here it was freezing cold at night, the heating barely warming the room before escaping through ancient window frames and under doors, out into the night.

The following morning I woke early, got up while the others slept and strolled to the village with the baby in a sling and tucked

beneath my coat like a hot water bottle. On the way, I passed another mother pushing a spotless twin pram. Our eyes met briefly as
we passed each other, and I saw in her eyes that familiar anxiety.

Back at home, Paul and Rachel were in the kitchen, drinking
coffee and gossiping about old friends as Paul's mother cooked
bacon and eggs.

'We're all going to meet up at the New Inn tonight. You should
come along,' she said to Paul. 'If that's okay with you, Simone, of
course,' she added quickly.

He looked at me. 'Oh, I should stay here with the baby,' he said,
'and help out a bit.'

'What's the New Inn?' I asked, and Rachel laughed in disbelief.

'The local pub. It's been here for – maybe five hundred years?'
she replied.

Paul looked at me, kindly, but I wished that for once he would
stand up for me, instead of being the nice guy in the middle,
always keeping the peace.

'Do you want me to take him for a bit, Simone?' he said, and I
handed the baby over. Against Paul's flat chest, he was still and
quiet, unbothered by the smell of milk that made him restless
when I held him. Fully awake, yet content, as if Paul was a warm
resting place, a dry timber cabin on level ground.

The morning passed quietly, with Paul's mother taking the baby
for a long walk while I read a book and Paul and his father cleaned
the glasshouse and pruned the collapsed, soggy remains of last
summer's flower beds. Around noon, Rachel returned from visiting
a friend, holding a newspaper-lined basket full of dead birds. She
threw them down on the zinc-topped kitchen table. They were
beautiful, with delicate, dove-like heads and dark brown feathers
with intricate lacy patterns, white fluffy feathers beneath the shiny
outer ones. She laughed at my horrified expression.

'They're partridges – game birds, Simone! A delicacy. I'll cook
them later on and you'll see how delicious they are,' she said.

In the afternoon Paul dozed on the couch with the baby asleep on his chest, and I napped upstairs. The air coming in through the half-open window was cold, but it was warm under the flannel sheet and heavy red quilt, and I could hear a bird calling, long and sweet and trilling, that tipped me into a deeper, softer sleep as the afternoon faded.

When I woke up it was freezing, the room grey and creaky in the dusk gloom. In search of the baby and warmth, I went downstairs to the kitchen, where Rachel was preparing the birds, now plucked and gutted, their heads and feet gone. She told me that Paul and his mother had taken the baby to visit a friend, so I pulled up a seat by the stove and watched her butcher the small bodies, boning the legs with quick, sure movements and carving each breast off in one smooth, unhurried slice.

'So have they been refrigerated? Do we know they're okay to eat?' I asked her, feeling queasy.

'They've been hung for two days. To help the flavour.'

'Where did you learn to do that? To prepare them, I mean.'

'Leiths. A cooking school in West London.' She looked at me. 'You haven't heard of it?'

'No.'

'Oh.' She looked at me again, a long, appraising look. 'It's a very prestigious cooking school. All the top chefs go there. I went a few years ago, thinking I might open my own café. I learned so much. We did the same recipes, over and over, all the classics. Until they were perfect.'

'But didn't you also study nursing?' I asked her, confused. She was two years older than me, yet she seemed to have started three different careers already. How did she find the time? And where did she get the money?

'I've done a few things.' She sighed. 'More than a few, in fact. You have no idea.'

Was she having a dig at me? I rubbed my eyes, trying to wake up and locate the energy for a cup of tea and perhaps a warm shower. Her hands were small and pale and fast, and she seemed unbothered by the freshness of death on her fingers as she piled the meat into a china bowl and put it into the fridge, then swept out of the room.

For dinner we ate the partridge cooked with apples and cream and cider, the pale meat covered in a layer of pinkish sauce. I was so hungry I finished my plate first and had another helping. The soft meat tasted unfamiliar in my mouth, chewier and earthier than supermarket chicken. We ate it in chipped antique bowls, with soft white bread and glasses of pale cider, which Paul drank fast, Rachel constantly topping up his glass. Afterwards, Paul's mother pulled a rhubarb crumble out of the Aga that had been cooking there all afternoon.

They were so comfortable with each other, so happy to be here, and I tried to join in but felt myself getting irritated at Paul's drinking, noticing with cool, sober eyes that he was starting to slur his words and bang on the table and laugh too loudly at things that weren't especially funny. London was full of high-functioning alcoholics, and his drinking had seemed unremarkable there, but now I found myself wishing he'd slow down a bit. I noticed Paul's mother glancing over at me now and then, and each time I fussed over the baby to avoid her questioning gaze.

'Do you mind if I go down to the pub with Rachel?' Paul asked me, bleary-eyed, as we cleared the table.

'Not at all,' I said shortly, and I meant it. I was so tired I wanted only to fall into bed, and hopefully be asleep by the time he got back so I didn't have to listen to his snoring.

'Simone can stay and have a cup of tea with me, darling,' said Paul's mother, smoothing over the tension between us. 'We need to catch up on everything. Go and get ready, if you like. We're almost done here.'

A few minutes later, the dishes washed and in the rack, she sat down with me, a pot of tea and two cups between us.

'So, how is it all going?'

'You know … I'm tired. It will get easier,' I replied vaguely, not wanting to sound too negative.

'Is it going okay with Rachel? She mentioned that you're still quite worn out after the pneumonia and she's helping as much as she can.'

'Oh. I guess so. Yeah, she did help look after the baby when I was in hospital so Paul could work. That was lucky.'

'We wanted to come and see you, but Paul told me you were all coping fine and not to worry. He said that Rachel was very good with the baby while you were in hospital.'

She poured me some more tea and I felt her kindness, her desire to help. Maybe there was some way of explaining to her that I didn't quite trust Rachel, that she made me uneasy in a way I didn't understand.

'She was. And it was great that she could stay, it meant Paul could keep working and not use up all his leave.' I cleared my throat. 'But I am a little surprised she still wants to stay with us. It's not the most exciting share house in London right now, that's for sure.'

'Well, she and Paul have always been close.'

'Yes. She has mentioned that.'

She looked at me as if she was trying to work something out.

'And Paul's okay? Not too stressed or anything?'

'He's – I think so. I feel like I haven't seen him much recently, what with his work and me in hospital.'

'He does tend to bottle things up sometimes. I worry about him. But you can always call on us. You know that.' She looked suddenly grief-stricken as she leaned over and stroked the baby's head. For a moment I thought she might cry.

'Are you alright, Penny?'

She nodded and reached for my hand, then took a deep breath.

'I'm fine, Simone. I never thought – I'm happy, that's all. I'm happy you've come along. We've worried about Paul for so long, but with you ...' She squeezed my hand and smiled at me.

I felt like I should clear things up, perhaps break it to her that I barely knew him, and he barely knew me. That the baby was an accident, and this wasn't a love story. But she clearly wanted it to be one, so it was easier to keep quiet.

Paul's father suddenly appeared in the doorway. 'Come on, Penny. Come to bed. You should get some sleep, Simone.'

Something passed between them, a warning or unspoken message, and I suddenly felt like an intruder.

'Okay. Well, goodnight.' I headed upstairs with the baby. Our room was warmer now, and I laid him down on our bed, wrapped in my cardigan, and went to the bathroom.

As soon as I shut the door and looked around, at the wooden-seated toilet, the fifties lemon-coloured tiles on the walls and the pale grey carpet on the floor, I felt nauseous. Kneeling in front of the toilet, trying not to think about the stained carpet beneath me, it all poured out – the dead partridge and the cream and the apple cider, my body rejecting it all as if I'd been poisoned. Something about the memory of the soft gamey flesh under the creamy sauce made me retch, again and again, into the stained china bowl, until my stomach was sore and empty. Afterwards, I stood under the shower, scrubbing my teeth and gargling with hot water.

The hallway was dark and the house was quiet. I made my way back to our bedroom and closed the door behind me. It was a lovely room, with its high ceiling and old floral rug and the light of the bedside lamp gentle on my tired eyes. I took my time getting ready for bed, sorting through the baby's things in our suitcase, finding my book and brushing my hair, grateful for the solitude, the quiet of Paul and Rachel being elsewhere, and the relief of finally being alone.

When I turned back from my suitcase I saw the baby lying on the high pine bed, and startled at the sight of him, at how beautiful he looked. For a moment I'd forgotten he existed, that he was in the room with me. Fast asleep, he wasn't a source of constant worry, but a living person. I loved him in a way I had never expected to love anyone. No matter how weird the situation was, no matter what happened between me and Paul, he was real, and maybe in his own way, he loved me too. I breathed him in, basking in his warmth, and felt comforted to realise that I wasn't alone in the room, that he had been there all along.

Sometime later I awoke to darkness. The house was quiet and the mattress beside me was cool and empty. I thought for a moment I heard the rumble of Paul's voice outside and I got up and looked out the window. The back garden was dark and I could make out the shapes of the chicken coop and tall hedgerows and the little wooden hut. I saw there in the window a sudden flash, like a lighter, but then it was gone.

The baby stirred behind me and I laid a hand on his back until he stilled and breathed deeply again. Where was Paul? I thought about going looking for him, but something told me to leave him, to stay with the baby. Eventually, I fell back to sleep.

In the morning, the bed was still empty and I wondered if Paul had been and gone. When I went downstairs, I found him and Rachel in the kitchen, close to the Aga, a pan of bacon and eggs sizzling on the stove and the aromas of coffee and toast drawing me in.

'Hi,' I said, uncertainly.

Paul jumped up when he saw me and found me a chair. He seemed different, somehow. Too attentive, too kind. Rachel, meanwhile, was avoiding my eyes.

The last time we'd all been here together, for his sister's wedding, I'd also woken up alone, I realised. A sharp, sinking nausea dug into my belly as I looked at the two of them and realised there was so much I didn't know about their teenage summers here, their shared history. That strange chemistry between them – how sometimes they appeared to dislike each other, while on other days they were like a long-married couple.

'How was your night?' I asked Paul, while Rachel watched me steadily.

'Oh, good. We went to the pub, then came back here. Nothing big.'

'I didn't hear you come in.'

'You were fast asleep.' He brought me a plate of food, set a cup of coffee down in front of me, and sat back. 'Eat. Before the baby wakes. We should get going after breakfast.'

On the way back to London, Rachel slept beside the baby in the back seat. Had she been with Paul last night? Or when I was in hospital? They were cousins, but more like brother and sister, according to him. Surely it was illegal? We hadn't slept together since the birth, and I wondered if he was one of those traditional blokes who compartmentalised his needs once a baby came along – the partner for childbearing, the girlfriend for sex. Except that she wasn't a girlfriend, she was his family. I felt queasy at the thought of them, telling myself it wasn't possible. But maybe it was some old pattern from their teenage years that they were falling back into?

I looked at him as he drove fast along the M3. Again, I had that lonely feeling that I didn't really know him, knew very little about his past, and that what he said to me might be totally different to what he was saying to Rachel. I wished there was a sign, some way of knowing – but perhaps that was the sign. It was all there, when I made myself look at it. His attentiveness to her. His willingness to accommodate her. We weren't actually that close at all. It had just felt like we were, for a while, because of what we'd done together, and because we shared a bed.

And something else was happening too. As I felt more sure of the baby, that he was really here, that he was going to stay, Paul and Rachel seemed to recede. There was something infantile about them, going out drinking and sneaking around. Did I even care if they slept together? A little. My pride was wounded, and I hated the dishonesty and the lack of respect. The fact that I was having the role of cheated-on girlfriend foisted upon me was unpleasant. But perhaps it was a message. Maybe Paul was mirroring my own growing certainty that we needed to go our separate ways, that this baby's arrival had revealed to us just how little we meant to each other, how temporary our attachment was?

'You okay?' he said, reaching for my hand, and simultaneously looking in the rear-view mirror at Rachel.

'I'm fine, Paul,' I said, and his hand retreated.

I stared out the window and practised my hypnobirthing breathing technique, which had been useless during labour but was surprisingly helpful now. What a disaster I'd made of things. Again I remembered landing at Heathrow, so certain of everything, so full of plans. Yet somehow I'd ended up here, with these people I didn't understand or particularly like. At some point soon I had to fix things up, to make Paul understand that I wasn't going to play the role of docile Australian girlfriend for much longer, that this arrangement couldn't go on. Ahead of us and on both sides, cars crawled towards London, and for the first time ever I dreaded going back there.

19

The next morning, back in the concrete warmth of the Barbican, I got up to an empty apartment. I felt different, a sense of relief at the prospect of freedom, as if I had caught a glimpse of my old self, and I might be able to somehow reclaim her while also moving forward into a new life with the baby. I decided to go to the mothers group at the child health centre again, and on the way back I stopped off at the Museum of Childhood to feed the baby. I settled in a quiet spot on the first floor, where the village of night-time dollhouses was gathered. And then to my left I saw a flicker of movement, the height and dark hair unmistakable. Rachel.

The one place I felt safe, the one place I thought she wouldn't turn up at, and here she was. That familiar stance, and now she was looking at me, heading over, her face set, as if to say, *Wherever you are, I can be there too. If I want to.*

She smiled at me.

'Hello! I thought I'd go out, and happened to end up here. I remember you mentioning this place, and so I took the baby here when you were in hospital, because I thought perhaps he liked it, too.'

'Why would you come here now, though? There are so many other places you could go without a baby to look after,' I answered her rudely, before I could stop myself.

'I don't know. Because I like it? Are you okay?'

'Well, not really.' I rubbed my eyes, knowing that as soon as I opened my mouth it would all come out. 'I feel so trapped. Things aren't great with Paul and it kind of feels like we need some space, like it's too much having you to stay, to be honest.' I lifted the wakeful baby from the pram and forced myself to meet her eyes. 'It's not really your fault. It's just not a great time right now.'

'All I wanted was to help you. I don't know what I've done.' She looked at me with a confused expression. She suddenly seemed so fragile, more fragile than me in some way I couldn't quite put my finger on. Perhaps I'd been too harsh.

'Look, I know you're trying to help,' I said quickly. 'It's just that I'm trying to get used to everything, looking after a baby and all. But I do think, perhaps, that it's probably time ...'

She looked at me and her expression changed again, from tears into something else.

'It's probably time you – I don't know – maybe went to stay somewhere else. Found somewhere else to live, I mean.'

She was moving about now, agitated, leaning towards me, muttering quietly as if to herself.

'I want to help you, and you won't let me. You make it so difficult. But you need help, with a newborn. And the baby cares for me now. He's attached to me, too, you know. And you don't really have anyone else, do you?'

I felt exhausted. The words repeated in my head. *You don't really have anyone else.* And maybe she was right.

'I don't need anyone else. I have the baby.'

She said nothing, just looked at me as I got up, put the restless baby back into the pram and walked away from her.

Back at home, the rooms appeared untouched, and there was nothing to eat apart from a stale loaf of bread, so I made toast then put some washing on from the weekend and cleaned the bathroom, the baby kicking his legs up in the air on a towel beside me. Later, while he slept, I wrote an email to my parents, asking what their plans were for visiting, and then I watched TV as the day faded outside. Just as I was drifting off to sleep, my phone rang.

'Simone. How are you? It's Christine.'

'Oh, Christine! Hi – how are you?'

'We're fine. Congratulations, by the way.'

'Thanks.'

'I was wondering if you could come in next week? We'd love to see you, and we need to have a talk about what's happening here going forward. Only if it's convenient, of course.'

Seriously? Say no, I told myself.

'Oh – sure, I can come in.' I heard myself saying after an uncomfortable pause.

'Great. Tuesday, ten am? See you then.'

'Hi, Simone.' Rachel appeared in the kitchen, put down her bag and keys on the bench. She looked pale and contrite, and I felt myself soften towards her.

'Hello. How are you?'

'I'm alright,' she put the kettle on. 'Who was on the phone just then?'

'Oh, work. Calling to remind me I've got to go in for my check-in day or whatever it's called. I think I've got three scheduled before I go back.'

'So soon! When are you due back at work?' asked Rachel.

'In four months. Dreading it. Wish I could be off for longer.'

'But what would you do if you didn't go back to work?'

'What I'm doing now. Looking after my baby. For a year or so, anyway. I need the money, though.'

From the hall came the sound of keys in the lock. Paul, home earlier than usual. He let himself in, calling hello, and went to the bedroom, where the baby was starting to stir.

'Would you be able to afford not to go back?'

'I've got some savings. And I get a maternity allowance.'

'But – what does Paul think? Paul?' She looked animated, intrigued, and I wondered what she was up to. Well-slept people had so much energy, such curiosity in them.

Paul reappeared from the bedroom, the baby tiny and awake against his blue work shirt. 'Huh?'

'We were talking about work, and I wondered what you thought about the fact that Simone's thinking of not going back.'

'Oh. What? Well, she is working. She's looking after the baby. And he's still so little, we don't have to think about that yet. Personally, though, I think she should quit. It's a bit of a dead-end job, and the pay is terrible.'

'Really?' I said. 'You never told me that before.' Aware that we were having this conversation in front of Rachel, I hesitated for a second, but then went on. 'When did you decide all this?'

'I was talking to Mum and Dad when we were back home. There's a family trust, you know. We can draw on that, whenever we want to, and they were certainly open to you – well, us – drawing on it now, to give you the freedom to look after the baby, if you don't want to go back to that place.'

Was that freedom? I looked around the apartment – the leather couch, the mid-century wall units, the smooth-closing doors and soft lighting, the garbage disposal that carried all the rubbish away to some unseen location, leaving only a faint whiff to remind you that rotten things even existed. The expensive, brand-new pram in an impractical pale blue that his parents had ordered for us, which I was yet to take out, because I was used to the old one. Beneath my feet, the heated tiles warm against my bare soles.

I thought back to the museum, how I'd suddenly sensed my former self. Giving up my job would be a step away from her, into the claustrophobia of Paul's family. I liked them, but I didn't really belong with them.

'They are so generous, your parents,' said Rachel fondly. And I wondered how much this mysterious family trust supported her lifestyle, too, all her courses. Imagine a family trust. Free money.

'Christine rang,' I said to Paul. 'That's why we were talking about my job. She wants me to come next week for a meeting.'

'Oh.'

'I think I'll go. I want to assume I'm going back, for now.'

'Fine.'

That simmering quiet again. Rachel played with her hair. 'Do you want me to come in with you, Simone, to look after the baby while you go in? Or are you taking him into the office with you?' she asked.

I thought about it. The office was not in any way set up for children. It was an overheated, silent arena of strained adulthood. Sound carried across the desks. I could imagine the baby sensing the hostile environment and staging some kind of primal rejection.

'I was going to take him with me, but maybe, if you don't mind, I could leave him with you outside during the meeting. It wouldn't be for long.'

'I could travel there with you and take him for a walk in his pram when you go into the office?'

'Only if you don't mind. That would be good, thanks.'

'I'm pretty good at it, pushing a baby round in a pram.' She wasn't looking at me, but at Paul as she said it, her face expressionless, while he stared back at her, as if frozen in place. In his eyes lurked something furtive and cold, and I looked away, wishing I could turn back time and unsee that expression.

'And also I was thinking, do you want to go to the pool tomorrow? I could hold the baby while you do some laps, or we could leave the pram by the pool or something?'

Rachel's voice was pulling me away from what I had seen in his face, and I was relieved.

'Simone? Do you want to do that?' She looked very small, suddenly. She was trying, I realised. Maybe it would be better if I went, for the sake of peace. She'd be gone soon.

'Yes. Let's do it. A swim would be good.'

As soon as I said the words a new movie premiered in my head – the pram rolling into the water and too many people trying to dive down and unbuckle the baby and getting in each other's way until finally he was dragged out open-mouthed and blue and gone. Closing my eyes, I let the scene run through my head. It replayed, and then I was in the water, holding my breath, finding my way to the familiar seatbelt buckle, undoing it. Focused. Swimming to the surface, lifting the baby out. A lifeguard performing CPR on the poolside and shouting between breaths for someone to call an ambulance.

And then I was back in our kitchen, looking at the baby, alive and undrowned in Paul's arms. 'You should go, Simone,' said Paul. 'He's old enough, and you love swimming. It will be good for you to have some time to yourself.'

20

The night felt like it would never end – a cycle of falling asleep and being woken again, sometimes with only half an hour passing according to the bossy red numbers on the bedside clock. Paul eventually shuffled off to sleep elsewhere and at around five I gave up and simply lay there, staring at the ceiling.

Around eight, Rachel appeared at my door, looking sleepy and relaxed.

'Pool?'

Too tired to resist, I got up and dressed the baby, found my swimming gear, my skull thumping with a headache.

We walked to the Ironmonger Row Baths. The air was warm and chemical, a mix of chlorine and stinging cleaning fluids wafting up from the puddled tile floors. Signs shouted from the walls. The water was warm and relaxing, almost steamy. Before the baby, before Paul, I used to catch the tube from Finsbury Park to the pool at Highbury Fields on Sunday nights, where I'd swim off the weekend. The pool felt different at night, not so hectic and dirty, and the long swim would leave me tired and tranquil. The lifeguards would play music, and I'd go into the fridge-like white steam room and warm myself, or float in the warm water of the baby pool, listening to the deep rumble of Tube trains passing beneath me, taking their passengers all over London to their own beds. This place felt different, though. In the plain morning light I was noticing bandaids and dead skin in the water, and a man blowing his nose comprehensively in the main pool. Everything appeared grey and washed out, as if my eyes weren't seeing colour as strongly as they used to.

I looked over at the lap lanes, and remembered how it felt to be cut off from the noise and outside world, nothing but watery blue silence and a pair of white kicking legs ten metres ahead in the cloudy gloom. I used to swim for what felt like hours. With a baby, though, there was no retreating underwater, but instead sitting in the warm water, or at the benches littered with soft-drink cans and chip packets and soggy tissues.

As we sat at the shallow end of the kids' pool, the baby on Rachel's lap, the conversation shifted to Paul and his family.

'Me and Paul, we were pretty close as kids, you know.'

'Really?'

'Yeah. I think it was because our mothers were both so distracted. Mine was living in Nigeria with my stepdad, that expat existence with the kids packed off to boarding school and servants and not really having to lift a finger, apart from to order another gin-sling. So in the summer holidays I'd go stay with Paul's family in Dorset and we'd run wild together. And as teenagers, too, you know.'

'So you'd stay at Paul's family house?'

'Well, not in the main house, no. I was in that little hut out the back with the bunk beds. You've probably seen it. We'd be out there doing God knows what and the parents would be inside drinking. We did a lot of our growing up together. Is this okay?' She gestured at the baby. 'He's just sitting here. Does he look cold?'

'He's fine. The water is warm.'

'And we didn't get that much attention from our parents, you know? They weren't demonstrative at all. Sometimes when I look back on my teenage years, all that happened – I don't know what Paul's told you – but I think that maybe all I needed was a bit of affection, so I didn't need to go looking for it.'

What did she mean by that? What was she trying to tell me? Paul seemed uneasy around her. Too eager to please, and unwilling to stand up to her, even when it was at my expense. Did she have something over him? He would never, ever tell me. I knew him well enough to know that if there was something between them, some secret past, I would never hear about it from him. From her, maybe – she seemed itching to talk about their shared childhood. But from him, never. I sat quietly, waiting for her to tell me more, but she moved on to talking about Paul.

'... And it's weird – when I see Paul now, he's not how I remember him. He seems kind of jaded, exhausted. I don't know if it's London or the baby or what. Have you noticed that, how tired he seems?'

'Yeah, he's tired. Of course he is. We're both exhausted.'

'Is he being supportive, or is he sort of going into his own head? He does that, sometimes.'

Our conversation was interrupted by some children getting into the pool – a girl, about fourteen, a bikini barely covering her rounded, pale body, and what looked like her two younger brothers. She too was holding a tiny baby. The two boys surrounded her protectively, both of them smiling into the baby's face, as she stepped into the warm water. All of them had a faint but noticeable air of nervous excitement as she settled down into the water, the baby on her lap. The girl appeared proud, responsible, and for a moment I was confused, looking around but not seeing an older woman, a mother, looking burdened and tired, in search of coffee or a place to sit down or a rubbish bin for a dirty nappy.

The girl had sat down beside Rachel, who was still holding my baby on her lap, so that the two tiny boys were now side by side, slumped in the water with their sloping shoulders and round bellies like miniature old men, unaware of each other. I noticed, through the water, stretch marks, still raw and red, on her bare white belly. Her teenage body had been rushed into motherhood, and I wondered how her birth was. I remembered my GP saying that young mothers were usually more relaxed than later ones: they got on with it, didn't obsess over every rash or elevated temperature, and they had more energy. I wanted to talk to her, swap notes about sleep and feeding, but Rachel was sitting between us.

'What's his name?' she asked Rachel, and Rachel told her, neglecting to clarify that I was his mother, not her.

'This one is Albert,' the girl said, looking down at him. 'He's six weeks old. He likes it here, we bring him quite a lot. Have you brought him before?'

'No, it's his first time swimming. He seems to like it, too.'

I waited for her to include me, but she and the girl chatted on, playing with the babies, and I sat to one side feeling irritable and left out.

'So where was he born?' the young girl asked.

'Homerton. And Albert, where was he born?'

'UCLH. It was so busy there. And when is his birthday?'

Rachel said nothing.

'The fifteenth of December,' I said, leaning in and smiling at her. She looked confused. 'Oh, he's your baby?'

'Yeah.' I could see her reorganising their conversation in her head, smiling uncertainly at me as Rachel gently stroked the baby's cheek with her thumb, ignoring both of us.

'Should we get out soon, Rachel? He's probably ready for a feed and a sleep.'

As we stood up, the girl's brothers gathered round the baby, all three siblings focused on him, adoring him, trying to make him smile. Finally he did, and they all cooed in encouragement.

'My God,' whispered Rachel. 'That mother can't have been older than about fourteen. It's so sad, isn't it? That she was allowed to keep him.'

'Maybe she'll be a good mother, though. She seemed good enough. And she had two little helpers.'

'Teenagers aren't fit to be parents,' she said, then stalked off to the change room.

The baby was hungry, opening and closing his mouth at me and chewing the air, so I fed him on the change room bench still in my bathers, using the towel as a shawl. Beside me, Rachel stood completely naked, rubbing cream into her arms. It was hard not to look – she was completely in her own world, unselfconscious, her body so flawless it belonged in some airbrushed movie, not this grim council changing room, where long hairs tangled under the plastic mats and the air was thick with cheap spray deodorant and fake-apple-scented shampoo. Again I noticed the tiny lettered tattoo on her inner arm.

I packed the baby into the pram and said to Rachel, 'I'm going to get dressed in the cubicle.' My own body felt so ungainly in comparison to hers, I didn't want anyone seeing it.

When I came out, an older woman, dressed in plain black bathers, a white towel around her waist, approached me.

'It's nice to see a mother breastfeeding her baby,' she said quietly.

Rachel raised her eyebrows and looked at me as if the woman was crazy, but I knew what the woman meant. I had vivid memories from childhood of being mesmerised by breastfeeding mothers, of their milky breasts spilling out of dresses on visits to the homes of more bohemian school friends. Or of my baby cousin, still and quiet under a lacy white blanket, my aunty looking down at him, unsmiling but not stern, simply absorbed. Afterwards, I'd pretend to breastfeed my own doll, assuming the same serious expression.

'Thank you.'

There existed a quiet, invisible network between women, I was discovering, where supportive words were expressed in undertones, quickly, between one errand and the next, from one stranger to another.

21

A week later my 'keeping in touch' workday arrived, and I dressed unhappily, knowing there was nothing I could wear that would hide my heavy, aching body that still hadn't healed fully. The body of a *mother*. It was such an old-fashioned, martyr-ish word. So not edgy. Nothing you'd put in *Dove Grey*, that was for sure. We did feature babies sometimes in photo shoots, but only in soft focus, as a pale, floral-draped ornament in some glamorous person's house, playing with a Danish wooden truck on a polished concrete floor or something. Most of the younger editors I'd come across had no children, including Christine, the deputy, and I'd seen the disdainful way she treated Anna, the features editor, who had two small daughters. I had no idea what those little girls were called, I realised, with belated guilt. She never talked about them at work.

Rachel was still sleeping when it was almost time to leave. I knocked on her door softly, then opened it a crack. She was lying in bed, the blinds down, and I could hardly see her in the dark room.

'Are you getting up? I have to go into work soon. Are you coming?'

She groaned and I heard her climbing out of bed. 'Can you leave him here? I didn't sleep very well last night.'

'Oh, I can't really. What if he gets hungry? I didn't manage to express enough milk.'

'Can he have formula? I could take him to the supermarket and get some?'

'Ah, no, not really. I don't know if he'll still take a bottle.'

'If he's hungry he will.'

'I'm kind of trying to exclusively breastfeed him again,' I said, knowing how precious it sounded.

'Ooh, *exclusively*,' she laughed. 'Okay, well, I'll get in the shower.'

'We have to leave in about fifteen minutes, though.'

'Okay, fine. I'm getting up.'

We left the house later than I would have liked because Rachel took so long getting dressed. I was aware that she was doing me a favour by agreeing to come, so I was hesitant to tell her to hurry.

A wave of nervous nausea hit, and I swallowed and closed my eyes, the bus rumbling along Clerkenwell Road. One of the old Italian diners had been done up, I noticed. The battered tables and pale green walls had been replaced with a Nordic plywood interior, white pendant lights and sleek bench seating. I would mention it to our food editor, if I saw her. That was the kind of stuff she took very seriously. Personally, after two years of working with the food department, I was never more in favour of baked beans on toast with a mug of tea. Taking cooking as seriously as our food writers did was surely a sign that we had become decadent beyond rescue. I'd read somewhere that dinosaurs, towards the end of their time on earth, had become over-specialised and ridiculous-looking, with strange adornments and extravagant horns. Maybe food journalism was the Homo sapiens version of pointless frills. Perhaps in a thousand years, if humans still existed, historians would look back at our era and talk about how we became obsessed, spoiled, over-nourished. How we ate only the best parts of animals and threw the rest away, flew asparagus all over the world in planes; how we didn't merely eat food for energy, but began to watch shows about it on television and write about it endlessly in books and magazines and on websites. And how, in fact, the day that an adult human wept on a reality TV show, because she had oversalted a risotto bianco and was being sent home, marked the beginning of the end of humankind as we knew it.

Already I was feeling tense, and we hadn't even arrived yet. As if reading my mood, the baby began to fuss in his pram, and I lifted him out and tucked him under my coat, leaving Rachel to hang onto the pram.

People were tumbling off the bus and onto the gum-stained wide pavements of Oxford Street, and we followed them, past the tourists with their empty suitcases sitting outside Primark, and turned down the side road into the quieter streets of Mayfair and past the security guard, through the dirty glass doors of the dingy brown brick building that was the unlikely home of *Dove Grey*. The whole building was a musty warren, and I'd got lost a few times when I first joined, because all the floors looked the same: tired, dark and claustrophobic. It all made sense when someone told me the building was originally a multi-level car park, before its real-estate value rose too high and it was converted into office space.

'So maybe you can wait here in the lobby – I shouldn't be too long,' I told Rachel. 'You could take the baby for a walk if he gets restless. Grosvenor Square is down there.'

'Okay. We'll go for a walk, I guess.' She seemed irritated.

'Thank you. I really appreciate it.'

She pushed the pram towards the exit and I was torn for a moment between following the baby and returning to my old working life, which seemed at that moment very foreign.

The mirrored lift full of immaculate colleagues confirmed my suspicion that I should have done more than slap on some foundation and mascara and run a comb through my hair. But I was already late, so I made my way to the *Dove Grey* editorial area, saying hello to people as I passed the various magazines, which were divided up by carpet-covered partitions and bulging filing cabinets.

It was weird being back, the familiar sounds of the phone ring-ing, the printer churning out proofs and someone laughing in the marketing department, yet it all feeling so different. Samuel, the fashion director, was at his desk opposite mine, and in the midst of an icy discussion with Thea, the art editor. They nodded and said hello, then continued talking as I tried and failed to get into my email account. I flicked through some mail while eavesdropping on them. Thea, who wiped the floor with me on a regular basis, was always exceedingly deferential to Samuel. It was a cycle of abuse, really, because she took his aggression without a murmur, then promptly dumped it on me.

'I came over to see how you are, Samuel. After the misunder-standing with Evelyn.' Her voice was low and gentle in a way I'd never heard her use with anyone else, like a doctor giving very bad news. She looked fabulous, as always. Hair in an artful bun. Thin silver hoops in her ears. Rust-coloured lipstick. Smokey eyes, matt skin. A black draped dress printed with tiny lime-green budgerigars hanging off one shoulder.

He barely looked at her, and over the low barrier that divided our desks I could see his lips were clenched into a thin line. 'I really don't want to talk about it with you.'

'Well, I wanted to explain to you that the deadline was an hour away, we still didn't have the prices, and I decided that the best thing was to contact her directly.'

Samuel took a long, controlled breath. Around them the office had fallen silent in the way that offices do when this sort of interesting conversation takes place. I wondered how the baby was doing; if he was crying. The office was always so overheated, and I felt my face begin to prickle.

'*I* am her contact. She *only* talks to me. I was speaking to her from Sardinia at the same time as you, pretending I was in the office, and your email made it clear that I was *lying* to her.' He snapped out each word in a clean little burst, like shot pellet.

'Well, I'm so sorry about this. It's a … terrible situation.'

'The thing you have to realise is that she's *not* a very nice person. She's tricky, and I *know* that, and now I'm going to have to *try* to sort it out.'

There was a pause. Thea gave it one last shot.

'And the thing *you* have to realise is that we had an hour to the deadline and *you* weren't answering your phone.'

The entire office held its breath, waiting to see how Samuel would take it.

'Well, yes, I do realise that,' he said in a bored voice, before delivering his final line. 'It's just that I thought the email you sent her was somewhat rude, and rather poorly worded. So there's that.'

Poorly worded. No greater insult.

She stood speechless for a long moment.

'Sorry!' he called as she turned her back on him and walked away. 'But it's *true*!'

I cleared my throat. 'Hello, Samuel.'

'Oh. Back from the lying-in hospital, are we? How are you? Safely delivered?'

'Yes, thanks.'

'Boy or girl?'

'Little boy. Thomas.'

'*Lovely*. I don't need to see a photo, but congratulations.'

'Thanks.'

'God almighty,' he said, flicking through the latest issue. I peered over to his desk, where a double-page spread showed a burly, tattooed celebrity chef standing bare-chested in front of a platter with a juicy piece of roasted meat on it. 'Andy looks like he's about to *rape* that hogget. Does it need to be quite so literal?'

This job is pointless, I suddenly realised. *This job is completely and utterly pointless.*

All we did was create obsessively styled pages that sold people things they didn't need, often to placate our highest-paying advertisers, in between expensive advertisements that also sold people things they didn't need, and didn't *know* they didn't need until they bought the magazine. How had I done it for so long? How could I ever unsee how pointless it all was and come back here to work? It had only been a few weeks since I'd left, but maybe a small break from the relentless forward momentum of a monthly production schedule was all it took.

My phone pinged. Rachel. *He's crying. I don't really know what to do? Will you be much longer?*

I texted back: *Maybe try giving him some milk?* I had expressed some last night, sitting in front of the TV like some listless cow, wincing in pain as the milk trickled into the bottle.

I tried that but he's already finished it.

I will be out as soon as I can. Try rocking him. I messaged back.

Sweat started to bead across my forehead, my cheeks, began to run down my back, and I imagined her trembling hands, spilling milk. My shirt began to feel drenched like an internal tap had been switched on. Some kind of weird post-pregnancy hormonal freak-out was visiting me right now, on the one day I needed to resemble a normal person. I headed for the kitchen, but bumped into Christine along the way.

'Hi, Christine. How are you? I was just going to make a coffee if you'd like one?'

'I'm fine, thanks. Look, I was going to have a quick word with you but we've got the editorial meeting and you're a little late. Why don't you get your coffee and come along to that and we can talk afterwards. How's the baby?'

'He's good. I was going to bring him in but I thought it might be a bit tricky. Another time, though.'

'Yes,' she smiled at me absently. 'I'll see you in a minute.'

Dismissed, I stopped past Thea's desk. 'Thea, would you like a coffee?'

'I'm detoxing,' she replied, not looking up from her screen.

That was it for the tea round. Samuel only drank takeaway espresso from Bar Italia and Anna was buried somewhere beneath piles of work, and always made her own drinks anyway.

After downing two glasses of tap water I made a coffee, left it on the counter, then went to the ladies to attempt to sort out my sweating, my frizzy, bus-steamed hair surrounding a flushed face.

When I came back here I'd need to try a bit harder. But right now, it was hard enough getting myself out of bed, let alone being a woman of effortless fashion like my colleagues.

The toilet flushed behind me and Laura emerged.

'Oh *mein Gott*, Simone! How are you? What's wrong – you're *schwitzing* like a *schwein*.' Laura's boyfriend was from Hamburg and she spoke a little German.

'I don't know. It's boiling in here. I need to cool off somehow.' I splashed my face with water, messing up my hastily applied mascara.

'Where is the baby?'

'He's outside with my boyfriend's cousin. I couldn't face bringing him in. It was hard enough getting myself here. Look.' I pulled out my phone and showed her a photo of him sleeping, wrapped in a yellow flannel blanket, his face pointing downward, as fine and pale as a china doll.

'Oh my God. He's adorable. Bring him in next time.'

'I will. How are you?'

'Oh, not too bad. Had an awesome weekend,' she smiled, whipping out a hairbrush and raking it through her peroxided bob. 'Drank way too much though. Green tea and lettuce leaves for the rest of the week. Ready for the meeting?' She looked at me closely. 'Are you sure you're okay? You look a bit red, and sort of sweaty.'

'Oh, no. I'm fine.'

'Maybe put some foundation on before the meeting. You know what Christine is like.' She gave her hair one last flick and walked out.

Everyone gathered in the meeting room, chatting quietly, until Christine swept in and we all fell silent.

'We've got a double shoot next Saturday,' said Thea. 'Urban foraging and Romanian handcrafts. It's the only time Lock can do it, and he's a brilliant photographer. I'm going to be there, but we need someone from features to come along, too.'

'I'm in Cornwall for an Ayurvedic spa review,' said Christine. 'So unless it's urgent I'd obviously prefer not to reschedule.'

'Milan,' said Samuel, sounding bored. 'Not that shoots are really my thing, anyway. I think it says that somewhere in my contract.'

Christine looked at Anna, her head tilted. 'Anything on, Anna? Goat farm? Rhyme Time?'

'I can't go on a Saturday shoot,' said Anna. 'I promised I'd help my mum pack for her move.'

'There's no "I" in team, Anna,' said Christine sweetly. 'Does anyone else want to go? Laura, perhaps? It might be handy to have the experience.'

'Mateo is DJ'ing on the Friday at a club in Leeds, and I've promised I'll be there,' said Laura.

'Couldn't you come back for the shoot?' asked Christine.

She shook her head. 'We've got something on the next day, too.' That was Laura-speak for *I'll be catatonic on Saturday*. There was a good chance she'd email in sick on Monday morning, too, with one of her ongoing 'chesty coughs'.

Anna spoke. 'I suppose I could do it.'

Cigarette smoke drifted in through the open window as someone lit up a sneaky fag on the fire escape. Christine got up, stalked over to the window and shoved it up a little higher.

'Excuse me? I'm so sorry, but would you mind not smoking outside our window? It smells absolutely revolting. Sorry. Thank you. Thanks.'

She slammed the window shut and everyone sat in silence.

'While we're on the subject of fashion, can I bring up something about the illustrations we did of those models, Thea?' Anna said, her face reddening.

'What about them?' Thea replied, in a dangerously flat voice, as

Samuel sat up straighter beside her, looking suddenly animated.

'Their arms, they're like bones. Emaciated. I don't think it's the right message to be sending, particularly for young women.'

'I'm not taking art direction from editorial.'

'It's something to think about, though, isn't it?'

'I'm *not* taking art direction from *editorial*.'

I cleared my throat, preparing to politely excuse myself, but Christine caught my eye and said she needed to talk to me in one of the soundproof glass meeting boxes that were used mainly for phone fights with boyfriends. Once we were both inside and seated, she told me that she was very sorry but my services at *Dove Grey* were no longer required.

'But – I thought I was coming back,' I said, faint with shock. 'Isn't that what we agreed?'

She blinked as if mildly surprised. 'Do you have an email saying that? Anything in writing?'

'Uh, I don't think so. No.' And even if I did, I was locked out of my email account. Although I had asked her several times, she'd never quite got around to renewing my contract before I went on maternity leave, and I'd forgotten to chase it up once the baby arrived.

'Look, I am sorry to do this to you when you've just had a baby. But it's out of my hands. The circulation is down, so are the ads. We've had to make some very difficult decisions. Obviously we'll pay you everything you're owed, holiday leave and so on, and I'll ask for a little extra given the circumstances. I thought it was better to tell you now so you've got time to work out what you want to do next.' She looked at me for a beat, head tilted, clearly expecting me to thank her for this kindness.

'Thank you, Christine.'

'You're welcome. And I will give you a glowing reference, of course, and we'll get you in for some freelancing at some point. You've been excellent. It's not personal.' She looked at her watch. 'I have another meeting. We'll be in touch.'

I went back to my desk to gather up my things. Samuel was on the phone to someone, probably his best friend Seb in marketing. 'If you get a chance, do check out Dom's outfit today. He's absolutely *embraced* dress-down Friday,' he said, in a stage whisper that only I heard beneath the chatter of the editors going over the cover options.

My phone lit up. Rachel. 'I think you need to come down now. He's really crying.'

'I'm coming.' I gathered up as much as I could of my work stuff, too shaken to say goodbye to anyone or share what had been said in that small room. I'd email everyone later, a measured and professional farewell, once I'd gotten over the shock. As I caught the elevator back to reception I tried to work out how I felt. A bit sad. Ready for something new. Free.

As I arrived at Grosvenor Square, I saw Rachel pushing the pram absentmindedly and chatting on her phone as the baby howled within. I looked into the pram and his terrified, unblinking eyes locked with mine. Behind me, Rachel ended her call.

'I don't know what's wrong. He cried and cried, as soon as you left. He had the bottle but I think he was expecting more, and that may have started him off, and then I put him back in there.'

'You need to hold him if he's crying,' I told her, reaching into the pram and grasping his tiny, stiff body. Lifting him up against my neck, I felt his gasps and warm tears against my skin. He'd been in this state the whole time I'd been gone, and I felt nauseous with guilt. Gradually, as I rocked him, he began to quiet.

'I was reading somewhere that they need to learn to self-soothe,' offered Rachel.

'It's okay. Sometimes he gets himself worked up and there's not a lot you can do.'

'Look, I tried everything.'

'I know. Thank you for coming in.'

'So, how did it all go?'

'Not very well.'

'Oh?'

'They don't want me back. She basically sacked me.'

'What? But you sound so calm. Are you okay?'

'I think I am. When I was in there, it all seemed so pointless. Magazines are a distraction, really. Fluff. I couldn't quite be bothered with it all. I don't want to be all, "Oh my God, everything is so meaningless compared with the wonder of a newborn baby," but actually, quite a lot of things are quite pointless. Such as magazines filled with pictures of expensive crap that no-one actually needs.'

She looked at me in confusion, like I was speaking a foreign language, and maybe to her I was. 'So, what will you do for money? It's not like you and Paul are married or anything, are you? You don't want to be financially dependent on him.'

'Well, I have to work out what to do next.' I thought about Paul's comments last week. The family trust. But I didn't want to rely on him.

'But you have a baby now. You can't assume that everything will work out, that Paul will support you. You have responsibilities.'

'Oh, I know I do. I just need to think about it.' I walked away from her, towards a park bench, and sat down so I could feed the baby.

'Wow. You are so relaxed. I envy you.' She sat down beside me and smiled, watching closely as I tried to get the baby into the right position. 'Is that an Australian thing? To be so laid-back about everything all the time?'

Suddenly I remembered what Samuel used to say sometimes, in relation to a conversation with someone he didn't particularly enjoy. *I was like, I'm sorry, but you are literally sucking the life out of me.*

All I wanted was to go home, put the baby in the bath, feed it, feed myself, put it to bed, put myself to bed. And sleep. For days. Weeks. I was too tired to even refer to it as *he*. It was another obstacle – like Rachel, like this city park, and the train journey home – between me and my soft, undemanding pillow.

As I settled the baby back in the pram, Rachel reached in and started stroking his face. I was still cooling off after the tense magazine environment, the shock of being turfed out without warning, the realisation that I hadn't particularly wanted to go back to that job anyway and therefore needed to figure out what to do next. I looked around. It was all office workers about at this time of day, barking into their phones, looking ahead to their next meeting. An unfamiliar world. When I looked back down at the baby I saw that Rachel had somehow allowed her index finger to slide into his mouth. Confused, I stared at her finger, while I tried to work out what I should say, if anything. Wondering where that finger had been on our long journey here and why she had chosen to insert it into my tiny, not-yet-immunised baby's mouth. Looking up at her, I saw again that she was staring at him, that small smile playing across her face. It was the smile of a clever little girl, tormenting someone quietly and skilfully, under the radar of everyone except her chosen target. Or was I imagining it? But I was simply too drained to question her, so I took hold of the pram and she removed her finger and I wondered what the hell that was all about.

'Let's get out of here,' I said, no longer even trying to sound polite.

22

The next morning Paul's parents rang and said they were staying in Camden and did we want to meet up? Paul said, 'Yes, of course,' nodding in my direction with his eyebrows raised.

I washed my hair, then went into my room and sorted through a pile of clean, wrinkled clothes for something to wear that looked okay. The baby wasn't in his cot so I went looking for him, assuming he was with Paul. But Paul was sitting at the kitchen table eating a bowl of cereal. Something dropped in my belly. He wasn't in the apartment. I could feel it.

'Where's the baby?' I asked Paul, breathing as steadily as I could while I felt my panic rising.

'Rachel went on ahead with him on the bus, in the new pram.'

I stared at him.

'Why?'

'Because she wanted to save you the bother. She suggested it. They are only five minutes away. We can drive there as soon as you're ready.'

'We need to go find him. I can't believe she left with him. He's a newborn baby, Paul.'

I still hadn't asked him what the story was between him and Rachel. It was easier right now to bury it. But still it was there, in my clenched voice, in the sudden frustration I felt for him, for this situation I was in and couldn't easily get out of, but knew deep in my belly that I needed to. He'd been nice about me getting fired, at least, promising to give me some money until I worked out what I was going to do next.

I threw on jeans and an old navy blue sweater and my trainers, no longer caring about my appearance. As Paul drove towards Camden, I called Rachel.

'Rachel, where are you? The baby is going to need to be fed soon.'

'We're in the markets. At some cafe. I just came here from the Tube station.'

I thought of the baby going down those long escalators at Angel and hoped she had strapped him in properly.

'Is the baby okay?'

'He's fine, Simone, don't worry. I know how to look after a baby. You'll find us. I can't really hear you, but give me a call when you get here.' She hung up. A few minutes later my phone beeped and I saw that Rachel had sent me a photo of the baby, strapped in his pram at the very top of the escalator at Angel station. A text message followed.

Here he is.

When we got to Camden, Paul dropped me on the street next to the markets and kept driving to find a parking spot. My phone was almost dead, I realised, too late, as I dialled Rachel's number. It rang and rang but went to voicemail. I tried again, and this time, with much fumbling, she answered.

'Hello? Where are you guys?'

'Where are *you*?'

'We're in a café. Sort of in the markets. Behind a record shop. Some clothes shops.'

'Can you be a bit more specific? What's the name of the café, so I can ask someone?' I looked around frantically, hoping someone would help me; that a friendly policeman would materialise and show me the way. No-one was nearby apart from a skinny bloke lurking in a doorway of a closed bar, looking very much like he did not wish to be spoken to.

'I think it's called Wiltons or something. Wilsons? I don't know.'

I looked around me for the pale blue pram, hurrying through a food court selling noodles and massive fake-looking pizzas and ice cream, past a pub spilling drunks and a gyrating man dressed in a white fur coat, who didn't appear to realise the night was long over. People stumbled onto the footpath, blocking my way, drunk and laughing. One of them snatched a hot dog off a man cooking them outside, shoved it into her mouth, then spat it straight out, close to my feet.

Still I searched, down long canvas-covered pathways between shops selling hash pipes and miniature bicycles and pet hamsters. I was certain that if I didn't find him this time, I would never see him again. He was too tiny, too vulnerable. I hadn't kept him close enough. It would be my own fault. Even if I did find him, he would be altered, somehow. It was ruined. All ruined. People ambled along, taking their time, stopping to browse at stalls, and I stumbled into them, swearing under my breath but still maintaining a precarious cool because if I lost it here, surrounded by Led Zeppelin t-shirts and pornographic bumper stickers, I might never make it back again. Camden Market was the kind of place you might never come back from at the best of times. I couldn't bear to think of my baby in here somewhere.

A café appeared between two shops, and I stumbled down two steps and into the warmth and chat of the small room busy with people and newspapers and puzzles and the clatter of coffee cups and the roar of the espresso machine. A long, narrow central table was crammed with relatives of Paul's: his jolly parents, his sister, some of their friends from Scotland.

'Oh, here she is!'

'Hello!' I tried to smile, but failed, and didn't take a seat. On the other side of the table I saw Penny holding the baby, his face hidden by an unfamiliar hat, and I made my way towards them, wilting in relief, resisting the urge to shove people out of the way in my need to have him back in my arms, folding into him and getting my breath back. The baby was crying, fussing, clearly hungry, and my bra filled yet again with milk at the sound of his cries. But when I looked closer I saw that it wasn't my baby.

'Hi, Simone,' Penny said. 'Look at this little fellow. It's Sarah's grandson.'

As always, Penny was lovely, making an effort to be kind and gracious towards me, and I felt obliged to admire the baby, before asking, after a moment, 'Do you know where Rachel is, with the baby?'

'Oh – she took him, I think, for a walk. In the pram. He was crying. She said something about walking him to sleep, he was a bit upset. I don't know where she would do that around here though – maybe down at the canal?'

'He must be hungry. Is that where she said she was going?'

'I don't know, Simone. Are you alright?' Finally, she was looking at me properly, seeing me, and for the first time I felt like she understood that things weren't great. Not bothering to answer, I took off again, back onto the street, searching for the closest canal entrance.

Passing a young man who looked both local and friendly, I said, 'Have you seen a woman pushing a pram? A pale blue pram?'

'A Bugaboo?'

'Yes!'

'Only about fifty of them. You ladies sure do love your Bugaboos.'

'Yes we do. Do you happen to know where the entrance to the canal is?'

'It's right down that street. Turn down there and you'll see the steps on your right.'

'Thank you.'

As I ran down the steps to the canal and onto the pathway, a man in front of me was blocking the path, pulling a thrashing fish on a line out of the water, then kneeling down on the ground with his catch. No concern about people trying to use the footpath, so focused was he on the small fish he'd pulled out, with its coarse, dirty-looking scales. He pulled a knife out and fell upon it, killing it quickly. Surely he wasn't going to eat something so drab-looking? He avoided my eyes as I passed him, and there was something sordid or furtive about him. The canals were always a little haunted and seedy. And I'd never liked the tunnels, the cold, dripping damp of them.

Then I saw Rachel, a hundred metres or so away, leaning into the pram and taking a photo, then turning away. The pram was right on the edge of the canal and she hadn't fixed the brake, and as I watched, she released it, almost carelessly, and then turned away, hunching over her phone and shading her eyes as if sending a message to someone. It wasn't safe, leaving it that close to the water, and as I ran towards her I pictured it rolling away from her, tipping into the canal, only the handle sticking out to show me where it was. Reaching down, pulling that tiny body out through that dark polluted water, his clothes clinging to fragile ribs.

My phone beeped in my pocket but I ignored it.

'Is he okay?' I asked her, reaching into the pram and peering in, needing to see him. His wet eyes met mine and for a long moment we stared at each other.

'He's fine, Simone. Are *you* okay?'

'What have you done to him? He looks strange.' And he did, with a bluish tinge around his mouth, his eyes sunken and glassy.

'Nothing. He's fine. He's been a bit crabby, but I think he's just tired.'

Was it just the light? Could it be that I was imagining the blue cast on his skin, his strange eyes?

'There's something wrong with him. I know it.'

'You're imagining things, Simone.' She smiled at me, shaking her head. 'He's absolutely fine. You're overreacting.' She was looking at me too closely, and I didn't want to waste valuable time on the conversation, so I cut her off.

'I'm going to take him to a GP clinic, just in case. Can you tell Paul to meet me there?' I searched my phone for a walk-in centre near Camden. 'St Mary's hospital is closest. Tell him I've gone there in a cab.'

Seizing hold of the pram handle, I turned away from her and went in search of a taxi to take me to that hectic, public site of chaos and illness that was paradoxically the only place in this whole city that felt safe.

In the paediatric waiting room, Paul stayed by my side but I barely registered him. He flicked through his phone and I saw that the last message he'd got was from Rachel, a photo of the baby and a single *x*.

The baby was taken away from us and a nurse came in to tell me they were assessing him and we would be able to go in shortly. When she returned she guided us to what looked like a bad-news room, with its box of tissues and insipid floral prints on the walls.

'So, what's been happening?' said the doctor, a young woman with a long dark ponytail and searching eyes. A gentle knock at the door, and another woman came in, holding the baby. As she passed him to me I thought that she looked familiar, and when she introduced herself I realised, with a sudden queasy understanding of how intricately the whole system was linked up, that she was the child health nurse who had come to our apartment.

'Is he alright?' I asked. 'Did he look blue to you?'

'He looks fine. I'm more interested in what you think, though,' she said in a calm voice, her eyes curious and kind.

I told them again about how he looked strange at the canal, his lips bluish and his eyes sunken and glassy, realising as I spoke that I was being assessed as much as the baby: for depression, postnatal psychosis, or something else.

The child health nurse studied me with that same prying face and tilted head, and wrote things down in a file with my son's name on it. But this time, I saw her not as the enemy but as an ally, someone who was on the baby's side, with her eyes trained on everyone around him, even me, to keep him safe. He was lucky to have her looking out for him. Someone had to, I told myself angrily.

The doctor cleared her throat. 'So, we've tested his oxygen saturation levels and they are normal. And I've examined him and he seems completely healthy. Now, very young babies can look blue around the mouth temporarily. It may be that he was a little cold – you said that he was outside – but you can see now that he's lovely and pink, and he's breathing normally. But we would like to keep him here under observation for one night.' She continued to look at me closely. 'You can stay with him. So if you want to go back to the waiting room now, someone will take you up to the children's ward in a little while.'

Paul remained uncharacteristically quiet as we returned to the waiting room. The baby had fallen asleep in my arms, which gave me the opportunity to say what I should have made clear weeks ago.

'Rachel has to go. Or I go. I don't even know why she's still here. Why is she a part of this?'

For a long moment he said nothing.

'Okay. I'll talk to her.'

'It would have been good if you'd had that conversation a while back.'

'I know. I'm sorry. I was worried about her, in London, on her own.'

'I've done it. Lots of people have done it. You go and find a job and a room to rent somewhere and get on with it. It's weird. Why did she take the baby without asking me? It's starting to feel like she wants to hurt him. Or take him away from me.'

He shook his head slowly. 'No. I don't think that's fair, Simone. She loves him like we do.'

'She sent me a text message and a photo of him, at the top of the escalator. It said, *Here he is*. With a full stop on the end. A full stop. It was a sign.'

He looked confused. 'A sign of what?'

'*I don't know*. Of something ending.'

He looked uneasy, almost embarrassed. 'Maybe you need to rest, Simone,' he said in a formal tone. 'You've been through so much in the last six weeks.'

'All along, she's been wanting to take him away from me. Why is she like that? What is all this about?'

I waited for him to tell me, to take the opportunity to be honest, but still he said nothing. We sat in silence, like two strangers. The baby slept on, warm in his blanket. After a while Paul's phone rang, and he stood up and walked out as he took the call. A few minutes later he was back. 'That was Rachel. She feels terrible about what happened, about upsetting you. She was in tears. I think – she really does care about him, Simone. More than you can imagine.'

I stared at the baby. Safe, sleeping. Alive. That was all that mattered.

'You need to talk to her. She has to leave.'

That night, I slept in a fold-out bed next to the baby's old-fashioned metal cot. Away from the apartment, the baby safe, the nurses at the front desk keeping watch through a glass window, I felt calm. By the early hours his warm body was close to mine, my t-shirt pushed up and my arms encircling him, feeling him breathing against my skin, feeding and sleeping, feeding and sleeping.

When I woke I remembered where I was and relived the day, what had brought us here, but this time the baby was awake and alert beside me, and yesterday's panic was absent. Already he was bigger than a newborn, getting stronger all the time. And as I lay with him, I thought back to the man at the canal with the fish. His meaningless kill, for the sport of it, because he had nothing better to do. The crack of the fish scales as his blunt knife carved into them, and how he'd turned away from me, not letting me see what was in his eyes.

23

A little later, I was in the ward playroom, staring out the window and holding the baby against me. There was absolutely nothing wrong with the moment. And maybe that was the lesson I needed to learn. To breathe, to be still and exist, like the baby did, in the present.

'Simone?'

I startled and turned around quickly. Penny stood in the doorway. She had come in so quietly.

'I wanted to see how you were.'

'I'm okay.' And I was. If I had the baby close to me, if no one was trying to get him out of my arms, I was fine.

'Have you spoken to Paul?'

'He's coming to pick us up at nine, once the doctor has seen the baby.'

'Well, I won't stay for long. I thought I should talk to you. Explain a few things. In confidence.'

She sat down and I noticed how pale she looked, how unlike her usual groomed self. No makeup or chunky silver jewellery. Hair flat against her head. Her eyes roamed around the room as she started to speak, almost as if she was talking to herself.

'Rachel was always wild. A beautiful little girl. So gorgeous. But she did go off the rails. The whole thing was terribly sad.' She looked exhausted, her hands were trembling, and I hoped the social worker wouldn't turn up.

'The *whole thing*?'

I needed to steer her. I knew, somehow, that if Paul arrived I would never hear this story. She looked like she'd come here in a daze after a bad night's sleep, and if she didn't say what she needed to right now that would be it, she wouldn't let her guard down again.

'The baby was too much for them.' She looked at me, wincing slightly as if she instantly regretted saying the words. 'Sorry.'

'This baby?' I asked, knowing what she was telling me but resisting it at the same.

'They had a baby together. As teenagers.'

'You said it was too much for them? What happened?' I asked, keeping my voice even.

'The thing is, we have always believed Paul. And I always looked out for Rachel. It was no wonder she turned out as she did, with her parents neglecting her like they did, but we always helped her with her studies, gave her somewhere to live, supported her financially. It was – well, she's been wandering for years.'

Will you get to the point? I wanted to shout, but I also wanted to cover my ears. 'What happened to the baby?' I asked again, keeping my voice as calm and even as I could.

'He died. A beautiful little boy. Eddie. Only seven weeks old. They – the doctors – at first, they thought he was shaken. That Paul shook him. But they were never able to prove it in court, and we managed to keep it out of the papers. And, of course, they were both so young. So that's how we handled it.'

I stared at her for a long moment, unable to speak.

I'd known all along. How Rachel had turned up and taken hold of him like he belonged to her. How Paul had never asked her to leave. And those words inked across her skin – *Only you return.* Her avid interest in my baby – her own son's half-brother. It had all been there.

'You have to understand that Rachel – well, she never got past it. I think she came back to London in the hope that it might be healing for her. To help you with your baby, to forgive herself, and Paul. Another chance.'

'Another chance?'

'Well, to be with a baby, to be a part of it. To make sure Paul didn't get so tired again. That's what she hoped, I think.' She shook her head. 'But there's nothing here for her except more pain.'

She picked up a green car off the floor and held it in her hand like an amulet, and for a moment I saw her as a new mother, spending hours in bright, toy-filled rooms like this one, wondering as she held her babies if she could keep them from harm.

She looked at her watch. 'I should go. Please don't mention to George that I was here. We feel differently, and he thought it was best to say nothing. He has always respected Paul's wish to put it behind him. But as a mother myself, I thought it best that you know. To understand why things might seem a little ... strained, at times.'

A little strained? I thought of Paul's hands, his younger hands. What they had done – what he had done – to a tiny baby. And how every time the baby cried he walked away, as if he was frightened of what he might do, as if he knew what he was capable of. I thought back to the doctor's face in the emergency room, when I'd been admitted with pneumonia. His wary expression when Paul got angry. A trained wariness. He would see that anger often in his working day, and know how to handle it.

'What you have to understand about Paul is that he will have his moments of anger. But he did love that baby. He never meant to hurt him. And you can always come to me for help, advice, support. He's told you about the family trust. Sometimes – you know what it's like, with men – you just have to be the forgiving one. Rachel has come to understand that.'

I wanted to run from her, from this room. From the whole family. But I looked at her and nodded, the baby alert and content in my lap.

'Rachel, at times she believed that Paul hurt the baby. They had a fight that night, you see. She left; he was alone with the baby. We were out – it was only one night, but I'll never forgive myself – and Paul was too young, too inexperienced, to be left with a newborn. We came back, and the baby was injured, it was too late. Rachel eventually came round to our way of thinking, that it was a terrible accident, but I'm not sure what she's said to you. Sometimes she doubts him. But we've always stood by her, and Paul. She's family, after all. We look after her. Like we will you.'

She came over to me and placed her hand on the baby's back, for a moment, and then was gone, as suddenly as she had appeared.

They had a fight that night. Paul and I hardly fought. But one night we did. That night I had been trying to remember, or perhaps forget. The night of the work drinks at Thea's weird basement club in Soho. I had bumped into a boy from high school, Ben, and we'd ended up chatting away and laughing about old school friends, getting closer to each other as the volume in the room increased. And then Paul had materialised next to me. Somehow he'd tracked me down, and was leaning over me and telling me it was time to go home.

Maybe I had been standing a little too close to Ben, and that's why Paul had taken my arm, claiming me. He was smiling and being his usual jovial self, but all the time his hand tightened. Through a cushion of alcohol I felt his thumb pressing against my inner arm, the tendon or muscle beneath shifting. I was drunk and tired and also confused, because Paul was smiling so calmly, as if that cruel hand belonged to someone else, as if he didn't even realise how much he was hurting me. Ben suddenly looked uneasy, and moved away, and Paul's smile disappeared.

'We're leaving,' he said, his voice so loud in my ear I jumped.

Then we were outside on the dark street, the yellow of a taxi light gliding towards us.

'Get in.'

In the back of the cab, he pulled me against him and I was engulfed by his expensive, foresty smell.

'Lucky I found you when I did.'

'How *did* you find me?'

'Were you having a nice time?' he asked, ignoring my question.

Even in my drunken state I knew my answer needed to console him.

'Not really. It was dragging on. I was about to leave.'

'Who was that bloke you were talking to?'

'Just someone from high school. He wanted to reminisce about home. Think he might be feeling a bit lost here.'

When we pulled up outside the soaring concrete tower, he held open the door and helped me out of the car, his hand on my arm gentler now. We fell into bed, and though I was too drunk, really, and half-asleep, we had sex because he wanted to and it was easier to go along with him. That was the night I got pregnant. I knew it. And now here we were.

If Paul hadn't appeared, Ben and I might have swapped numbers and met up, though it was impossible to imagine an easy, tipsy night like that ever again. I had a new life now, rising up around me and looking more real by the day. The baby, who was a miracle. But also Paul and his parents, Rachel, the family trust, the fortress-like architecture of the Barbican, the expensive blue pram. Circling me, walling me in, making me forget who I used to be.

Twenty minutes later Paul appeared. I understood now why he was on edge in hospitals, around healthcare workers and people trained to spot trouble. I couldn't meet his eyes, couldn't look at his hands. But he was oblivious. He was always oblivious.

'Rachel is leaving,' he told me.

Despite myself, I felt a tug of grief for her.

I remembered what she'd said to me that night in the bathroom, right before I'd got sick: *I'm on your side.*

'I think it's time, don't you?' he said, taking the baby from me and heading for the exit, and I followed him closely, watching his hands, watching the baby.

When we got home she was there, waiting. She looked terrible – pale and red-eyed and haunted. How exhausting it must be to live in her head.

What I needed to do was edge away, somehow. I couldn't stay with Paul, now that I knew who he was. Would we even have stayed together past the winter if there wasn't a baby?

Rachel gathered her toiletries from the bathroom, packed her bags in her room and slowly dragged them out to the hallway.

'So, where are you heading to?' Paul asked her politely.

'Oh, I'm going to go and visit a friend I studied with. I bumped into her the other day at Old Street and she ended up inviting me to stay with her for a bit. She's in Hammersmith.'

'Do you want a lift to the station?'

'That would be great.'

I went to the door with her, holding the baby, and when she reached out her hands I gave him to her. She held him against her for a long minute, breathing against his warm head, and for once I didn't feel like snatching him back.

'Do you have a coat?' I asked her.

'No,' she said.

I took mine off the hook. 'Here, have this. And take care of yourself.' Then I held out my hands for the baby. 'Come and see us soon.'

She slipped the coat on, my grandmother's diamante brooch bright against the grey wool.

'Thank you for letting me stay so long,' she said. 'Part of me just needed to see him. And then when I got here, it was like I couldn't leave.'

'I know,' I said quietly, and our eyes met.

Paul shifted impatiently, looking at the two of us with a wary expression, and picked up her bag. 'Okay. We should get a move on, Rachel.'

And just like that, she was gone. Paul glanced at me as he shut the door and I saw something familiar in his eyes. Fury. He knew I could leave. And maybe I would, taking the baby with me.

I made some dinner and when he returned we ate together, talking about nothing in particular. But my mind was active, more awake than it had been for months, as I tried to work out what to do next.

24

A week later I put the baby in his pram and went wandering down towards the East End, where I thought I'd like to live one day, out of the city a bit, closer to London Fields and the paddling pool, where I could take the baby on summer afternoons.

At the apartment things were stilted between Paul and me, the atmosphere cool and empty. I knew that it was going to be harder, once I told him I was leaving and we became opponents, so I wanted to work out a plan first. My parents were lending me some money, and I knew how lucky I was to have that lifeline.

London smelled like petrol puddles and road tar. The homes here were long, curved rows of Victorian terrace houses, with small gardens and tall windows. I walked through London Fields, a bare-treed triangle where daffodils in garish yellow were pushing their way through the ragged sodden grass – tiny glimpses of the warmer days to come. The children's summer paddling pool was drained, the gate padlocked, but I could see the steam rising off the London Fields Lido.

Feeling too underdressed for Broadway Market, with its crowded footpaths and stacks of *Guardians*, I turned down Westgate Street, passing the children's centre and through the viaduct to Mare Street, and then Cambridge Heath Road.

Eventually the museum came into view, filled with its stories from other childhoods, swiftly lived through and then abandoned as those boys and girls grew up and moved toward independence.

Whatever happened next with Paul, I would do my best to keep the baby safe. To surround him with picture books and primary colours and playgrounds and a home where he felt secure and loved.

I wanted to find Jennifer, to talk to her about everything that had happened since I'd last seen her. That fog of the early weeks had thinned a little, and I wanted to find out more about her, and how she somehow knew all the right things to say to me. She wasn't around the museum displays, though. In the café I ordered a cup of tea and sat to drink it, the baby on my lap, slumped against me. I realised I was waiting for her, because the other times I'd visited she'd seemed to know I was there, and to find me. But this time, even as I ordered a second cup of tea, she did not appear.

Eventually I wandered down to the back of the museum, and let myself through the unlocked heavy door into the dim hallway that led to her office. I was expecting to see a closed door, with the light shining out from under the bottom, but instead I found the door standing half-open, and no lights on inside. I peered in.

All of her things were there in the half-light – the furniture, the books, the leather armchair. But the paintings were stacked by a chair, and the flowers were dead in the vase. The green hellebores outside were still flowering lush and pale in the winter air, though. It was a room that had been abandoned in a hurry, its owner too distracted to clean it properly. I recognised the quality of the mess. There was something familiar about its look of unexpected abandonment.

Someone was standing behind me.

I turned, hoping it was her, but it was another woman, of around the same age, also with long grey hair and no makeup, wise blue eyes and a gentle expression.

'Is Jennifer here today?' I asked, knowing already what the answer would be.

'She's not, I'm sorry.' She looked at me for a long moment. 'Jennifer fought breast cancer for a long time. And only last week, she lost that battle.'

I had no idea of what to say. I thought of her, standing outside the hospital that day I saw her on the way to the library, looking as small as a child against the huge building.

'We are talking about setting this room up as a space for young mothers. She always befriended them when they came in here. She was a real help around the place, but she wasn't working here, towards the end. Not technically employed, anyway. She kept her office, and she used to help people, by listening, giving them a space to talk.'

I looked at the room again. Her beautiful books, her pot of winter flowers on the windowsill, those dark, scrawling pictures.

'Would you like to take something?' the woman asked me. 'Maybe a plant, or one of her books?'

'That's okay.' I didn't like the thought of anything being removed, of her room being emptied. 'I had no idea that she was so unwell. I liked talking to her.'

'No-one realised. We thought we had a bit more time.' She sighed. 'She was a gift to a lot of people.'

Gift. It was a strange image and I tried to focus on it so I didn't burst into tears, picturing a box tied with a pink silk ribbon. I remembered the whiteness of her hands. Now, though, I saw what was familiar about the room's state. It had been left by someone who was sick, suddenly very sick, and didn't have the energy to clean up, or even shut the door.

Walking home along the back streets of Bethnal Green towards Hackney Road, I passed a young child at the window of a terrace house, staring down at me. He looked eerie and winter-pale, watching me. All the way home I thought about Jennifer. How calmly she'd appeared to live her life – peaceful, steady, getting on with her work and forming connections with people. Not creating drama, or skidding from one crisis to another. What a relief it would be, to live like that. A year ago I wouldn't have even come across someone like her. Now I missed her.

My phone rang. Soraya.

'Look. I'm just ringing to say, if the only thing keeping you in a shitty situation is money, then I have money. I have a spare bedroom. You can stay, for as long as you need to.'

'What have you heard?'

'It doesn't matter.'

Rachel, I thought.

'Should I leave?' I had no idea what the right thing to do was. I knew Paul would talk me out of it, talk over me, confuse me with moments of kindness and insistent, endless sentences.

'Of course you should. You're not safe. If he hurt a tiny baby, he can hurt Thomas or he can hurt you. Maybe he already has?'

I was silent. On the other end of the line she waited patiently, then spoke in a clear voice, enunciating every word so they all went into my overloaded head.

'Go home. Pack. Make yourself a cup of tea. I'll be there in an hour.'

At Soraya's flat in south London, the rooms were warm and cluttered with books and plants and framed photos. In her usual businesslike way she'd come up with a solution – a small, light-filled flat in Hackney, owned by a friend of hers who had moved up north, would be vacant in two weeks time, and I could rent it.

In the meantime, the days stretched ahead with no structure, no meals or predictable naps or breaks to hang the hours on. Somehow the baby and I got to the end of another windy March afternoon. We were both warmly dressed, the lamp was on and I'd made myself tea. Soon Soraya would be home, and she'd hold the baby and tell me about her day while I served up the dinner I'd made in stages throughout the day.

Ever since I'd left the Barbican for what I hoped was the last time, I'd been building a picture of my life with me in charge. Without Paul.

He didn't know it – he thought we were taking a break, that I was thinking things over – and something warned me not to tell him too soon. But slowly it grew more vivid. I had a small payout from work and the loan from my parents and a stack of university brochures and funding application forms to get through in the pockets of free time I had when the baby napped. My plan was to retrain in something useful. Maybe childcare, maybe midwifery, maybe teaching. I wanted to be like the people I'd met over the last few months, in the hospital and out in the world, people who solved ordinary problems, laughed, offered practical support.

I settled the baby in his bouncer and sat beside him, watching the news to see what was happening beyond this bubble we'd been living in. It was such a relief to see the old newsreaders, to lose myself in their stories again.

After a moment, I became aware of that pricking sensation of someone's eyes on me. That odd jolt on the Tube or in a shop, when you realise that someone is observing you.

I looked down at the baby – Thomas – and his face was turned to me, with an expression of frank affection. He wasn't smiling, exactly; it was all in his bright eyes. With his expression so alert, so quietly thrilled, it seemed rude not to respond.

I said hello, and laughed nervously. He was silent, apparently needing nothing more than to gaze fondly at me.

How strange it was to feel that I was enough for someone, simply by existing. It made me shy. It was as if I was being introduced to someone I'd admired from afar, whose approval I'd longed to win. A secretly loved teacher, or someone I'd gone to school with, but never known. We'd been travelling towards this ordinary dusk together for months, and now – with only a look to mark the moment – we'd arrived.

ACKNOWLEDGEMENTS

So many dedicated people work to open doors for aspiring authors, and I have many to thank – first of all, my editor Georgia Richter at Fremantle Press for seeing the potential in my manuscript, knowing all the right questions to ask, and calmly steering me and this book to publication. Thank you Armelle Davies for your encouragement and insightful copyediting, and to Alicia Lutz and Dr Morgane Davies for your close reading of the manuscript and helpful comments.

Thanks to Jane Fraser, Claire Miller, Tiffany Ko and everyone at Fremantle Press for your support and enthusiasm for this book. The Hungerford Award offers a unique and necessary opportunity to aspiring WA authors, and I thank Fremantle Press and Delys Bird, Cate Noske and Richard Rossiter for their time and energy in judging the 2018 awards and shortlisting my manuscript. Thanks to the City of Fremantle for supporting the prize. And thanks, again, to Cate Noske and Delys Bird for publishing in *Westerly* 61.2 my short story, 'To the Motherland', from which this novel then grew.

The Australian Society of Authors and Katharine Susannah Prichard Writers' Centre provided timely advice and practical support – thank you.

A nod to Perth's wonderful writing community, too many of you to mention; to Fred Nenner, Laurie Steed, Alan Fyfe and Kyra Giorgi for writerly kinship, and to Bella Carlin and Mary

Torjussen for reading and commenting on an early draft. I must also mention Marion May Campbell, whose brilliant creative writing workshops at Murdoch University have guided me ever since, and the dedicated creative writing staff and fellow students at Bath Spa University for a life-changing and illuminating year.

To my friends Kerry, Ben, Steph, Anna and Carly, thank you for many words of encouragement over many years, and to Melanie for being my Northern Hemisphere voice of reason through 2020 – I can't wait to see you all again.

Thank you to my parents, Heather and Leon, for your lifelong support, and for raising me in a house full of books and dogs, allowing me to read whatever and whenever I wanted, and always letting me follow my own path. Thanks to my sisters, Ashe, Renee and Emily, for a lifelong four-way conversation that has schooled me in drama, intrigue and dark comedy like nothing else. And hugs to my nieces and nephews, Matilda, Jack, Grace, Maxi and Valentina – we're so lucky you all showed up.

To my darling Felix, *vielen Dank* for taking the brave marital step of suggesting I put aside my first attempt at a novel and start something new, and for always providing the love, support and ideal light in which to do so. Finally, thank you to my beautiful boys, Tilo and Rafael, for blasting into our lives and bringing so much of everything with you.

MORE THRILLING READS

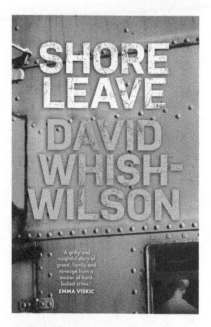

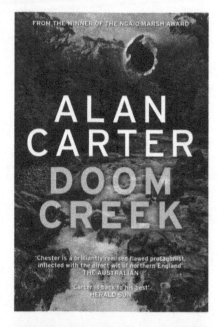

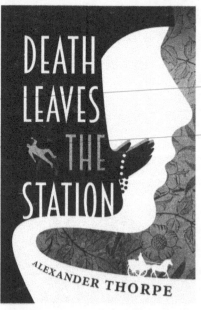

AVAILABLE AT FREMANTLEPRESS.COM.AU

FROM FREMANTLE PRESS

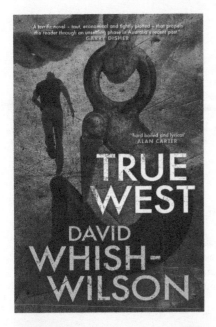

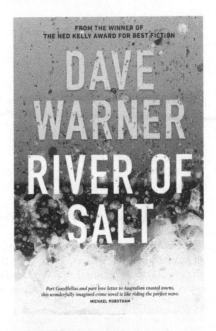

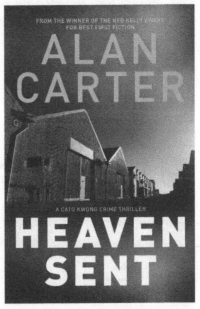

AND FROM ALL GOOD BOOKSTORES

First published 2021 by
FREMANTLE PRESS

Fremantle Press Inc. trading as Fremantle Press
25 Quarry Street, Fremantle,
Western Australia 6160
(PO Box 158, North Fremantle WA 6159)
www.fremantlepress.com.au

Copyright © Zoe Deleuil, 2021

The moral rights of the author have been asserted.

This book is copyright. Apart from any fair dealing for the purpose
of private study, research, criticism or review, as permitted under the
Copyright Act, no part may be reproduced by any process without written
permission. Enquiries should be made to the publisher.

Cover photograph by Simone Hutsch / Unsplash
Cover design by Nada Backovic, www.nadabackovic.com
Printed by McPherson's Printing, Victoria, Australia

 A catalogue record for this
book is available from the
National Library of Australia

ISBN 9781925815634 (paperback)
ISBN 9781925815665 (ebook)

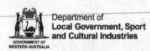

Fremantle Press is supported by the State Government through the
Department of Local Government, Sport and Cultural Industries.